I0598781

The Clockmaker's Son

by
Susan Buffum

Susan Buffum

Copyright Susan Buffum 2018

Published by

Inklings, a division of Dark Ink Press

All rights reserved by the author. No part of this book may be used or reproduced by any means graphic, electronic, or mechanical, including photocopying, recording, taping, or by any information retrieval storage systems including file sharing, without the author's express written permission, except in the case of brief quotation embodied in critical articles or reviews.

Please contact the author at sebuffum415@gmail.com for permission.

This is entirely a work of fiction. All characters, names, incidents, organizations, and dialogues in this novel are either the products of the author's imagination, or used fictitiously and are not meant to represent anyone currently living or deceased.

ISBN-13: 978-0-9997016-3-8

ISBN-10: 0-9997016-3-0

<u>Dedication</u>

To my family and all of my friends, and especially to Dorothy Karlstrom who became a mother to me during the writing, proofreading, editing, and revisions of this novel! You're a wonderful lady!

<u>Acknowledgement- Cover Design</u>

To my good friend who doesn't mind late night messaging, who is always there for me, author Melissa Volker. You can visit Melissa and view her work at **www.melissavolker.com**

Susan Buffum

Chapter One

Before the three boys had gone on that fateful camping trip up at Turkey Pond on the side of Clay Hill there had been incidents of mutilated farm animals having been found out in the pastures located on the outskirts of town, mostly dairy cows and goats. However, these things had happened in surrounding towns, too, not only in Pine Haven. People were inclined to write it off as the work of a pack of coyotes, or a pack of feral dogs. Hunters had found the torn open carcasses of deer in the woods that had further pointed toward the coyote/feral dog pack theory. No one really thought much about letting their kids hike in the woods back then, or even go camping up at the pond. They figured the coyotes or dogs wouldn't bother or attack a noisy group of kids when there was other prey in the woods and fields that they could hunt.

The livestock and deer killings were just random occurrences that no one had given much serious thought to until those three boys went camping and did not come home when expected. It was then that what had been a nuisance to farmers and an annoyance to hunters had become a widespread community concern.

When the two bodies had been found with their throats torn out, their bellies ripped open, and their hearts missing up near the pond, and the third boy's body had been discovered missing from his bloodied and tattered sleeping bag the attitude toward coyotes and feral dogs had taken a hard shift toward the elimination of them all.

The regional high school is located on Foster Road on former farmland donated specifically for a school to be built upon years before I had even been born. The land had been cleared quickly, but the funding hadn't come through for the new high school to be built until I had been in third grade. My father, Edward Rumford, had been the attorney who'd cleared up the last legal issues with the one distant relative who had protested the will in which old man Foster had deliberately left the land to the town for the purpose of building the new school, his only son, Thomas, having been the only student to die when the gymnasium bleachers had collapsed in the old school during a pep rally. Thomas had been nearly decapitated in the tragic incident that had injured dozens of other students. He had fallen so that his head had become wedged between the risers below him so that the weight of the risers above and the tumbling students falling over him had crushed his neck.

Of course, I hadn't heard all the gory details until I'd been older, many years after the old high school had been razed after the completion of the construction of the new high school.

The Department of Public Works had erected some metal Quonset huts and a huge, brick garage building on the former high school's land once the site had been cleaned up.

The Clockmaker's Son

It was common enough, when hanging out with friends, to have someone bring up the story of the ghost of Thomas Foster haunting the DPW yard, especially as Halloween drew near and the shadows lengthened earlier with the sun setting sooner. The whole shocking business of that ill-fated camping trip up at Turkey Pond on Clay Hill was still a year away, although we'd gotten our introduction to Thomas Foster's ghost this year, the year my friends and I were in fifth grade.

That's what we were doing on Halloween afternoon when I was ten-years old. My best friend, Ripley Forbes, our mutual classmate Ashley Taylor, who lived down the street and around the corner from me, and I were sitting on the front porch of Ripley's house where I was having supper before changing into my cat costume and then going out trick-or-treating with Ripley's older sister Sara supervising us. We were telling childish ghost stories, until Ashley leaned closer to us and asked, her voice hushed as she furtively cast her eyes about as if there might be someone listening to fifth grade girls talking and trying to scare one another with silly stories that were making us giggle more than shiver, "You want to hear a real ghost story?" Ripley and I glanced at one another, such close friends that we could communicate with our eyes and facial expressions without a spoken word crossing our lips. Simultaneously, we'd nodded. We were basically kids still. What in the world kind of a ghost story could Ashley know that required hushed tones and furtive glances? "This is a true story, cross my heart and hope to die," she intoned.

"Well, cross your heart, but you can skip the dying part or we'll be telling a ghost story about you haunting my front porch next Halloween," Ripley responded.

"This is serious," Ashley admonished. "If you don't want to hear it, I'll go tell it to Olivia Cusson over on Willow Street." Olivia Cusson was a strange girl from a broken home. She was into cutting, something we weren't supposed to know about, but girls talk in the gym locker room the same as boys do, only we talk about different kinds of stuff, girl stuff, I suppose you'd call it. My older brother calls it 'little girl gossip' or, worse yet, chick talk in preparation for hen talk when we're older, sitting under hair dryers in Betty's Magic Mirror Beauty Salon over on South Main Street.

I shot Ripley a look and she shrugged. "Go ahead," I encouraged her. "Tell us."

"I heard my father talking to his friend Greg this past weekend when he stopped to have the truck's suspension looked at. They forgot I was in the truck up on the lift and started talking about Greg's brother Gary who works for the DPW. Gary saw a gruesome ghost out near one of the sand piles. He said its head was all wobbly and bloody, and that the ghost couldn't hold it upright. One of its eyes had popped right out of its socket and was dangling down its cheek!"

"Oooo!" I cried, shivering at that image, and also feeling a little roil of nausea in my stomach.

"It was Thomas Foster," she stage-whispered, making her eyes large and round. "You know who he is, don't you? He used to live where the new high school now stands. He got killed in an accident in the gym at the old high school. He got crushed when the bleachers collapsed during a pep rally right around this time of year. Greg told my dad that lots of guys at the DPW don't like to work there because they see the ghost a lot and it's really scary! It moans and staggers around. Sometimes they feel an icy cold hand touch them, or they smell a really bad stink, like rotting meat!" With a captive audience, Ashley was really getting into her recitation of the gruesome facts she'd overhead while slumped down in the passenger seat of the pickup truck so her father would keep talking and she could hear more. "There's a stain out in the yard about where the old gym once stood that they can't get rid of. It's like a big old blood stain and it's still a little gooey. They've put sand on it lots of times to cover it up, but the next day the stain is back!"

"Maybe it's oil from one of the trucks, or something," Ripley suggested.

"It's blood red!"

"Oil can look red at times. It depends on how the light hits it. I've seen rainbows in oil spots on our driveway."

"This is all red. Dark red, like, you know, blood clots." I wrinkled my nose and hugged my knees harder. "It's like those buckets of blood when old man Keach slaughters his hogs."

"Oh, come on!" I cried, jumping up. "You're making me sick with all this blood stuff!"

"Charlotte, you're such a baby!" Ashley admonished as she rolled her blue eyes. "Why don't you run home to Momma and cling to her apron strings!"

"Her Mom is in Great Barrington at an auction," Ripley replied. "She's hanging out here until she gets back and picks her up." My brunette friend looked up at me. "Why don't you go see how much longer it is until dinner?"

I was relieved to be sent inside away from Ashley and her horror story. The screen door slammed with a flat bang behind me and I closed the inside door because it was chillier out now with the sun lower in the western sky. The house felt warm and safe, as familiar as my own home, and much cozier.

I say it felt cozier because Ripley's parents had all normal, modern furniture in their house—couches and chairs you could sit on, a coffee table you could kick off your shoes and put your stocking feet or bare feet up on without anyone freaking out about it like my mom did in our house that was chock full of pricey antiques. Even my bedroom had an old iron bedstead that had been painted snowy white with rosettes on the headboard. It was a twin-sized bed, kind of narrow. I really wanted a double bed like Ripley had in her room. I had always liked sleepovers at her house because we would dive into her bed and huddle under the covers whispering late into the night.

At my house, she had to sleep on an air mattress she had to bring over with her. My father hated fighting that thing to deflate it and then pack it back into its carrier bag when it was time for Ripley to go home, cursing a blue streak in his courtroom voice, making us uneasy and afraid that he would ban any further sleepovers because he really hated that air mattress. So, most of our sleepovers were held at Ripley's house nowadays.

Mrs. Forbes was taking a meatloaf from the oven when I walked into the kitchen. "Hey, honey, dinner's almost ready." She set the loaf pan on the counter and then turned, giving me a long look. "What's the matter with you?" she asked. I shrugged a shoulder. "No tell me. Were the boys down the street teasing the two of you again?" The boys she was referring to were the Nelson twins, fifteen year-old skateboarders with shoulder-length hair who thought they were gods of some sort. I shook my head. "Then what's that face for?" she probed as she lifted the lid of the pot in which she was boiling potatoes, prodding them with a long-tined fork.

"Ashley was telling us a gross ghost story."

"I see. That girl has a very vivid imagination." She set the lid back on the pot, put down the fork, adjusted the gas flame under the pan, and then turned back to me. "What kind of a ghost story was it? Was it related to something her parents let her watch on TV? Some parents have no common sense whatsoever."

I shook my head again, and then looked away. "About Tommy Foster."

"Oh." She went to the refrigerator and took out a stick of real butter and the gallon jug of milk. "Mr. Forbes will be home any minute. I could use some help getting the table set while I mash the potatoes. Can you go and ask Ripley to come inside now? I'm sure you girls want to eat dinner and then go upstairs and put on your costumes. Mrs. Sliwa worked so hard to make them for you. That woman has a gift with that sewing machine of hers! I can't even hem curtains with mine! I'm absolutely hopeless with it!"

That wasn't really true, I thought, as I walked back down the hallway to the front door. Mrs. Forbes sewed clothes for Ripley and she had made a sundress for me a couple of years ago. It had been a little big, but it fit me fine now. "Rip, your mom needs us to set the table. Your dad will be home soon."

"Okay." Ripley jumped up, probably happy to get away from pretty, but morbid, Ashley with her glossy, long, blonde hair. She was going to be a Disney princess again for Halloween. She was always a Disney princess. Ripley and I were going to be alley cats with patched up fur and ragged ears this year. I couldn't wait to see us when we were dressed and made up. Mrs. Forbes was doing our faces and we had cat-eye masks with stiff white plastic whiskers. "We've got to go in and eat. See you 'round the neighborhood, Princess!" she said as she headed to the door I was holding open for her.

"Oh, I'm not a princess this year," Ashley said as she got to her feet. "I'm going to be a dancer like my cousin Heather over at the Renegade Club. Ta, girls!" She dashed down the steps and walkway, leaving us standing there with our mouths hanging open.

"Holy smoke," Ripley muttered as she elbowed me in the ribs while passing me in the doorway.

I closed the inside door as I snapped my mouth shut. I might have been ten-years old, but I knew a little about that club. It was across town, maybe half a mile or so from the former machine shop that R. Hollis Beresford had purchased a number of years ago. He had fixed it up and turned it into his clock making shop. He made beautiful clocks for homes and businesses. His clocks were really nice, and were also very expensive. European royalty special ordered clocks from him for coronations, jubilees, royal engagements and weddings, as gifts to foreign dignitaries, and to celebrate the births of princes and princesses.

Mr. Beresford was the richest man in Pine Haven. He lived in a sprawling brick, stone, and timber mansion at the opposite end of Pine Haven from the shop. His wife had been a Randolph. The mansion had been in her family originally and she'd been allowed the use of it when she'd married Mr. Beresford. But, once he was richer than any of the Randolph's, he'd bought the house from them and then the property next door to it so that he could build her a gorgeous formal garden with a tea house at the center where she could entertain the Garden Club ladies. My mother was a member of the Garden Club. She always put on an expensive dress from the Charming Woman boutique in Stockbridge when she went to high tea at Randolph Hall.

The Beresfords had one son, a boy named Julian Rand Beresford, who preferred to be called J. Rand, or just Rand. He was thirteen and currently in his last year of middle school. I didn't know him, but I had seen him riding his bike around town with his two best friends, Cody Underwood and Austin Peck.

Cody lived at the end of our street. I didn't like him. He was worse than mean to me. Austin lived a few streets away from the Beresfords in a nicer neighborhood full of big, older homes. My mother wanted to live on Juniper Avenue or Rosemont Boulevard, but my father continued to insist that his great-aunt's old Queen Anne Victorian house was good enough for the Rumfords. Well, I liked it well enough anyway, even if it was stuffed full of antiques that I wasn't allowed to touch.

Halloween this year, my last year in elementary school, was fun. We were a perfect pair of stray cats in our costumes—me the tiger cat, Ripley the tuxedo cat with white belly, mittens and socks. Everyone had thought our costumes were great.

We ran into Ashley in her short-shorts, halter top, and knee high boots with heels, her hair pulled up, knotted on top of her head, and dangling behind her back in a long ponytail, her face made up so that she looked way older than ten. Ripley and I quickly looked at one another and shook our heads, both of us wondering how Ashley's mother could let her little girl walk out of the house dressed like that.

We didn't learn until later that Ashley had walked out of the house in a dowdy bathrobe with a shower cap hiding her hair. She'd had bedroom slippers on her feet, her boots and makeup stashed in the bottom of her shopping bag candy sack. She'd dolled herself up at Nicole Miller's house. Nicole's mother worked nights at the convenience store. Her father worked second shift at the mill in Windsor and didn't get home until eleven-thirty most nights, unless he stopped off someplace for a couple of beers with his buddies, then it was closer to two o'clock when he got home. Ashley was supposed to have been supervised by her older sister, Jennifer, but Jennifer had been fifteen years-old that year. At age thirteen, she had started sneaking out of the house to hang out with her girlfriends and some older boys near the pizza shop downtown. No one really watched Ashley anymore, which was apparently how she got away with stuff like this.

Ripley and I saw her talking to a man on the street corner when we turned onto Falcon Lane. Ripley told me he looked like the new gym teacher at the high school, Mr. Gunther. She'd seen his picture in the newspaper. He had moved to Pine Haven from Germany about a year or so ago and applied for the position when Mr. Tucker, the longtime gym teacher, had badly injured his back in a car accident and gone out on permanent disability. Mr. Gunther lived out toward the Renegade Club. He was probably in his early thirties—tall, lean, but strong looking. I'd heard my mother remark that he was a handsome devil, so I kept twisting around to look back at him and Ashley over my shoulder, until I tripped over an uneven section of sidewalk, crashing to my elbows and knees, candy sack spilling across the concrete. "Watch where you're going, not where you've been," Ripley chided me.

And then Mr. Gunther was suddenly there to see if I was all right. When it was determined that I'd only scuffed up the fur over my knees and elbows, he'd helped me pick up my scattered candy and then helped me back onto my feet. "Be careful, ladies. In those cat costumes you might find yourselves being chased by big dogs!" He smiled at us, a wide smile full of white teeth.

"Thank you," I said.

"It's getting late, girls. Finish up your trick-or-treating and then you'd better get yourselves home before your parents start worrying about you."

"There you are!" Sara cried, coming around the corner. "You two are in big trouble for running off on me like that!" she scolded us.

Mr. Gunther laughed and said, "I had my eye on them, Sara."

She turned her head and gave him a look but then, recognizing him, she smiled. "Oh, hi, Mr. Gunther. Sorry if they were bothering you."

"They weren't bothering me. The little tiger took a tumble and spilled her goodies all over the sidewalk. I came over to help her pick them up and to make sure that she hadn't hurt herself. I was just going to help them find the adult they're out with."

Sara drew herself up taller. "That would be me," she said, as if fifteen-year olds were suddenly full blown adults.

"Very good. I return them to your supervision, Miss Forbes. As I was pointing out to the girls, it's getting late."

"Yes, it is. Charlotte's father will be coming to pick her up soon. Thanks again for helping her. See you in gym class!" She gave us both a shove to get us moving. "Bye, Mr. Gunther!"

"Goodbye, Sara."

My last glimpse of him was as I turned up the Vernon's walkway, glancing back toward the corner where he had returned to Ashley, who had been sulking there. I saw him put his hand on her shoulder, saw them begin walking up the street, and then I couldn't see them anymore because I was behind some shrubs. I didn't really care anyway. He was a teacher and he was probably telling her also that it was time to go home.

When, two days later, Ashley was officially reported missing in the newspaper, her most recent school picture smack dab in the center on the front page, I really didn't think much about it. I saw her picture in the paper. I heard my parents talking about how she had disappeared on Halloween night in hushed voices at the far end of the kitchen counter where we ate breakfast, how Ashley's parents weren't fit to raise children, and that she'd probably be taken away from them once she was found.

No one asked if I had seen her on Halloween night, so I didn't feel any need to mention it. She'd been out trick or treating like the rest of us. I'd seen a lot of my classmates on Halloween. I'd seen her talking to a teacher who'd most likely been suggesting to her that she head home. I hadn't seen anything other than that.

In late November, when a deer hunter came across the remains of a young girl in the woods behind the Renegade Club, my parents had burned the newspapers in the fireplace. I was told that my friend was dead, but death to a ten-year old doesn't really mean much. My goldfish had died. My kitten had died. It didn't mean much more to me than that.

On the day of Ashley's funeral, the principal came on the PA system and asked us to bow our heads and think of our friend Ashley who was no longer with us. I didn't know what to think about her, but later, when we were outdoors after lunch, Ripley, all wide-eyed and secretive, pulled me around the corner of the building into the doorway leading to the custodian's room and hotly whispered in my ear that Ashley had been torn to pieces by a feral dog. She'd heard Sara talking about it when she was on the phone with a friend of hers who had heard it from her uncle who was a cop in town. "You can't tell a soul what I just told you," Ripley hissed, glancing around to make sure that she hadn't been overheard.

I'd been bitten by the Hanover's terrier when I was little. It had bitten the back of my calf. I'd had to go to the emergency room to have the bite treated, and Fritzi had had to go to the vet where he'd been quarantined until the Hanover's could retrieve his vet records from where they had moved from, his rabies tag having fallen off his collar at some point during their move to Pine Haven. They'd fenced their yard in, put in a gate, and brought a batch of brownies to our house, apologizing again and again to my parents for their dog having bitten me. At least they hadn't tried to blame me. I'd just been skipping home from Ripley's house when it had come charging off the porch yipping and yapping, jumping on me, and then suddenly biting the back of my leg.

It wasn't until the following year that the horror of a human body being torn to pieces by a feral dog would mean a little more to me. It wasn't until the three boys camping up near Turkey Pond were attacked that Pine Haven began to comprehend that the feral dogs were getting more vicious. But, by then, it was already too late for Ashley and those boys, because even the boy who survived the attack was never the same as he had been prior to that fateful camping trip.

Susan Buffum

Chapter Two

The summer before I started sixth grade at William Blake Middle School was idyllic in many ways. I'd turned eleven-years old at the end of May. The Forbes had thrown me a surprise birthday party. I had been to New York City with my parents for two weeks while my mother had scoured the city for certain antiques that a client was interested in for their summer house in the Adirondacks and my father had gone to court every day, not as an attorney, but as a spectator. One of his old law school buddies was prosecuting a notorious murder case and had invited him to come watch him work.

I'd chosen to follow my mother around from one antique shop to another rather than sitting in a boring old courtroom. But, I really hadn't had a choice anyway, since my father had argued with my mother that the case was not fit for the tender ears of an impressionable pre-teen. My mother had not been happy about having to watch me, so I'd tried to prove to her that I was capable of taking care of myself, that I knew my way around antiques.

And that's how I'd broken the little boudoir clock. It was so pretty that I'd had to pick it up to look more closely at it. It had slipped from my hand when I'd been trying to return it to the table that it had been sitting on. A sign clearly read, *If You Break It You Own It.* The clock had cost close to four hundred dollars. My mother, ever the antiques dealer, had stated flatly and emphatically that the little clock wasn't worth even half that much. They had argued rather vehemently, but she'd won and gotten the cost of the clock lowered to one hundred and fifty dollars, which was basically all the spending money I'd had with me. I'd meekly handed over the crumpled cash and stuffed the broken clock into my canvas shoulder bag, deeply disappointed by my own clumsiness, the clock having been broken, and all my money having been spent on something that was broken.

Outside on the sidewalk my mother had looked at my face and said, "I did a favor for Mr. Beresford once, locating a certain clock that he wanted. Perhaps he can give you a decent price on the repair of the clock, even though it is of far inferior materials than what he normally works with."

"I can use it as a paperweight," I'd glumly replied.

"It won't hurt to see what he has to say."

So, that was how I'd met R. Hollis Beresford in early August. At that time, he had been working at his clock shop that he'd made from the partially renovated old machine shop at the base of Clay Hill out on Clay Hill Road. Mother had taken me to see if she could persuade Mr. Beresford to repair the clock for me since I had mentioned it again to her, that I wished it was working, and she had grown tired of hearing me say that.

We'd entered the shop through the front door and seen no one behind the counter, but we'd heard a man arguing with a younger man whose voice occasionally cracked. They had been somewhere farther back in the building. Mother had flattened her lips at the arguing, walked to the counter, and briskly rung the call bell that was there.

A boy in his early teens with longish, dirty-blonde hair had come up the long corridor to the front of the shop, a sullen expression on his face. He'd ignored my mother, but his eyes had pinned me in place. My eyes had met his. He had eyes that seemed to hold every earthy color in their irises- grays, greens, browns, in several shades, and gold. His eyes had mesmerized me. "What are you staring at, Carrot-top?" he'd grumbled before brushing past us, shoving the door open, and going outside.

Mr. Beresford had then come along the corridor, pulling on a suit jacket, straightening his bow tie. I'd always had this thing for bow ties. I'd thought they were cute so I'd smiled at him, which had caught him off guard, and had seemed to fluster him. "Mrs. Beresford," he'd said, shifting his eyes to my mother and managing a smile.

"Was that Julian? He's grown so tall since I last saw him."

"Yes, he's gone through a growth spurt this summer. Now, what can I do for you, my dear?"

"Charlotte has a broken clock. She fell in love with it when we were antiquing in New York City. Unfortunately, the clock was broken when we arrived home. It fell out of her bag and onto the driveway. She'd tucked it into one of the outside pockets of her duffle bag and it had worked its way half out. When Edward grabbed the bag, it popped out of the pocket, fell, and broke. Charlotte spent her whole savings on the clock and is heartsick over it." Here, two things had happened. The boy named Julian had come back

21

into the shop as my mother had been talking, and his father's eyes, the same color as his son's, had met mine.

"Is that so, young lady? This is an old clock. It should have been carefully wrapped up and protected inside your bag, not stuffed into a side pocket, especially if you spent all your money on it." I'd felt my face grow hot at his admonishment.

Then, the boy had grabbed the clock from his father's hand and shaken it. "This belongs to the kid?" he'd asked, glancing at me sideways. "How much did you pay for this piece of crap, Copper-top?"

Humiliated, and not wanting to compound the situation by bursting into tears, I'd turned and quietly slipped outside, closing the door behind me. Tears spilled down my face once I'd reached the parking lot. I couldn't have stood there and been insulted further once my mother had told them how she'd gotten the price down to a hundred-fifty dollars. That had been a small fortune to me. Maybe to the Beresfords it was only a piece of junk clock, but I'd liked it. I'd thought it was pretty. It had a white enameled metal case painted with violets and ivy. The crystal of the clock was set in a gold-colored bevel. The clock was wound with a brass key that stuck out of the back. There was a piece of old purple satin ribbon tied to the key, somewhat the worse for wear. The numerals were very curly, the hands ornate with delicate filigree. There was a spray of tiny, hand-painted violets in the middle of the clock face where the hands met. The clock had no second hand.

Behind me, the door had opened and the teenaged boy had come outside. He'd thrown down the skateboard that he'd brought out with him and ridden around on it in the parking lot, doing a few tricks. I'd just sat on a log that prevent vehicles from driving into the front of the building, moving bits of crumbled asphalt around with the scuffed toes of my sneakers, keeping my head bent so that he wouldn't see my tears.

Finally, he'd come right at me and jumped off the skateboard, using the tail fin to bring it upright right in front of me, wheels still spinning. It had startled me because I'd thought he'd meant to run me over. I'd leaned back and raised my head, looking up at him. He'd looked down at me. As I'd started to lower my head, he'd said, "If the damn clock means that much to you, then give me two weeks to get a few parts made in the shop. I'll fix it. My father's too busy making a clock for some duchess or whatever. He doesn't have time to fix it. But, I'll do it for you. It'll run like new. You'll see." I hadn't known what to say because he'd sounded so sullen and still angry about something. "What grade are you in, Red? Fourth? Fifth?"

"I'm going into sixth," I'd replied.

"I just finished middle school. I'm starting high school at the end of August." I'd nodded. "What do you like so much about that stupid, old clock anyway?"

"It's pretty," I'd answered.

"It's too girly for my liking. But, for what it's worth, it's French, late eighteen hundreds, hand-painted. There're probably a million tiny parts inside—gears, jewels…all sorts of stuff you probably broke dropping it out of your bag."

I'd shaken my head. "No, I dropped it in the shop and had to buy it because it broke," I found myself saying. "It cost almost four hundred dollars, but my mom argued him down to a hundred and fifty. It didn't fall out of my suitcase or anything." He'd stood there just looking at me. I'd glanced at him and then looked back at the ground. "I hope you can fix it."

"Of course I can fix it. I've been around clocks my whole life. Come back in two weeks to pick it up."

"I don't know if my mom will drive me back here. This is a busy time of year for her. She goes to shows and stuff."

He'd blown his breath out as he'd dropped the skateboard back onto the asphalt and stood on it. "Well, I can drop it off at your house then. Where do you live?" I'd told him my address. "That's easy enough. I can ride my bike over. But, once I fix it, try not to be such a butterfingers. Don't ever drop it again."

"I won't."

He'd done a turn around the parking lot and returned. "Hey, what's your name anyway?"

"Charlotte."

"Charlotte. Jesus, that's a punishment. Too old-fashioned. I'll just call you Cherry, because of your red hair." I'd lifted my head until my eyes had met his again. "For what it's worth? A hundred-fifty for that sweet little clock? You got yourself one hell of a deal, girl. My old man would have paid the four hundred for it."

"But I broke it."

"Doesn't matter. He can fix it. But, so can I. I'll have it running like a charm in two weeks."

"Thank you, Julian."

He'd leapt off his skateboard and strode right up to me, standing over me. "J. Rand. I don't want some little girl calling me Julian. I don't want anyone calling me that. You can call me J. Rand, or just Rand. Don't ever call me Julian again."

"Sorry," I'd whispered.

"You'd better be," he'd muttered as he'd jumped back on his skateboard and pushed off. "But, I'll get over it, this time," he'd called back over his shoulder as my mother had opened the door and come out.

"J. Rand has offered to repair the clock for you," she said, watching the teenager do some tricks near the road.

"Was he bothering you?" she'd asked as I'd stood up and followed her to the SUV.

"No," I'd replied.

"According to his father, he's reached that age where he's disagreeable and wants to be more independent. They were arguing because J. Rand wants to camp up on the hill with a couple of his close friends before school starts. The Beresfords own the hill. It's part of this property, but he doesn't like the idea of three fourteen-year old boys camping alone up there. There isn't much around here except for that wretched roadhouse just up the street." The roadhouse she'd meant was the Renegade Club. "Well, that's for him to deal with. I don't know what J. Rand will ask for the repair work. That will come out of your savings, young lady. I don't have money to waste on fixing broken clocks." Internally, I'd groaned. Now, I'd have to go to the bank with her and get some more of my savings out to pay him with. "We'll just have to wait and see what the bill is when the work is finished."

"He said the clock is worth four hundred dollars," I'd said when she'd gotten behind the wheel.

She'd pursed her lips as she'd started the car, and then she'd nodded. "He knows his clocks. It's a little beauty all right. I just wish you hadn't broken it."

"I didn't mean to."

"You need to learn not to touch things, to be more careful while handling them."

"I'll be more careful from now on."

"It was a costly accident." She'd glanced at me sideways and then totally floored me when she'd said, "I'll pay for the repair work. You've invested quite a bit of your own money into that little clock. I think you've learned a lesson with this little accident. Let's just hope that boy knows what he's doing and doesn't gouge us a small fortune."

25

"I think he likes clocks."

"Well, let's hope so."

Exactly two weeks later I'd been sitting on the front porch picking gravel from my skinned knee when J. Rand had ridden his bike up the walkway and let it drop on the lawn. He'd had a messenger bag, half size, like a rucksack, across his torso, the bag resting against his hip. "Hey, Cherry, what the hell happened to you?"

"I tripped over the hose and fell on the sidewalk."

He'd shaken his head. "That was graceless." I'd looked away. "I have your clock. This should cheer you up." He'd opened the flap on the bag, unzipped it, reached in and pulled out a purple velvet bag with a gold cord drawstring that had tassels on it. "Here, check it out." He'd come farther up the walk and handed it to me.

I'd taken it in both hands, set it on my lap, opened the top of the bag, and looked inside. I'd seen the top of the clock. I had also heard it ticking. Carefully, I'd pulled it out of the bag and examined it, then held it to my ear as if I was listening to a heartbeat. "You did it!" I'd cried, grinning happily at him. "You fixed it! It *is* as good as new!"

"It's better than new," he'd replied.

"Thank you!" I'd set the clock back on my lap, picked up the velvet bag, and held it out to him. "Here."

"No, you keep it. When you need to move the clock or bring it in for service or repair, put it in the bag and it'll be protected."

"It's pretty."

He'd shrugged. "My dad has them made to send clocks to princesses in."

"Real princesses?"

"Yeah. Hey, I've gotta go."

"J. Rand, wait!" I'd cried as he'd headed back to his bike. "How much do I owe you?"

He'd stood his bike up and mounted it. "Nothing. You don't owe me anything."

"But…"

"I needed the practice. See ya around, Cherry!" He'd turned his bike and pedaled off.

I'd hugged the little clock to my still undeveloped breast, feeling quite happy that it was ticking away, keeping time, that it had been saved from the trash bin by an amazing, talented, fourteen-year old boy. It had made me forget all about my abraded knee as I'd stood up, carrying the clock and its special velvet bag inside. To me, J. Rand Beresford had been the hero of the day and I would be forever grateful to him for repairing my beautiful clock.

And then, only a few weeks later, J. Rand and his two best friends, Cody Underwood and Austin Peck, had gone camping and fishing up at Turkey Pond on Clay Hill behind his father's clock shop. They'd hiked up from behind the shop on a trail J. Rand and his friends had cleared, just a narrow path with a few yellow plastic strips tied around saplings to mark it, intending to camp out Friday night and Saturday night, to fish, hike, and swim before meeting Mr. Beresford's driver, Peter Sanborn, at the shop. Sanborn would drive them home at around two o'clock on Sunday afternoon. The boys would be starting high school at the middle of that week.

Only, on Sunday afternoon, when Mr. Sanborn had arrived at the clock shop to pick them up there had been no sign of them. He'd waited nearly an hour, figuring that boys would be boys and they'd been swimming, or had hiked farther than they'd thought they would go, and had lost track of time. He'd tried reaching J. Rand on his cellphone and not gotten an answer. He'd blown the horn several times to try to catch their attention, to let them know that he'd been waiting for them, it had been time to be heading home. But as three o'clock had come and gone, he'd grown somewhat irritated.

At quarter past three, he'd started following the narrow trail, the yellow plastic markers leading him up toward Turkey Pond. It had taken him about twenty minutes to reach the pond, to arrive at the scene of a shocking sight. The boy's camp site had been trampled and trashed. Two of the boys had been there, one still in his torn up sleeping bag, the other one just a few feet away from his own sleeping bag. Both of them had been obviously dead, their throats torn out, their bellies ripped open. Sanborn had been unable to look at either of them for long, just long enough to see that one was a brunette and the other one had pale blonde hair. Neither had been his employer's son.

He'd walked around in a daze, in shock, calling for J. Rand but he had been unable to locate him, or his body. Then he'd been ill and had staggered back down the trail to the parking lot where he'd called Mr. Beresford to report what he had seen, to inform his employer that J. Rand was missing. Mr. Beresford had told him to wait there. He had called the police, and then he'd had his butler drive him out to the clock shop.

Mr. Beresford had insisted on accompanying the police up to the camp site. He'd called for his son repeatedly, but had received no response. He'd been deeply distressed, terribly shaken by the brief sight he'd had of the two dead boys' bodies before the police had steered him away from the crime scene. They'd said something about a pack of feral dogs, how they must have attacked the boys once they'd settled down and fallen asleep. The camp fire was cold. No one had attended to it for a while, although there had been a small pile of branches and sticks nearby that the boys had gathered for fuel. Their backpacks had not been disturbed, even though all three boys had taken plenty of snacks and food to supplement the fish that they'd caught. There had been a five gallon pail with some live fish in it, fish they'd probably intended to bring home with them to share with their families. The police had dumped the fish back into the pond while they'd waited for the crime scene unit to arrive from the state police barracks. The scene had been more than the local police department could handle.

Meanwhile, the police had called in the fire department and put out a call for volunteers who had come up and begun searching for J. Rand. Sanborn, Beresford, and the butler, a man named Adair Druce, had retreated from the bloody, horrific scene to the clock shop where a female officer had stayed with them. Beresford had answered her questions. The boys had planned the trip when they'd gotten the idea for a campout back in June. They'd ridden their bikes out to the shop on weekends and cleared the trail, marked it, and cleared the campsite of ferns and whatever else had been growing up there. They had all been swimming in the pond before, just like hundreds of other teenagers had throughout the years. It had once been a popular high school party spot when the machine shop had been closed and abandoned

When Beresford had purchased the property and renovated the shop to use as his clock making and repair shop, he'd posted No Trespassing signs because he'd also purchased the surrounding property which consisted of a large section of Clay Hill, including Turkey Pond and the land all the way up to Big Pond.

He had not been popular with teenagers for several years. They'd broken windows in the shop and had spray-painted nasty words on the sides of the building. He'd hired a security guard who'd summoned the police whenever teenagers showed up after dark. The police had gone out and given the kids trespass warnings and then taken them home to their parents.

Soon enough, the teenagers had grown tired of that and they'd found another place to party and swim just down the road on the far side of the Renegade Club in an area known as The Swamp. It hadn't really been a swamp, just lower and wetter than the area near Clay Hill, however there had been a pond out there as well—Rifle Pond, called such as it was located on land that had once been owned by a gun club. Several old rifles had been found in the muck at the bottom of the pond when it had been dredged after a girl was thought to have drowned there. However, the girl hadn't drowned. She'd gone off with an older man and had been found almost a month later living in his trailer home in Tylerville when several of her friends had grown uneasy about her text messages. The police had gone to remove her from the trailer since she had only been sixteen years old at the time. The man had been arrested for statutory rape and other charges.

That girl, Virginia Sweet, had been Pine Haven's one and only murder victim back in the seventies. She had been rebellious and wild. She'd dropped out of school and, while still underage, had managed to talk her way into a dancer's job at the Renegade Club. She'd taken over a tiny, abandoned cottage nearby where she'd entertained men. It had been one of those men, someone probably just passing through town, who had strangled her and left her dead, naked body on the saggy old bed.

That was a story that I'd heard, but not until I was older and almost through with high school. The horror story of what had happened up on Clay Hill to Cody, Austin, and J. Rand had been all over Pine Haven and had been unavoidable by the time school had started near the end of that summer. J. Rand had been found up near a cave at Big Pond, deep in shock, deep gouges and bite marks all over him, his face scratched, and there had been something wrong with his eyes. He'd been hospitalized after being treated in the ER and had only said that it had been a wolf that had attacked them. From the size of the tracks found at the scene, the police had had to admit that a wolf or wolves were a possibility, even though no wolves had been sighted in Massachusetts for quite some time. But, there had been no denying the size of the bites on J. Rand, or the fact that something large had pinned the other two healthy fourteen-year olds down on the ground and done that kind of damage to them. There had been no signs of scuffling, no indication that the boys had struggled much or attempted to get away. The beast, or beasts, had done their terrible work quickly and efficiently.

Of course there had been plenty of rumors going around that J. Rand had fled like a coward and left his two best friends to be killed by wolves, even though he himself had suffered serious injuries. Others had pointed out that he must have known there was nothing that he could do to help his friends and had run in an attempt to save his own life. Somehow, he had managed to get away while bleeding heavily from bites and deep scratches. It had been a miracle that he hadn't died of blood loss and shock, that he had been found when he had been or else the town would have lost three fine boys that summer.

However, it hadn't mattered what you'd thought, there had been those who'd insisted that J. Rand was a coward and a lucky rich boy who had been more familiar with the property since his father owned it and he had always been up there hiking around, whereas the other two boys had not been as familiar with the area. But, that actually hadn't been true. Cody had talked to my brother lots of times and described how the three of them were always prowling around the hillside—exploring, building a fort here, a lookout there. They'd been all the way up to the crown of the hill past Big Pond and crowed like jubilant discoverers of a new world when they'd seen the thick woods on the far side of the hill.

All I knew was that that fateful camping trip had stolen the boy who had repaired my clock and left a silent, somber, almost reclusive lookalike in his stead. He'd missed the first three weeks of school and suffered virtual disdain and animosity when he did join his classmates in ninth grade at the high school.

He wouldn't look at anyone, wore darkly tinted glasses all the time, dressed in black jeans and black, long-sleeved t-shirts, black sneakers or boots every day. His hair had grown long and shaggy. Sometimes he'd pull it back in a ponytail, but most times he'd just let it hang like a curtain across his still handsome face. There had been only faint scars along his jaw and down one side of his neck. I had been sure that he had other scars also, and that had been why he always wore long-sleeved shirts and long jeans while everyone else ran around in t-shirts and shorts.

Although he was three years older than me and had never been in my social circle, I hadn't been able to stop thinking about how it might have been better for him if the wolf or wolves had killed him too. He had no friends to speak of. People shunned him. He'd become a loner.

The year I'd started as a freshman, he'd been a senior. I'd see him skulking in the stairwells between classes, standing in a stairwell staring out a window between classes when I was sent to the office or elsewhere to run an errand for a teacher during class time. I'd always said, "Hi, Rand," when passing him, but he'd never answered me, although twice he'd turned his head and looked in my direction, but it was hard to see his eyes through the dark lenses of the glasses he habitually wore, so I really couldn't tell if he had been looking at me, through me, or past me.

About three weeks before the seniors were to graduate, I'd been sent to the nurse with a bloody nose. I had a wad of tissues clutched in my hand in case the bleeding resumed, as it was prone to do when I had these massive nose bleeds. It had slowed to a trickle for the moment.

I'd nearly collided with Rand who had been coming from around behind the back of the staircase. His sudden appearance had startled me. "You're bleeding," he'd said. And then he'd sniffed at the air like a dog and said something that had rattled me thoroughly. "It's not menstrual blood. It's not your time of month. This is fresh blood." And then he'd taken another step closer. "What's wrong with you?" he'd asked, his voice low, terse.

"Bad nose bleed. I get them every now and then."

"Going to the nurse for an ice pack?" I'd nodded. "Better get going then." I'd started to go around him, but he'd suddenly reached out and grabbed my arm just above the elbow, gripping it hard. "Cherry, the clock, it's still running?"

It took me a moment to work through the flash of fear that his grabbing me like that had caused, to work out what he'd asked me. As he'd started to let go of me and turn away I'd figured it out. "Yes. It's been running like clockwork since you fixed it." It had been the stupidest thing to say, but I had been fifteen-years old and hadn't known what to say to a boy who had been so damaged that it had broken my heart anew every time I'd seen him around the school. "I love that clock." I'd had a crush on the fourteen-year old boy who had repaired my clock and not charged me for his work. That had been the only way that I could relay my feelings for him to him, but I'd thought he was too psychologically wrecked to understand what I had really been saying. However, he'd hesitated, his fingertips still touching my sleeve.

He'd kind of poked me in the arm. "Not much meat on your bones," he'd said, and then he'd given me a sort of sardonic smirk. "If I was a dog, I'd bury you someplace and then dig you up to enjoy later on, after you've aged a little more." He'd sort of chuffed a laugh through his nose as he'd shaken his head. "Tap is running again," he'd said, pointing toward my nose. "Get the fuck out of here, Cherry, before I start licking blood off your face."

"Can't you ever stop being so weird, Julian?" I'd flared, calling him by his real first name because I was angry with him. "Maybe people would like you better if you weren't such a psycho!" I'd cried as he'd turned and walked away from me.

"Only you can call me that and live to draw another breath, Charlotte Rumford." He hadn't said it very loudly, but I'd heard him. It had made me catch my breath as I'd neared the nurse's office; when fifteen-year old me had realized that eighteen-year old J. Rand Beresford had just held a brief conversation with me, even one as unsettling and strange as it had been. However, his last remark had to have meant that he liked me, if he was going to allow me to get away with calling him by his first name! I could call him Julian if I wanted to, but I probably wouldn't be doing that ever again.

At least not for ten years as it turned out, because J. Rand Beresford had snatched his diploma from the Principal's hand, leapt off the stage, and had stalked out of the auditorium, the middle finger of his left hand raised as he'd given everyone in the auditorium his long-restrained opinion of the townsfolk and his classmates gathered there. And that had been the last that anyone had seen of him because he'd just seemed to have disappeared from Pine Haven after the double doors at the back of the auditorium had banged shut behind him.

Chapter Three

Within six months of J. Rand's disappearance from Pine Haven, the clockmaker's shop on Clay Hill Road closed. Mr. Beresford moved the business to the mansion on Juniper Avenue and even he was seldom seen in town. My father had told us at dinner one night that J. Rand had argued bitterly with his father about college, stating that he'd been treated like dog dirt since the incident at the camp site and he wasn't going to live anywhere near this place, that he was moving far away.

Evidently, that's what he had done on graduation day. He'd walked out, shedding his cap and gown in the lobby of the high school as if he was a snake shedding its skin. Then he'd gotten into his black pickup truck and driven off, a few bags already with him in the back. He'd driven to Bradley International Airport, checked in his baggage, parked his truck in long term parking, and, a few hours later, gotten on a plane and left the country. Mr. Beresford's business manager, Christian Stroud, and his attorney, Ellard Bean, had managed to determine that the eighteen-year old J. Rand had obtained a passport, had booked a one-way flight to Strasbourg, France, and a suite at a hotel there. However, by the time his father had sent a telegram to the hotel, J. Rand had moved out, had moved on, leaving no forwarding address. He'd also canceled his cellphone. Gradually, his father had accepted that his son was gone, but with that acceptance came an equally gradual decline in his state of health.

By the end of my sophomore year of high school, hardly anyone mentioned J. Rand anymore. Ripley and I remained best of friends, but she had started to date, whereas I hadn't. Boys occasionally asked me to school dances and I sometimes went, but I really wasn't interested in dating then. Charlie was away at college. My parents had drifted even farther apart and were seldom home at the same time. There was always tension in my home, so I began staying after school to help Mrs. Claxton, the school librarian. Sometimes, when I was shelving books, Mr. Gunther would come into the library to check out the games area. He was a gamer, I guess, and the boys talking about the games they were playing online had no problem with the handsome gym teacher joining in their conversations. Mrs. Claxton would give them scowls when they grew boisterous, but they'd just smile and wave at her as if humoring her.

I sometimes saw one or two sophomore or junior boys climbing into Mr. Gunther's SUV. I assumed he was just giving them a lift, maybe to the convenience store down the street where kids usually hung out after school. However, one day, while shelving books, I overheard a couple of these boys talking in low voices about going to Mr. Gunther's house where he let them smoke pot while they played video games, and how he never supervised them very closely if they brought girls there. He'd stay upstairs and chat with other kids in the house, while couples went down into the basement and made out. I was shocked that a teacher would encourage high school kids to smoke pot and have sex in his house.

When I shared what I'd heard with Ripley, she'd looked at me as if I had two heads and thought I was making it all up. But, less than two weeks later, she'd pulled me aside in the girl's bathroom, waiting until the other girls had left before hissing, "You were right. I went with Billy to Mr. Gunther's house and everything that you told me was true!"

"You went there!" I'd cried. "Are you crazy?"

"I didn't do anything. I had a soda and sat outside playing a game on my phone. Mr. Gunther came out and asked me if I wanted to watch a movie or something, but I just shook my head and said that I was waiting for Billy to finish playing a game, that I had to be home for dinner at five o'clock because I had to help my mother with a project after dinner. He'd nodded and then asked me if you were seeing anyone. When I said no, you weren't into dating yet because of stuff going on in your home, he'd nodded again and then walked off with Jillian."

"Oh, my God! His house is nearly as bad as the Renegade Club! And why in the world would he ask you about me? That's downright creepy!"

"Probably because everyone knows we're best friends," she'd replied. "Oh, and I'm willing to bet his house is even worse. It's much worse! I think he's sleeping with Jillian," she'd whispered. "He couldn't keep his hands off her!"

We'd looked at one another but hadn't said anything more because we'd needed to get to our classes.

Although we'd talked about the situation going on out there past the Renegade Club and the once again closed old machine shop, Ripley and I never told anyone about what we had discovered was going on there. Neither one of us felt that it was our place to rat out the charismatic gym teacher. We were certain that, one day soon, his actions would slip the noose around his own neck and he'd end up hanging himself.

Then, toward the end of our junior year, Jillian Poole went missing. Ripley and I huddled in the near darkness in her bed, whispering back and forth half the night. My stomach was upset from the greasy pizza and worry about what might have happened to Jillian. There were so many places around Mr. Gunther's log cabin-style house where a teenaged girl's body could easily disappear and never be found.

Her disappearance hung over the town like a thunderhead. We all walked around, waiting for the lightning bolt to strike like it had when Cody and Austin had been torn apart by what was still believed to be wolves or large feral dogs. But the lightning strike didn't come until a month before my class's graduation the following year. That was when a man out training his hunting dog to retrieve small game and fowl he shot stumbled upon a shallow grave in the woods about a half mile beyond the old machine shop on Clay Hill. It was an area owned by R. Hollis Beresford that had not been posted. Hunters were welcome to hunt there in season. It was a popular location with deer, wild turkey, and pheasant hunters because those species had been plentiful years ago. However, these days there were far fewer deer in those woods. Only last fall hunters had found several torn apart deer carcasses in the woods and, once again, the rumors had run rampant that the wolves had come back. People kept their small children and pets indoors. The police forbade hikers and swimmers from going up Clay Hill to Turkey Pond and Big Pond.

The police had been called by the man with the dog, and they'd excavated the grave, uncovering the bones of a female skeleton. Items of clothing and jewelry found in the grave were gathered and compared to any missing persons reports filed within the past ten years. Of course, in our town, only one person had gone missing. Her mother had been called to the station and had identified Jillian's class ring and a gold necklace that she had been wearing, plus several of the items of clothing, those that had not been too badly decayed in the acidy soil beneath the pine trees where the grave had been dug.

Jillian's funeral overshadowed our graduation, casting a pall over all of us. I sat in my seat in the auditorium, my eyes occasionally falling on Mr. Gunther who was sitting on the stage in a navy blue suit beside Mrs. Claxton, who looked rather prune-faced, her having been seated beside him. It had always been evident that she disapproved of him, so I could understand how being seated next to him must rankle her.

Ripley was going to Amherst College not all that far away in Amherst, Massachusetts. My father had walked out on my mother and me halfway through my senior year. He'd moved to New York City to work in his brother's law office. Mom's ego balloon had deflated with his departure, at least until Sam Drake, an antiques dealer from Maine, had swung by on a buying trip in April and thoroughly charmed her.

Anyway, I was going to the nearby community college, studying to be an administrative assistant. It was nothing like what I had ever imagined I'd be pursuing a degree in, but my life had become a steady barrage of disappointments. Therefore, I was just happy I could say that I was going off to Great Oak Community College, instead of, I'm going to go work as a cashier at one of the outlet stores in Lee.

I worked as a page in the town library during the summer. This was my third summer doing this. One day, Mr. Barowski surprised me by asking if I wanted to lend a hand in the research area. I'd readily agreed, so he'd stolen me away from Miss Davies and put me to work in the research room. My job there was to scan foreign newspapers to discs.

And that was how I came across photographs in a German newspaper of an amazing mechanical clock tower that had been commissioned from a new master clockmaker in the nearby city of Geheimnis. The clock was a technical marvel with a multitude of moving mechanical figures set in realistic tableaus. The clock gave me goosebumps it was so incredible. However, it was the last photograph, the one of a young man with longish hair and an unshaven jaw, wearing a leather jacket over a band-collar shirt that caught my full attention. It was the dark glasses he had on that drew my attention and convinced me that I knew that young man before my eyes had dropped to the caption, written in German, but his name, J.R. Beres, had leapt out at me and made my heart pound. Rand was in Germany! He was a clockmaker like his father. No, not like his father. He wasn't making mantle or table clocks or even case clocks fit for kings and queens. He was fabricating tower clocks for town squares and parks!

Newspaper committed to disc, I was supposed to recycle the print version. I carried it to the paper bin, but couldn't bear to throw away the page with the clock photos and J. Rand's photo. He'd modified his name. He was living in Germany. He was making clocks. Instead of recycling it, I folded that page and tucked it into my bag when I took a break.

That night I started a scrapbook and Googled J.R Beres on the internet. I found pictures of several more amazing mechanical clocks attributed to his skillful craftsmanship, but found very little in regards to the clockmaker himself. What I did find was in German, which wasn't a language I could translate. I printed out pictures of the clocks he'd made, printed out a map of Germany and put a thumbtack in each town or city where one of his clocks was located, those that were shown on the internet anyway. I had no idea how many he had actually made. There were six pictured. He'd been gone just over three years.

That made me wonder how he had become a master clockmaker so quickly. But then I remembered how easily he had crafted the parts to repair my little boudoir clock in his father's shop and realized that his father had been training him all of his life. J. Rand had learned at his father's knee, had diligently studied the intricacies of clock movements. And now he had gone on to pursue his own interests in the field of clock making—mechanical movement clock towers that were like something out of fairytales. I never would have taken him for someone who could create such magical clocks. It was almost as if I needed to keep pinching myself to make sure I was awake and not just dreaming this stuff up. My scrapbook was real enough. The newspaper photograph of J. Rand was real enough. At twenty-one or twenty-two, he didn't look much different than he had during his senior year of high school. He was a genius!

But I couldn't tell anyone about what I'd discovered because, for whatever reason, I felt loyal to him. Friends did not betray one another. I didn't even share my discovery with Ripley when she came home from Amherst at Thanksgiving.

She and I went out for pizza and to catch up. She was dating a boy from Plymouth named Miles Worthy. I thought that was an absurd name, but she liked him, so I didn't say anything to her about the weird name. I had talked to a few guys at Great Oak, but hadn't gone out with anyone yet. I was too busy working part time and going to classes full time. I was still in the research room at the library, where, every time I worked, I scanned the German newspapers, hoping there would be something more about Rand's clock towers, but there never was anything else about his work. It had just been a fluke that I had come across that page that day.

Just after Christmas, the little clock I cherished stopped working. It had an unusually strong effect on me. It was as if I was mourning the loss of a loved one. I missed its comforting, gentle, steady tick-tock on my bedside table. When I was twelve, I'd imagined the tick-tock was Rand's heartbeat. It had helped me to fall asleep when I'd been feeling stressed, especially when my parents were fighting and not speaking to one another. That had always bothered me. Now, Dad was in New York City dating a juvenile court judge named Winona Dyer. Mom was often away from home on buying trips with Sam. They were traveling all over the country. Her longtime close friend, Chase Quinn, was running the antiques store. I helped Chase on weekends, unpacking cartons and crates that Mom was shipping from wherever she and Sam were.

When spring arrived, I summoned up a reserve of courage I hadn't known I possessed and drove over to Juniper Avenue, turning into the long, curved driveway in front of the brick, stone, and timber Beresford mansion. I had the little clock with me in its purple velvet bag with the gold tassels.

I stumbled on the front steps, somehow managing not to drop the clock. With a trembling finger, I pressed the button to ring the bell. It took the man in the black livery and crisp white shirt nearly three minutes to respond to the bell. "If you are soliciting for some local charity, Miss, I can assure you that Mr. Beresford supports many…"

"My clock is broken," I said, cutting through his obviously well-versed speech.

"I beg your pardon?"

"My clock, it's stopped working." I held up the purple velvet bag. He looked at it, frowned, and then looked at me more closely.

"Where did you get that bag?" he asked. Not where had I gotten the clock. He was more interested in the purple bag.

"Um." I hesitated, not sure what to call him. "Mr. Beresford's son repaired my clock for me years ago. He returned it to me in this bag. He told me to put the clock in the bag whenever I transported it anyplace."

"Did he?" He seemed suspicious, and I began to feel as if he thought I'd stolen the bag.

"Mr. Beresford was still out on Clay Hill Road when my mother brought me to the shop to see if he could repair the clock. He was too busy, so Julian..." and here he stiffened and puckered his mouth as if he had just bitten into a lemon, "I mean, J. Rand, offered to repair the clock for me. And he did. He had to make some of the parts that he needed, but he got it working again. He delivered it to me at my house in this bag."

"I see. Well, Miss, Mr. Beresford is not in the habit of repairing household clocks."

"No, it's not an ordinary clock. J. Rand told me it was worth about four hundred dollars, that it was French, late eighteen hundreds. Here, look." I carefully opened the top of the bag and lowered it enough to reveal the top of the clock. "See?"

"Yes, I see, but it's not something Mr. Beresford would be interested in looking at."

"Please? Can't he just take a quick look at it? I love this clock. It's been on my bedside table since I was eleven years old. I'm going to be nineteen soon, in May. Maybe it just needs to be cleaned? If that's all it is, couldn't he just tell me how to safely clean it so I don't break it?"

"I'm sorry, Miss, but Mr. Beresford..."

"Druce," said a quiet male voice from somewhere behind the man. "Let Miss Rumford in. I will see her in my study."

"Yes, sir." He gave me the cold fish eye, but stepped back to allow me room to enter the vestibule between the front door and the door into the reception hall beyond. "This way, Miss."

I could tell that he was not at all happy with my intrusion on Mr. Beresford's privacy, but that Mr. Beresford had known who I was had surprised me and given me a little boost of confidence. He probably remembered me because of my mother being in the antiques business. Or, maybe, he just remembered me because of my red hair. There weren't many redheads in town and my hair was the richest red. When J. Rand had called me Carrot-top, he'd been wrong. My hair wasn't orange at all. When he'd said he'd call me Cherry, he had been more accurate.

"Come in, Miss Rumford. Please place the bag that you're carrying on my blotter and then have a seat here before the desk." Mr. Beresford was sitting behind a massive mahogany desk. I crossed the thick oriental carpet, leaned over, and placed the purple bag dead center on his pristine blotter. Then I sat down in one of the two leather chairs before the desk. "Druce, would you bring us some tea. You do drink tea, don't you, Miss Rumford?"

"Yes, sir. I do." He nodded and the penguin man departed, heels clacking on the polished wood floor of the hallway.

Mr. Beresford opened the bag and carefully removed the little clock, holding it in his hands. He examined it, listened to its sad silence, and then set it down on the blotter, moving the bag out of the way. From his deep burgundy-colored, satin smoking jacket pockets he removed a small case and a jeweler's loupe. He opened the case, revealing an array of tiny implements. With one of those delicate tools, he opened the back of the clock case to expose the clockworks within.

Murmuring softly to himself, he opened one of the desk drawers, taking out a padded board that he laid on the blotter, moving the clock so that it lay face down on the pellet-filled cushion; was nestled in it. "This keeps the clock from being scuffed and also holds it in place without damaging it," he said aloud.

"That's clever." His eyes rose briefly to meet mine before he returned his attention to the clockworks.

"My son designed it." He proceeded to gently probe the interior of the clock with a thin pick-like implement. "I can see which parts J. Rand fabricated. The brass and steel bits are still new looking." He poked and prodded a bit more, then took out a pair of tiny tweezers and removed a sliver of metal, laying it carefully on the blotter. "This fragment of broken gear was the culprit, Miss Rumford. Rand's keen eyes missed it when he was cleaning out the broken bits prior to installing the newly fabricated gears. If he was here, I would chastise him for such sloppy work." A small sigh seemed to slip from between his lips as he used a tiny bellows to puff air into the clockworks. A little bit of dust came out of the clock interior in a wispy trail. "He never cleaned it properly either, lazy boy."

"He's not lazy anymore," I said before I could stop myself. His head came up and his eyes, so much like his son's, met mine. He just stared long and hard at me for several moments before he returned his attention to replacing the back panel of the clock.

"This should run well for you for the next twenty-five years or more. Bring it back every few years and I will clean and lubricate it for you." He gently wound the key and then set the clock down on the blotter facing me. His eyes fell on me again, noting the delighted smile that lit my face when I heard the sweet tick-tocking of my little clock once more.

"Thank you so much for taking the time to see me, and to look at the clock. I truly do appreciate it, Mr. Beresford. It was very kind of you."

Before he could respond, the man named Druce returned, bearing a tray on which was a china tea service. Mr. Beresford replaced the cushioned board in the desk drawer, put away his tools and loupe, and moved the clock forward towards me so that Druce could set the tray on the blotter. "Shall I pour, sir?"

"I can manage, thank you, Druce. Please close the door on your way out. I will ring when Miss Rumford is ready to be shown to the door. I would like to have a chat with her, since she's here."

"Very good, sir." He made a slight bow and turned to leave. Again, I didn't fail to catch the imperious and disdainful look he gave me down the slope of his nose. He clearly was not pleased that I had invaded their privacy. The door clicked quietly closed behind me.

"I no longer entertain, Miss Rumford. It's a rare occasion when we have a guest drop by. I thought I would be spending a quiet afternoon playing solitaire before dinner, however, I can't say that I am displeased to see you. How is your mother?"

"Oh, she's running around the country antique hunting with a man named Sam Drake. My father moved to New York. Although they aren't divorced yet, they're both with someone else."

"That must be rather awkward for you." I nodded. "So, what are you up to these days? You must have graduated from high school by now."

"Yes. I'm taking Administrative Assistant classes at Great Oak Community College. I'm also working in the research room at the library here in town. I still help Chase in the shop on weekends." He nodded again as he finished pouring tea into two cups. "One sugar and a little milk please." He fixed my tea and then passed the cup and saucer across the desk to me. "Thank you."

"English breakfast tea. I never cared for bergamot. Earl Gray was my late wife's favorite tea, but I can honestly say that I do not miss the odor of it in this house." He saw my expression and a sly smile curved the left corner of his mouth. It reminded me of that sardonic little smirk J. Rand had given me in high school years ago. "However, I do miss my wife. Grace was the joy of my life. Besides clocks, that is."

"She was beautiful. My mother always enjoyed the high teas she hosted in the formal garden here." I sipped my tea.

He was quiet for several long moments as he gazed toward the window, and then he suddenly began to speak. "My son was close to me. Oh, I know you heard us arguing the day that you and your mother brought this little clock into the shop and asked me to repair it. I was busy. And I was angry with Julian. Teenage hormones had kicked in. He was testing new boundaries that we were in the process of establishing. He wanted more independence than I was willing to allow him.

"However, I gave in to his persistence and allowed the venture to take place. I will regret my acquiescing to his insistence that he was old enough to go up there camping with his friends to the day I die. I lost my son that weekend. I got him back physically, but he was not the same boy. He had witnessed something truly horrifying. He had been attacked and looked death in the face. It changed him." He shook his head, lifted his cup in both hands, and sipped. I noticed that his hands shook as he set it back into the saucer, the china chattering due to his tremor. "When he came home from the hospital, he had terrible nightmares. He would scream in mortal fear. The doctor gave him sedatives to help him sleep. Sometimes they worked, but often they did not.

He would wake screaming and then be unable to fall back to sleep. He would pace the house like an anxious animal.

"It was his decision to move into the unused west wing. We hired a contractor to come in and soundproof the walls between the west wing and the main house. A new door was made, very solid. Julian locked it from his side. I allowed him his eccentricities. He was psychologically and emotionally damaged by his ordeal. It did not help that so many people in this town felt that he should have died that night like his friends had. I felt great pity for my son, great remorse for my not having done more to help him when he was so lost after the whole business.

"I attended graduation. It did not surprise me that he left as soon as he had his diploma in hand. It did stun and shock me how he rather dramatically made his exit from the auditorium. I found his diploma on the hood of the car. He'd thrown it there before leaving." He leaned back in his chair. "We tracked him to Strasbourg, France, but from there, he seemed to have done a disappearing act." His eyes traveled slowly around the room before coming back to settle on my face. "A little while ago, what did you mean when you said he was no longer lazy?" He saw me hesitate. "He's my son, Miss Rumford. He's still young. I worry about him constantly. I'm fearful of his mental status. I worry about him begging on the streets, cold and starving. I want to talk to him again. I need to see him. I want to do something to help him.

"There were so many things I could have done, but I was still reeling from the loss of my wife. I am ashamed that I neglected to do my best for him. If you have any information in regards to my boy, I would beg you, Miss Rumford, to share this information with me. I am not a well man. I would like to reconcile the differences between us before I leave this world. If you have any knowledge of my son, please share it with me."

"I have to go home," I said, setting my cup and saucer down on the desktop as I stood up. "May I go?" The crestfallen look on his face tugged at my heart. "I have to get something that I want to show you. I'll be back in less than half an hour. Can I go?"

"Very well. Yes, you may go. But, please, Miss Rumford, will you join me for dinner this evening? We dine at five o'clock, earlier than most people."

"I would like that, Mr. Beresford. Thank you for asking me. I'll be back by four o'clock, if that's all right with you?"

He agreed and summoned Druce, informing the man that I would be returning, and asking him to inform Helen that there would be a guest for dinner.

I'd been shown to the door, but as I stepped outside, Druce grasped my arm and stopped me. I turned my head and looked back at him. "I don't know what sort of a game you're playing at, young lady..."

"I'm not playing any game," I snapped. "Mr. Beresford wants to know where J. Rand is. I have a clue I can share with him."

He seemed surprised by what I'd said, that I might have information about J. Rand. "He has health issues," he warned me.

"I mean him no harm. I have only a little bit of information that I can share with him. What he does with it is for him to decide."

He was obviously displeased with me, but allowed me to go.

Susan Buffum

Chapter Four

I wore a dress to dinner at Randolph Hall that afternoon and I carried the scrapbook with me. I'd found a few more clocks that J.R. Beres had made—one in Switzerland, one in France, and the third in Brussels. However, the majority of the pages were still blank.

I again met with Mr. Beresford in his study where my little clock was still sitting on his desk, my having forgotten to take it home with me. It was back in its purple bag. The scrapbook had been placed on the blotter, but he had not opened it yet. Instead, he talked to me at length about clock making. He still had a burning passion for his craft.

He told me how he had learned clock making from his father and grandfather. It was a family trade continued down through generations. He had begun teaching J. Rand about clock making when he was just a little boy, about three years old. He had given him some old clocks to take apart and attempt to reassemble again. Gradually, the small boy had learned how to assemble what he had dismantled. He was obviously proud of the fact that J. Rand had proven himself to be as gifted and talented with clock making as his ancestors.

At five o'clock, he postponed the remainder of his story until after dinner. He offered me his arm and escorted me to the dining room. He was sitting at the head of the table, but he held the chair to his left out for me. "My wife always sat to my right, my son to my left. You may sit in his seat this evening. I'm not ready to see anyone else in Grace's chair yet."

"I understand. This seat is fine."

For an unexpected guest, I was served a five course meal that included a fruit cup followed by a palate cleansing sherbet. There was soup next, a consommé, I guess you'd call it. It was light and delicious. Next, there was a small, tossed garden salad with a light vinaigrette dressing. Then we were served a piece of flaky white fish that was very tasty. The fifth course was the meat and potatoes with vegetables, in this case roast chicken, mashed red potatoes with creamy butter, and bright green, tiny peas, tender and sweet. There was also cranberry sauce, which I was happy to see. We had coffee after the meal.

Then, Druce carried in parfaits—vanilla ice cream with layers of strawberry sauce, finely diced pineapple, and chocolate sauce drizzle over all, a few fresh raspberries nestled in the thick, real whipped cream on top. We had more coffee and then adjourned to the study, where he once again sat behind his desk and I sat in the chair across the desk from him.

This time, he put his hand on the cover of the scrapbook, but he hesitated before opening it. I could see that this was causing a stir of emotions deep within him. "I can leave the room, if you'd like," I said quietly.

"No. Please stay." He resolutely opened the cover and looked at the array of photographs on the first page. All of the images were of the exquisite, magical, mechanical clock tower that J. Rand had built for the town in Germany. Mr. Beresford studied the pictures, taking out a large handheld magnifying glass to more closely examine the images. He nodded and then leaned back in his chair. "I am disappointed that he did not follow in my footsteps," he said.

"He's the next generation. Maybe he has his own path to follow."

"Perhaps. I hope it's that and not a rebellion against all that he should be."

"I don't think he's rebelling. He's expressing his heart and soul in his work. Turn the page."

His eyes met mine before he turned the page to reveal the picture of Julian Rand Beresford, identified underneath it as J.R. Beres. His eyes grew moist. He had to draw a handkerchief from his breast pocket to dab at his watering eyes. It was obvious to me that he truly did love his son and that he missed him. This house was huge. I thought it must feel so empty to him, more so with his not knowing where his son was, or even if he was still alive. He lightly ran his finger over his son's image as if he searching for a physical connection via the static image. It made my heart ache.

Slowly, he turned to the next page, closely examining the four clock towers pictured there. They were each remarkable and intriguing works of art. I watched as his fingers traced these images, and then he was dabbing at his eyes again. "I thank you for giving me this glimpse of Julian. I am grateful to know that he is still alive, that he has made something of himself. A young master clockmaker. I am proud of him, although I am not a fan of clock towers and street clocks. I much prefer the kind of clock that you brought to me this afternoon to clean and restart."

S usan Buffum

"I like your kind of clocks, but his kind are pretty amazing, too."

"You are a born diplomat, Miss Rumford, not choosing sides between father and son, but rather being judicious to both."

"He's apparently still in Germany. Maybe you can track him down now, although when I did an internet search on J.R. Beres I honestly didn't find much there."

"I have the means to send a man to Germany to track him down. I would very much like to see him again." He turned the page back to the photograph of J. Rand and studied it. "Can you make a copy of this picture for me?"

"Yes, I can do that."

"Make several. I'll have to give a current picture to the man I hire to look for him in Europe. Meanwhile, having this more recent image of him will help me sleep better nights, with less worry in regards to his well-being."

He then turned the conversation to me, asking me what I planned on doing after college. I had no plans other than to find a job earning enough so I could afford a small apartment. I had the feeling my parents were anxious to sell the house and move on with their separate lives. I was in their way living at home, even though neither one had said as much. Not yet, anyway. He'd nodded, telling me that my parents had placed me in a difficult position, but he was certain that someone would hire me because I was bright, energetic, and efficient.

I went home that evening feeling a little bit better having brightened his life some by letting him know his son was still alive and was making something of himself wherever he currently lived. I set my clock on the bedside table and then went to get ready for bed.

Lying there in the dark, the steady, quiet tick-tocking of the clock soothed the underlying anxiety that ran like a dark river beneath the surface of my life. My brother Charles had been given all the advantages of being the first born and a son, the heir. He was going to be an attorney, like Dad, and was in a steady relationship with Melissa Peck, the late Austin Peck's sister. The Pecks had money, although not as much as the Beresfords had. It didn't matter though because Charles was going to be fine.

I was the one who had been handed the short stick in life, my family having fractured and me having to scramble to revise my plans, forgetting about a four-year college, having to choose something less for the time being, and always having to worry about making my way in the world. I was, basically, already living alone, since my mother was seldom home.

With a weary sigh, I closed my eyes, unaware then that the day to follow would bring fresh terror into all of our lives.

As it was Saturday, I got up early, made myself some scrambled eggs and cinnamon raisin toast, had a cup of tea, then grabbed my bag and ran out the door. I was driving my mother's SUV since she wasn't in need of it. Therefore, I got to the The Remains of Yesterday promptly at seven-thirty. I had picked up a cup of French vanilla coffee at the Big Dipper for Chase, who was always running late on Saturday morning, so I had that in my hand as I approached the rear entrance to the store from the municipal parking lot behind it. Chase's Toyota sedan was in her usual parking space.

I knew from talking to Chase on Thursday afternoon that Mom had shipped a ton of stuff for us to unpack, price according to her directions, which were usually handwritten and tucked inside an envelope included in each carton or sent via email, and then put out in the store. We'd most likely be rearranging things to make room for the new stuff today as well. We had a busy day ahead of us.

55

I let myself into the receiving area and saw that we had indeed received a bunch of cartons. The smaller cartons were stacked up on the long, sturdy table underneath the back window, the larger ones along the opposite wall. Chase had already opened several of them and begun unpacking them, probably yesterday afternoon. "Hey! Good morning!" I called as I set her coffee down on the edge of the table. "I'm here!"

I heard a scuffling sound out front and then a weird sound, like a wet snort. I thought that maybe she'd come down with a cold. Some sort of virus was going around at the college. I'd been lucky so far not to have caught it. "I have your coffee! Let's see what treasures Mom's discovered in her travels."

When I heard nothing but the soft creaking of the floorboards from out front, I started toward the curtained doorway that separated the work area in the back from the store front. I grabbed the coffee, intending to bring it to her, figuring that she was working up front for now.

Pulling the curtain aside, the first thing I noticed was that there were items lying on the floor in the main aisle. We sometimes moved inventory around while cleaning or changed displays, so that wasn't unusual. However, we were usually more careful about it and kept things out of the center of the aisles. These things looked like they'd been swept off the shelves and tables. "Chase?"

I took about six steps further into the shop, but a soft snarl followed by a low growl froze me in place. Chase owned a German Shepard. Sometimes she brought Ranger to the shop, but he normally stayed in the back even though he was friendly. He was never allowed up front because he was apt to accidentally knock something over. He just didn't understand about pricey antiques. Also, some people were afraid of dogs. "Ranger?" I queried. And then I saw a shadow move from the corner of my eye. It came rushing

56

toward me. The impression I got was of a tall figure in a fur coat and a wolf mask before I was literally picked up, spun around, and thrown halfway down the main aisle.

I landed with a sickening crunch on my bent left arm amid a number of things that my flailing arms had knocked off the shelves before I'd hit the floor. I had also struck my head on the corner of a shelf and seen stars, but I landed where I could see the curtained doorway.

What I saw rip the curtain off the rod and hurl it to the floor as it made a rapid exit through the rear entrance, leaving the door wide open in its wake, was the stuff of nightmares. To my dazed eyes, it had looked like a tall, lean wolf walking upright. It'd had a tail. It'd had the shape of a wolf from head to foot, but I didn't know how that could even be possible. Feral dogs, wild animals did not walk upright. They did not grab people, pick them right up off their feet, and hurl them like rag dolls twenty feet down a shop aisle as if they were pitching a baseball across home plate.

I don't know how long I lay there trying to clear my head, fighting the waves of nausea that the sharp pain in my arm and head were causing, but I finally made myself move, made myself take inventory of the rest of my body. I knew I'd have bruises from the hard landing, but my legs were all right, shaky but they moved. No broken bones. My left hip was sore.

I was doing all right getting myself up, until I saw my arm. My breakfast rose like debris filled floodwater up the back of my throat in its rush to get out of me. I leaned over and managed not to vomit on myself, but a few things that had tumbled from the shelves got hit. I groaned.

It took me another few minutes to get myself up onto my feet. There was a cordless phone on the counter at the left front side of the store. I headed there, stumbling as if drunk, dizzy from striking my head.

As I came around the end of the aisle, I saw Chase and totally lost it. No one should have to see what I saw by the pale rays of the morning sun streaming through the front window. There was blood and gore everywhere around her. She had literally been torn open, her clothes shredded.

Thankfully, I had my keys in my pocket. I dropped them four times trying to find the key to unlock the front door. I could only use one hand and it was shaking like crazy. There was no way I was going to leave by the back door the beast that had done this to her had departed by. Finally, I jammed the correct key into the lock and twisted it.

I stumbled out onto the sidewalk. It was still early for this town, but I saw the town SUV cruiser parked down the road in front of Casey's Coffee Shop and I just screamed. I couldn't move any further. Every movement jarred my arm. All I could do was stand there and scream for help. Within a minute, Officer Mike Emery was running up the sidewalk toward me.

He made me sit down on the bench in front of the shop and then radioed his dispatcher to send an ambulance and a back-up unit. I was hysterical and my nose had started to bleed. My arm was killing me and I couldn't look at the bone jutting through my shirt sleeve. I would totally lose it if I looked again. I didn't want to be screaming and vomiting in front of Mike Emery, although I couldn't stop keening and shaking.

He stepped into the store to see what had gotten me into such a state, and how I might have gotten hurt, took one look and came stumbling back out through the door, staggering to the curb and vomiting in the gutter. The fire department ambulance had arrived a moment ago and I could hear the siren of another vehicle rapidly approaching, whether it was police or fire, I didn't know.

Officer Emery was ashen pale and perspiring as he spoke quietly to the male paramedic at the curb. The female paramedic came over to me, looked at the damage to my arm and then hurried back to the ambulance to open the rear doors. "Frank! Let's get her on the cot. We'll be transporting her. She's going to need the orthopedic doc and be given something stronger than we can give her for pain. We need to have her lie down. She's in shock."

Frank glanced over his shoulder at me and then jumped to grab the cot from the back of the box van. Together, they moved me from the bench to the cot that they'd rolled onto the sidewalk. Meanwhile, customers from Casey's had begun to wander over to see what was happening at The Remains of Yesterday. Officer Emery had pulled the door shut and was standing in the entranceway not letting anyone past him. No one needed to see the remains of Chase. Her body was the stuff that nightmares were born of.

The female paramedic, whose name was Becky, started an IV in the back of my right hand and hung the bag of saline solution from a slender steel pole attached to the back of the cot behind my head. They used gauze roller bandage to stabilize my arm so it wouldn't get jostled too much during the ride to the hospital. They jammed pillows covered with absorbent pads around my whole left side while I held a cold pack wrapped in a disposable towel to my face to try to control the bleeding from my nose.

The Chief of Police arrived in his private vehicle, glanced at me, a look of concern mixed with curiosity on his face as he gave me a nod before going to talk to Officer Emery. They spoke in low voices, and then stepped into the store. I heard the Chief's shocked cry of, "What the fuck!" as another officer in street clothes arrived, his badge clipped to the waistband of his faded jeans. He went up to the partially open door, stuck his head in, turned white and came out to sit on the bench, his head down between his knees.

"Were you in there?" he asked me when the near fainting spell had passed. I nodded once. "You're Patricia's girl, aren't you?" I nodded again. "She's not in there, too, is she?"

"Kenny, for Chris'sake! She's in shock. Her arm bone is sticking out through her shirt! What the hell is wrong with you?" demanded the female paramedic.

"I know her mom, and her father. My wife drags me down here all the time to find stuff for the house. You remember me, Charlotte? You were classmates with my daughter Olivia." Olivia, the unhappy girl who cut herself.

"Mr. Cusson," I said from behind the cold pack. My lips felt numb so I eased it a ways back from my face. The bleeding seemed to be under control for now.

"That's right." He swept his broad hand across his damp brow and then ran his fingers up through his short dark hair. "Did you have a fall?" he asked me. I shook my head, not sure I was even able to begin to relate what had happened to me inside the store without getting wildly hysterical again. I was still shaking uncontrollably, but the keening had slowed to hiccups and occasional moans as any movement sent a jolt of searing, white hot pain through my entire body, and the bump on my head now felt as if someone was trying to push a screwdriver through my skull.

The Chief came out and looked at me again, then at Frank. "She needs to get to the hospital. I've called the ME. He's on his way over. Cusson, I want you to go with her to the hospital. Stick close to her. As soon as things are under some sort of control here, I'll swing over. I'm going to try to reach Patty and let her know what's happened here. The Staties are also on the way with a dog to try to track the son of a bitch…" And here a wild sort of laugh erupted out of me as an image of the great gray wolf standing upright flashed through my mind. "…who did this." He was looking at me again, but now tears were spilling down my cheeks and I was shaking my head, even though that only made it hurt worse.

"It was a big...." I began to say, but my tongue didn't want to proceed any further because my brain was already pointing out to me how ridiculous it would sound, how wrong it would sound. But I made my mouth form the word and pushed it past my lips anyway. I needed to tell someone. I needed to let someone know what it was that I'd seen, what it had been that had lifted all one hundred ten pounds of Charlotte Rumford and hurled her like a ragdoll halfway down the length of the store. "...wolf."

I saw the Chief exchange another look with Frank, and then he came over and crouched down beside the cot. "Honey, you know that's not possible. How would a wolf get into the store? Were either of the doors open when you got here?" I shook my head. "Did you have to unlock the door?" I tried to think. Yes, I'd had to unlock the back door because the store didn't open until eight o'clock. Chase was alone inside.

"The doors were locked. Both doors."

"Was it a large man, perhaps?"

"No. It wasn't a man. It was a beast!"

He very gently touched the hand that had the IV in it, just lightly stroking my fingers. "I'll come and talk to you later at the hospital, all right?" I agreed. "I'm going to call your mother. Is she at home?"

"No, she's..." I wasn't exactly sure where she was. She and Sam were heading westward, but I'd lost track of their exact location. Maybe she had sent me a text message. "My phone's in my bag. I left it in the back room when I came in. I had Chase's coffee..." I had no idea where the coffee had landed. It suddenly seemed overwhelming to me; the bloody mess at the front of the store, the broken objects, the blood where I had landed, the spilled coffee dripping God only knew where. I squeezed my eyes shut. "My keys are in the lock. Can you lock the shop when the police are through? My house key is on the ring, and Mom's car key. I'll need those. And, can you turn off the lights? Can you…"

"Sweetheart, we'll take care of everything. I'll bring you your bag, phone, and your keys when I come to see you in a little bit. You just worry about you and nothing else right now, okay?" I nodded once at his fatherly tone, the ever obedient daughter. "All right, folks, back up and let them get Charlotte over to the hospital now!" he said loudly as he stood up, surveying the small crowd that had gathered on the sidewalk. "Move back!"

I was soon in the back of the ambulance and then we were moving rapidly down Main Street. The last thought that ran through my mind was that I hoped Mrs. Brown's husky wasn't running loose again. He liked to dash back and forth across Main Street visiting all the shop owners. We all kept dog biscuits and treats under the counter for Sparky with his one pale blue eye and one warm brown eye. I blinked…

…and woke up feeling groggy and nauseous in a room with a bright light shining down in my face. I thought I might have died because the glare was terrible and all I could sense was cool air, a shadowy person moving around behind me and just on the edge of my peripheral vision. I could hear voices but they were at a distance. "Where…."

"Welcome back. Doctor gave you something to keep you unconscious while he examined your arm. It was just a light sedative. He said to just let you rest and you'd come out of it quickly enough. How do you feel?"

"A little sick."

"Like you might throw up?" I nodded. "I'm going to raise the head of the bed a little so you won't choke and give you a little basin. This might jar you a bit, but Doctor also gave you some morphine, which may also be making you feel queasy. Your arm shouldn't be anywhere near as painful now." She lifted the head of the bed, tucking a stainless steel crescent-shaped basin in the crook of my right arm. "What we're waiting for is your mother to sign and fax back some forms giving the doctor permission to operate on your arm. She has to get to the hotel where he'd faxed the forms to first." She glanced at the clock. "They should be coming back to us shortly. So, you're going to stay here with me until everything is in order and they're ready to take you up to surgery. Doctor Maroni is the orthopedic surgeon who'll be working on your arm. Dr. Gail Sawyer will be assisting him. She's also very good. Doctor Young sent her some pictures of the arm and she said she'd be here in an hour. She's here and upstairs with Dr. Maroni now. They're planning their strategy so everything will go like clockwork when they get you into the surgical suite."

Clockwork. Everything like clockwork.

Susan Buffum

Chapter Five

I had just finished my breakfast of lumpy gray oatmeal, hard, too bright a shade of yellow, eggs, a sausage patty that I'd had to stab with the fork and eat like sausage on a stick because I couldn't cut it, lukewarm orange juice, and watery coffee, when Chief Mitchell Adams came into the room. He was in street clothes, but had his badge attached to his belt. "Good morning, Charlotte. How are you doing?"

"I would kill for a huge sugary donut from the Big Dipper," I said before realizing what I was saying. I flushed, embarrassed and a little horrified that I'd used a phrase like that when Chase had just been murdered.

He only smiled and shook his head. "Next time I come over, I'll smuggle one in for you." He drew a chair up beside the bed and sat down. "I'd like to have a little chat with you this morning, if you don't mind?" I shook my head. The nurse had told me that someone from the police department would be coming to see me this morning. They needed to obtain my statement.

He took out a pocket notebook and a pen before settling back in the chair, just holding the items as he looked around the room. "Not especially five star accommodations," he commented. "But, you do get room service." I smiled. He smiled back at me. "Such as it is." I nodded. "I spoke to your mother this morning. She's managed to get a ticket for a flight that should be arriving this evening. Her friend is dropping her off at the airport and then driving himself back to be with her. I wasn't able to reach your father. He's apparently in Europe someplace with his girlfriend." I rolled my eyes, grimacing. "Exactly," he said, and then he opened his notebook and clicked his pen. "So, you were going to work as usual on Saturday morning?"

"Yes."

"The same time as always?"

"Yes. Chase is usually there a little earlier than I am. I always stop and get her a coffee or iced tea on my way in. She keeps a bag of biscotti in the breakroom downstairs. That's her usual breakfast every day. There's a coffeemaker down there, too. She uses that during the week, but likes something special on Saturdays when I work. I was bringing her a large French vanilla."

"That's nice of you. It's good to have, you know, nice things you do for one another." I nodded. "So, you parked out back in the municipal lot. You grabbed your bag and the coffee and walked through the lot to the back door. Tell me what you did from there."

"I shifted the cup to my left hand so I could use my right hand to unlock the back door with the key on my ring. I opened the door and stepped inside. Then I closed the door and made sure it was still locked so no one would come in when the store wasn't open yet. I put my bag down. I saw that Chase had been opening cartons of stuff Mom had shipped to the store. It looked like we had a lot of stuff to unpack, price, and find room for out front. I was thinking we were going to have a busy day."

"Did you call out to Chase?"

"Yes, just to tell her that I had her coffee, but I figured she'd know it was me anyway. The curtain was drawn across the doorway as usual. We never tuck it aside or push it aside. It's just the way it is. I thought she was up front dusting or shifting things around to make room for something she'd unpacked and wanted to put out right away for the Saturday shoppers.

"I took her cup and walked to the curtain, moved it aside, and entered the shop. She had just the one bank of lights on down the right side aisle. I started to walk forward and heard something, a sound I didn't recognize."

"What kind of sound was it?"

"Um, a snort. Like someone with a bad cold sniffing, maybe?"

"Okay, then what?"

"I called to her and she didn't answer. I took a few more steps forward, and then something huge picked me up and literally hurled me down the main aisle. I landed hard. I still had the cup in my hand, or thought I did, so my left arm got bent. I think I hit my head on a shelf when I fell. I saw stars."

"Did you lose consciousness?"

"No, I don't think so. I saw bright flashing lights, but my vision began clearing up right away. I heard a growl and raised my head. That's when I saw that...thing. It was big. Huge. Tall and lean. It had gray fur and a long muzzle like a dog, and eyes that were....I don't know how to describe them! They were golden brown. The pupils weren't round. They were more oval, you know, like lizard eyes can be sometimes?"

"You saw all that? How close was this creature from where you were lying on the floor?"

"It was back near the curtain. It looked over its shoulder at me before it tore the curtain down and went into the back room. It used its paw to open the door and then it left. It was kind of shadowy, but I know what I saw."

"I'm sure you know what you thought you saw. Could it have been a man or a young man in a costume, perhaps? We have a lot of cos-play teenagers and young men in town. Could it have been someone in a wolf or wolf-like costume? Maybe a werewolf mask?"

"If it was that, then it was the most frighteningly realistic costume and mask that I've ever seen."

"Some of these kids really get into it. They spend all their money on very detailed, elaborate costumes. I know this because we've responded to some parties that have gotten out of control now and again. Think carefully about what you saw, Charlotte. Could it have been a man in a costume?"

I thought, summoning the terrible, terrifying image into memory. It made me start shaking. But, I looked at it. I examined it in my memory and saw that the leg joints were definitely not human. No human being could bend their legs into that shape. And the torso was long and lean. The fur was too real. The eyes, they were larger than human eyes and they moved. They were expressive and evil. "No!" I cried. "No! It was some kind of a huge wolf or something, not a person! There was no way it could have been a person! And didn't you see with your own eyes what it did to Chase? It tore her throat out! It shredded her clothes and tore her open and…"

"Charlotte!" he said sharply, drawing me up short. "I saw all that, honey. I saw her."

"Did she suffer?' I managed to ask as tears flooded my eyes. "Did she…?"

The Clockmaker's Son

He set his pen and notebook down, reached for and gently took my right hand, being careful of the IV line. He rubbed my arm, his fingers loosely laced through mine. "Sweetheart, it's all right. When someone is attacked like that their adrenalin starts flowing. They're pumped up and don't feel pain right away. And then, when they suffer grave, mortal injuries like that, even if they don't die right away, the body goes into deep shock and then death swiftly follows. I don't think she felt it. I think it caught her off guard and before she could even figure out what was happening, it was already beyond the point where she would have felt anything. It was fairly quick and she then was beyond awareness of it and at peace." I nodded, wanting desperately to believe him, but what if the beast had mauled her first, scratched her and cuffed her around before biting her, tearing her open like that? It was still too much for my mind to manage and I burst into tears. "Hey, now, hey. Look at me, Charlotte. Look at me, please. That's it. Just look at me and listen to me, okay? Focus on what I'm saying, and don't let those other thoughts sneak into your head. All right?" I nodded, my blurred eyes locked onto his blue eyes. "What's your favorite antique? You must have quite a few in the house, probably as many as there are in the shop. Am I right?" I nodded. "Which one do you like best of all? You must have a favorite. Tell me about it."

I found myself telling him about the little clock with the violets and ivy painted on it that I had broken in New York City and paid for with all the money I'd had at the time. I told him how my mother had taken me to the clock shop and Mr. Beresford had been too busy to even look at it, but how J. Rand had offered to repair the clock. I told him how Rand had made the parts that he needed for it himself and that it had been running like a charm ever since, until recently. Then I told him how I'd bravely driven over to Juniper Avenue to ask if Mr. Beresford could look at the clock and figure out why it had stopped working. He seemed surprised by my going over there uninvited, but I said I'd been rather desperate because I'd missed the comforting sound of the ticking of the clock at night.

And then I'd told him that I'd found some pictures in a German newspaper of J. Rand who was making amazing clock towers in Europe. Again he was surprised by this information. But talking about the clock, J. Rand, how Mr. Beresford had kindly looked the clock over, found the problem, and gotten it working again, and then how he'd invited me to dinner...all of the talking steered my thought train off the track to terror and tears and onto the track to a better place in my own head.

He asked me questions about customers, if anyone had any issues with the shop or anything. There was no one I could think of who was mad at any of us. Of course, I didn't know everything that went on in the shop every day because I was in college or at the library, but I was sure that, if there had been any kind of problem with someone, Chase would have mentioned it, if not to me, then to my mother. He said he would be talking to Mom tomorrow after she'd seen me and gotten some rest.

Finally, he asked me if anyone had been bothering me, might have known that it would be just Chase and me in the store early on Saturday morning. I shook my head. He patted my arm and then sat back in his chair, taking up his pen and notebook again, jotting a few more notes while the nurse who had come into the room took my vitals for the second time since I'd woken up this morning.

Finally, he smiled at me, thanked me, and asked if he could talk to me again if he had any additional questions. I said he was always welcome to talk to me. Then he asked me if I could describe as accurately as I could the wolf I had seen. I'd suppressed a shudder and nodded. "Not right now. Maybe next week or so."

"I'll never forget what I saw, so even if it's a year from now I'll still be able to tell the police artist what I saw in a fair amount of detail."

"You take it easy, Charlotte, and get some rest now before they come back to poke and prod you some more." He reached into his pocket. "Here are your house and car keys and whatnot. I tried the keys on the ring and removed the shop keys so the state police could have them. They'll be returned to you as soon as all the evidence has been collected. No one can go inside right now. It's still a crime scene."

"Okay. Thank you."

As he was leaving, an older man came into the room with a white porcelain bowl full of violets and English ivy. "Miss Charlotte Rumford?" he inquired. I was the only patient in the double room. I nodded. "This is for you. Bed tray or window sill? Bedside table?"

"Can you put it here on the bed tray, please?" I already had a windowsill nearly full of flowers. Ripley had sent a vase of hot house daisies and ferns with a note saying that she'd come and see me soon, she had end of term finals and then she'd be home on a short break. Mrs. Claxton had sent me some roses. Miss Davies from the library had sent carnations and spider mums in cheerful colors. Mrs. Forbes had sent a philodendron plant. Charlie and Melissa had sent me a vase of assorted flowers and two balloons. There had been nothing from my father, but I wasn't sure he even knew what had happened, since he was still out of the country. Mom, who wasn't speaking to him, probably hadn't even texted him about it.

As the older man left, a young man closer to my age came into the room carrying a vase of pink and white roses. "Charlotte Rumford?" I nodded. "Hey, I remember you. It's the red hair. You were a junior when I was a senior. Do you remember me? Joe Fields?"

"Yes, you played baseball." He smiled, nodding. "Second base." His smile widened into a grin. "I remember."

"Damn, girl, what the hell happened to you? All over town people are saying wild and crazy things."

"I don't think I'm supposed to talk about it yet. The police are still investigating."

"Heard your arm got busted up bad." He set the bowl of roses on the bed tray beside the violets and ivy. The nurse would have to move them later so my lunch tray would fit there, but I liked looking at them. He plucked the little envelope from the plastic trident holding it, pulled out the card and handed it to me. "You have an admirer."

"Do you routinely read all the cards in the flowers you deliver?" I asked, taking the card from him.

He laughed. "Sometimes, but I happened to be in the shop when this guy came in to order the flowers for you. He wrote on the card and left it on the counter, not in the envelope. After he left, I picked it up. Knowing it was going to you, I was kind of curious as to what an almost forty-year old single cop would write to a girl close to my age. I think he's sweet on you."

I looked at the card. He'd crammed quite a bit onto it in tiny cursive writing. It slanted downhill. Basically, he was sorry such a terrible thing had happened to a nice girl like me. He hoped I was feeling better, and concluded his note with an invitation to go out for pizza when I was feeling up to it. It was signed Mike, Badge 37. I smiled. "He and I have weak stomachs," I said.

"I can do him one better. If you want, I can take you to Max's Grill and Tavern. You're probably not old enough to drink yet, but they make awesome non-alcoholic drinks, and really thick shakes."

"Are you asking me out?"

He shrugged. "Yeah, I guess so."

"But I hardly know you."

"Well, we have to start someplace, right?"

He was cute. "I guess so." He took my cell number, wrote his down on the back of the little envelope. "Text me when you get out of this place and we'll figure something out, okay?"

"I will."

He gave me a little salute before walking to the door. There, he paused, and then turned back to me. "Mike Emery is way too old for you, you know."

"I know. I'll have to let him down gently though."

He nodded. "You're going to break his heart though, no matter how gentle you are."

"I'll have pizza with him and talk about girl stuff and he'll figure it out, that I'm too young for him."

He grinned again and left. Sheesh! You get thrown around by an enormous wolf-beast and guys come crawling out of the woodwork to date you! That was the weirdest phenomenon I'd ever experienced. However, having two guys interested in me at the same time gave me something better to dwell upon than the horror that I'd witnessed.

Susan Buffum

Chapter Six

The white porcelain bowl of violets and ivy was from Mr. Beresford. His simple card had wished me well. I had tucked all my cards into an envelope that the nurse had given me to take home with me when I was released.

By the beginning of the following week, I'd been released and my mother had taken me home. Within a matter of days, I'd realized that she was a changed woman. She looked haggard, drawn, and acted aimlessly, as if she'd lost all sense of direction in her life. I sort of felt the same way, so spent much of my time sitting on the front porch staring across the street at nothing in particular.

Sam Drake arrived a few days after my return home. I heard my mother crying and then she became hysterical; Sam's deep rumbling voice trying to soothe her, her sharp voice telling him to get out, as if everything that had happened here had been his fault. He'd come out onto the porch looking shell-shocked, grim-faced. He'd glanced at me and then gone down the porch steps. However, he'd stopped on the walkway, turning back to me. "I'm sorry, Charlotte," he said before turning and continuing on to his SUV and departing.

Joe Fields stopped by late that same afternoon. I had managed to make myself a microwavable bowl of mac and cheese. My mother was in the throes of a terrible migraine so I'd been left to fend for myself. "You look pretty damn glum," he remarked as he came up the walkway and right up onto the porch. "How's the arm?" I shrugged. "You haven't called me."

"It hurts if I move it too much." He sat down on the porch railing. I was glad it was sturdy enough to hold his weight, although he wasn't heavy. He had a baseball player's tall, lankiness to him. His feet remained flat on the floor while sitting on the railing. "Sorry. Things have been...difficult here."

"You hungry? I just got off work. I hauled a bunch of flower arrangements over to the funeral home for your Mom's friend's funeral tomorrow." I winced. Chase's funeral had been delayed because of all the evidence collecting and forensic testing that had been done. Forensics police all the way from Boston had come out to take samples from Chase's body. I'd heard about that from the paperboy when he'd delivered the newspaper the other day. Mom and I weren't reading the papers, just throwing them, still tri-folded, into the recycle bin.

"I am," I replied, "but I don't want to leave my mom alone. She's got a wicked bad migraine."

"What would you like? I'll run downtown and get it and bring it back here." I didn't know what I wanted. I hadn't been eating right since I'd been home. He looked away when I didn't answer immediately, and then stood up. "I'll surprise you."

He left and I thought the surprise would be that he wouldn't come back, that he thought me worse company than a mannequin would be.

I sighed and let my thoughts drift back to darker things. I was struggling to work through the horror without therapy. I knew what I'd seen that Saturday morning, but no one was taking me seriously. They all had their own theories as to what had happened to Chase. It rankled that no one truly believed me. I was not a fanciful girl prone to making things up.

Joe returned, but I didn't even notice until he set a heavy rectangular takeout container on my lap. "Chinese," he said. "Golden fingers, pork fried rice, vegetable lo mein. Here, take your fork." He stuck a plastic fork in my right hand, and then sat down in the chair beside mine to eat his own dinner. "I don't care if you eat with your fingers, just start eating, okay? You're scrawny as all hell." I had lost weight. "I got you a Coke." He nodded toward the porch railing where I saw two takeout cups sitting. It was a surreal moment. It was as if I had stepped outside of the present time and he had come, laid everything out, and then summoned me back. "Eat, Charlotte," he said quietly. "Just start eating. Part of it is that your body needs fuel. You'll feel better with something in your stomach."

I began eating, ever the obedient girl. The food tasted vivid on my tongue, and my stomach clenched with hunger. I couldn't remember if I had actually eaten the mac and cheese or if I'd just left it sitting on the counter and had just thought that I'd eaten it.

A few tears trickled down my cheeks as I ate like a prisoner of war who'd just been released and was tasting real food again for the first time in years. Beside me, Joe shushed me and quietly continued urging me to eat. He brought me my soda and held it while I sipped from the straw. He was so good to me, so kind and gentle, so concerned and thoughtful that it made me feel bad, but also good. "I'm so full of contradictions!" I cried.

"Yeah, I can tell. But, you actually have a little color back in your cheeks."

He took my leftovers inside to put them in the fridge, and then returned. "There's a container of mac and cheese on the counter. Did your Mom come down and make that and then forget to eat it?"

"No, that was my dinner."

He snorted, shaking his head, as he opened a fortune cookie packet. He snapped the crescent-shaped cookie in half, tugged out the little strip of paper, and read it aloud. "'An adventure awaits you.'" I raised my eyes until they met his. "What if I take you to see a movie next weekend? An adventure movie."

"Can you call me mid-week? I don't know how my mom will be."

"Yeah, sure. But, let me tell you something. Don't get mad at me, all right? Just take it for what it is, okay?" I nodded. "You suffered some serious trauma, physically and psychologically. You'd known Chase since you were a kid, right?" I nodded. "It must have been shocking as all hell to find her dead. I know people are saying that you saw a huge wolfman thing. But, you know what, Charlotte? If you look back, there have been reports of feral dogs and possibly wolves in this area for years. Didn't the kid down the street, what's his name? Cory?"

"Cody Underwood," I supplied.

"Right, him, Austin Peck, and J. Rand Beresford were attacked by something. Two of them got killed and Rand got bitten and scratched. He was never the same kid. Something happened to him. He must have seen the wolf that attacked his friends and him. People thought he was mistaken, but how many cows, goats, deer, and stuff have people found mutilated around here over the years? I'm inclined to think there's something out there.

"How it got into the shop, I can't explain that, but I believe you. I believe you saw what you saw. You're not the kind of girl who'd ever make stuff up." He took a breath and then he continued. "I want to tell you something. A few months after those guys got killed up at Turkey Pond, well, me and a couple of friends hiked up there. There were torn ribbons of yellow crime scene tape around the area still. The ground was all scuffed and dug up. The fire pit they'd built was still there, and a few other things, like a sneaker. Kyle and I went up to Big Pond. I knew where that cave was. We saw more yellow tape where they'd found J. Rand. And, you know what? I went inside the cave and I found this." He set his soda down on the porch floor, leaned back and slid his right hand into his front pocket. He pulled out a little round, white plastic container, like the kind you can get at the pharmacy counter to carry a days' worth of pills in. He looked at me before handing it to me. "Don't freak out, okay? Just look at what I found in that cave. You can touch it, if you want to." There was worry in his eyes as he put the little container into my hand. I couldn't get it open, so he opened it for me.

At first, in the waning light, I thought it was a clump of downy feathers or dust. Or maybe some sort of finely shredded fabric. I thought it might be a scrap of something the beast had torn off one of the boys clothing, or worse yet, a clump of hair from one of their scalps. But it had no flesh attached, just a little debris from inside the cave.

I lightly touched it with the tip of my forefinger. It was coarse and reminded me of dog fur. With a gasp, it struck me what it was he was showing me. He had found a scrap of gray wolf fur in the cave! My eyes shifted to meet his. "You found this where J. Rand was found?"

"I don't think he went up there to hide. I think the damn thing carried him up there, or forced him to walk up there. It mauled him there, like it was full from the other two boys and took him with it to play with, kill, and eat later." I grimaced. For a wild animal to do something like that was unusual. It might kill its prey and carry it away to eat later, but it would be totally weird to think that a wolf would march a live boy up a hill to its lair and torture him while it digested its previous meal.

"Here, take this." I didn't want to hold it anymore.

He took the container, snapped it closed, and returned it to his pocket. "If I could find a scrap of fur in that cave, then you'd better believe that the Staties and the cops also found evidence of a wolf up there. There's a cover-up, Charlotte. I'd bet my life on that."

"Shh! You can't go around saying stuff like that!" I hissed, although deep inside of me I agreed with him.

He picked up his soda and sipped some, then stood up. "Is it all right if we go inside, or should I just go home?"

"If you're quiet you can come in. I can make some brownies, if you help me."

"Yeah, that sounds good. I have to head home about ten at the latest though."

We went inside. He basically made the brownies. At nine-thirty they were still warm, but he cut us each a large square, poured us glasses of milk and we sat at the kitchen table eating our late snack. I discovered that I liked Joe Fields. I had always thought the high school athletes were too full of themselves, but he was basically a down to earth guy working for Blooming Delights as their delivery driver while taking night classes at Great Oak.

He was going for a degree in Business Administration with the goal of taking over his father's printing business in the near future. His parents wanted to move south, closer to his mother's family. Joe would rent the family home from them for the time being and run the business. If he kept it going then he would buy the house from them, although he thought that, if he did that, then he'd buy the house from them, but in a few years sell it and build his own house, maybe over in Windsor.

He had plans and goals. I liked that. He told me that he'd hire me as his administrative assistant, if I didn't have a better job offer when I graduated. He gave me a lot of new things to think about when I was alone with too many of my former thoughts haunting me.

And then Officer Mike Emery came calling. He brought me a bouquet of pretty, bright-colored flowers. I blushed like a schoolgirl, which I basically was, although I was in college, not high school.

I had gone back to my classes, but it wasn't my mother driving me out to Great Oaks Community College. It was actually Peter Sanborn, Mr. Beresford's driver. Sanborn had shown up one morning, shortly after I'd come home from the hospital, with a letter from Mr. Beresford stating that his driver was under his direction to chauffeur me to my classes and safely back home again for as long as I was unable to drive myself. My mother had said no at first, but then her own problems had emerged and she'd been in no shape to drive me, so I had called the Beresford mansion and accepted the thoughtful and much appreciated services of Mr. Sanborn, sending a letter stating as much to Mr. Beresford, since it was Druce who had answered the phone and spoken with me.

Mike looked disappointed to discover that I was in a relationship with Joe Fields. "He's a decent kid, but I don't think he'll amount to much. His parents spoil him," he told me.

I kept my mouth shut, served him coffee that I made using the Keurig, and a brownie. While we were sitting at the table, Mom came downstairs, having heard voices.

"Mike, what are you doing here?" she asked, surprised to find a cop sitting in the kitchen with me. "Do you have more questions for Charlotte?" A faint frown creased her brow.

"I came to see how she's doing. And to see how you're holding up. How are you, Patty?"

"Oh, I've been better," she replied before going into the pantry to fix herself a cup of coffee. Then she joined us at the table, which had surprised me. Her headache wasn't so bad, if she could sit here and chat like this. And before long, I began feeling uncomfortable with the direction their conversation was going, so I excused myself to go upstairs to text Ripley about it. She was still in a relationship with Miles Worthy. Now, I actually had stuff to tell her, about Joe and this evening, about Officer Mike Emery chatting up my mom.

Life took strange turns every now and then, and this was one of those times.

Chapter Seven

I dated Joe for over a year. He got his Business Administration degree and, as planned, took over the printing business. His parents moved south like they had planned to do. Meanwhile, my mother and Mike Emery had grown closer. He was two years younger than her, but that didn't seem to bother them. But it did bother me when he moved into our house and began living with us.

I became the live-in third wheel, although neither of them came right out and said so. I stayed in my room a lot. Joe was busy at the printing plant, but said I could move in with him, there was plenty of room. My relationship with him had developed, but I could tell he was growing frustrated with me because I was not the kind of girl who jumped into bed with guys, even though we'd been dating for over a year now. I suspected he was getting what he wanted from someone else, but he did care about me and was willing to wait until I was ready to notch our relationship up to that level.

But then the girl he was being intimate with told him that she was pregnant. Decent guy that he was, he broke up with me and moved her into his house, thinking that he was doing the right thing, except, whenever I saw him, he didn't look happy. He was always telling me that he missed me and regretted the mistakes he'd made and how they'd messed up his life big time. I couldn't be what he wanted me to be, the other girl now. No matter how much I liked him, I just couldn't do that.

I was getting closer to graduation. Mom had closed the antiques store downtown, moving the business over to Windsor. There were just too many bad memories here for her to keep the shop open in Pine Haven. I was working over there when I didn't have classes, saving my money. I knew that when I was through with college I'd have to move out. Mike and Mom wanted their privacy. They were talking about getting married, now that my parent's divorce had been finalized. I continued to be in their way.

One April morning, when I was leaving for class, I saw the familiar vintage Bentley parked in front of the house. I walked down the driveway to talk to Mr. Sanborn, to find out why he was there. He came around and opened the back door for me. "Mr. Beresford would like to speak to you."

"But, I'm on my way to class."

"Yes, he'll talk to you while I drive you to your class."

It was then that I had noticed the passenger in the rear seat on the driver's side. I slipped into the empty rear seat on the passenger side. Sanborn closed the door, then walked around the car and got behind the wheel. I was nervous, not having seen Mr. Beresford in person since he'd cleaned and repaired my little clock and our dinner together.

"Good morning, Miss Rumford. How are you today?" he asked.

"I'm fine, Mr. Beresford. How are you?"

"Not as well as I wish I was. I'd like to talk to you about possible employment. I understand that you'll have your associate's degree as an Administrative Assistant." I nodded. "I'd like you to consider working for me at the house. I still make clocks, as you may already be aware. I have other business affairs, as well. I have a business manager, Mr. Stroud, and an attorney, Mr. Bean, who handle the majority of my business, however, there are many other things that need to be attended to such as correspondence, research, filing, and maintaining schedules so that I don't fall behind or miss due dates. Those are things I could use help with. I believe there would be enough work to keep you busy. You would have weekends off." He turned his head and looked directly at me. "I would like you to live at Randolph Hall. You would have a comfortable suite all your own. You would dine with me in the evening; however you would take your breakfast and lunch in the staff dining room. I have a much smaller staff than I had when Grace was still alive. Sanborn is at your disposal should you need to run any errands. You may keep a vehicle of your own. There is plenty of room in the carriage house and carports. I would pay you a salary that would allow you to save for your future. I would cover your room and board while you are under my employ. You'd just have to purchase your own clothing and cover your own entertainment expenses. We have a laundry room where you can do your own wash. I believe Druce has a schedule posted there. You'd just need to add your name to the schedule. You can do your own housekeeping or you could ask either Rose or Caroline to clean your suite for you."

I was overwhelmed by his offer and didn't know what to say. "I think...I'll need to think about this kind and generous offer," I managed to say.

"Yes, of course. I have business in Stockbridge this morning, so I asked Sanborn to pick you up so that I could speak to you. I know this must appear to come out of the blue to you, but I've been thinking about things. I understand that your mother wishes to remarry?" I nodded. "You'll be twenty in May?"

I nodded again, and then said, "Yes," aloud, not wanting him to think I was an idiot who couldn't speak.

"J. Rand has, of course, declined to come home at this time."

"You've been in contact with him?" I was surprised to hear this. I'd hoped he'd been able to track his son down and that they'd opened a line of communication between them again.

"Yes. We've had several brief conversations since my man was able to track him down and persuade him to agree to contact me. He was surprised to learn that it was you who had discovered the article and photograph in the German newspaper. He remembered repairing the clock. I told him the clock had stopped and that's what had led you to seek me out, that you had brought your scrapbook over." He sighed. "My son is still very resentful about how he was treated after the incident when he was fourteen years old. The last time I spoke to him, I mentioned what had happened to you. He asked if you had been bitten and I told him no, you hadn't been, just injured when the beast you claimed to have seen had picked you up and thrown you some distance." His eyes narrowed as he studied my face, watching my expression. "You see, Miss Rumford, my son has always claimed that it was a tall, lean, wolf-like creature that killed his friends and tormented him, biting and scratching him, but for some reason not killing him. The description he gave me back then is very similar to the description you gave the police. I don't feel that you are a fanciful girl inclined to embellish tales, especially when in shock and pain as you undoubtedly were. Therefore, I can only conclude that whatever this creature may have been, it is the same creature, or a related one, that attacked J. Rand and the woman running your mother's shop."

"I know what I saw," I said quietly.

"Those are the exact same words he said to me."

He stopped talking, and so did I. As Sanborn pulled into the long curving driveway leading to Great Oaks Community College, I said, "Mr. Beresford, I would be happy to accept your offer of employment."

"Very good, Miss Rumford. I would like to see you two weeks before your graduation. Send me a note with that date, will you? I'd like you to have dinner with me. Afterwards, we'll complete some paperwork and get you on the payroll. Mr. Stroud will need your checking account number so he can set up a direct deposit of your paychecks. I prefer to pay my employees in that manner, if that is all right with you?"

"Yes, that's fine." I just didn't know how much he was offering me and was too polite to ask.

"Are you at all curious about your annual salary, Miss Rumford? I don't believe I have mentioned what I will be paying you annually."

"No, you didn't mention it, but it has to be more than I'm making now with two part time jobs."

He smiled. "Yes, dear girl, it is much more than you're making with your current jobs." He took a small notebook from the inside breast pocket of his suit coat, and a pen from the same pocket, opened it to a blank page, wrote something on it, tore the page out, folded it in half, and passed it to me. "I hope you will find this figure satisfactory. I prefer not to mention salary amounts in front of my employees." He gave a slight nod toward Mr. Sanborn in the front seat. "Look at that at your leisure, Miss Rumford, and then we'll fine tune all the details when we have dinner and your pre-employment meeting."

"All right. Thank you, Mr. Beresford. I truly appreciate this." I slipped the still folded paper into a pocket of my messenger bag. Mr. Sanborn came and opened the door for me.

"Have a good day, Charlotte. Sanborn will be here to pick you up and take you home later on."

That was how, just after my twentieth birthday, I found myself moving into Randolph Hall a few days after my graduation ceremony. I was shown several suites in the east wing, but of course I chose the suite decorated with sprays of violets on the wallpaper, dark violet drapes, and a bed fit for a princess with a violet-patterned comforter and pillow shams. The bathroom was fitted out with purple towels and my sheets were lilac purple. Caroline, one of the maids, told me that the colors of the linens and towels matched the suites so they could be returned to the proper suite.

The first thing I unpacked was my little clock with the violets on it, setting it on my bedside table. The first thing I noticed, when returning to my room after dinner with Mr. Beresford that first night, was a beautiful mantle case clock with a small brass pendulum visible through a window under the clock face. The white painted case was decorated with hand-painted sprays of violets. English ivy trailed through the sprays of flowers. The clock could have been a big sister clock to my sweet little boudoir clock, but I had a feeling that Mr. Beresford had made this mantle clock for me, knowing that this suite would be the one that I'd choose. I was deeply touched that he cared that much to want to make me feel so welcome in his home.

I went to bed that night determined to be the best personal assistant he could ever ask for. His thoughtfulness and generosity had altered the course of my life and had freed me from Joe Fields' continued attempts to persuade me to be his mistress, to help him escape the misery of his unhappy marriage. He had to find his own way out of that predicament, if he wanted my attention again.

My mother hadn't said much about my taking the job at Randolph Hall. Mike Emery had told me that I really should have thought more about the offer before accepting it. I'd told him that I was happy with my decision, that I had a comfortable suite, good food served three times a day, use of the estate pool and tennis court, and use of certain other rooms in the mansion during my off duty time, such as the lounge on the first floor of the east wing where there was a big, flat screen TV, a cabinet full of DVDs, a table to play cards at, and a stereo system. And I could also make use of the mansion's library in the main house on the first floor, if Mr. Beresford wasn't using it. I liked to read. I wasn't a complicated girl. I swam in the pool, played tennis with Caroline, Rose, and Ethan Sinclair, the handyman, in the evening after dinner all summer.

I liked my work. I was efficient and caught on quickly to what my duties were. Mr. Stroud met with Mr. Beresford on Thursday mornings to discuss business affairs. I typed letters in the study while they met in the library. Sometimes, I was sent on errands with Sanborn while they met, if it was going to be long and tedious and involved taxes and stuff I didn't understand. However, when I showed curiosity about his clock making business, he freely spoke to me about it. During the bleak days of early January, I asked Stroud to bring the books to show me.

I could tell that Christian Stroud wasn't happy about discussing previously private business with a young woman still only just out of college, but I had helped my mother with The Remains of Yesterday, running the monthly statements, invoicing purchases, handling international sales and shipping. I actually knew more than I'd thought I did. He'd also been surprised by my knowledge and ability to learn new things quickly.

"Christian, I feel that we can trust Charlotte. She is my every day right hand these days. I chose wisely when I selected her to be my assistant. If I trust her, then so should you. She is an asset to this household and to my affairs."

"Yes, of course, Mr. Beresford."

"Tomorrow, Charlotte will be writing a letter asking J. Rand to come home. I have a number of things to discuss with him about the estate and the business."

"Are you sure you don't want me to handle contacting him? He can be quite difficult, as has been proven time and time again."

"No, I believe she is the one who should contact him on my behalf."

"Very well. If that is all, I should be heading back to Boston."

"Yes, that is all. Thank you for staying later than usual, Christian. My best to your wife as always."

The next day, I found myself writing to J. Rand, or J.R. Beres as he was still calling himself. He was in France now, according to the last report his father had received as to his whereabouts. I worded the letter simply, asking him to please make time in his busy schedule to come to Pine Haven to meet with his father in regards to estate business and the clock making business, that it was important, and had best be done sooner rather than later. I did not reveal that R. Hollis Beresford had received a grim prognosis recently. He had inoperable cancer. He had received chemo and radiation treatment and was now on medicine treatment, but the consensus was that nothing would be able to stop the cancer from spreading. It would only slow down what was inevitable. Therefore, before the inevitable happened, he needed to mend the rift between himself and his son and begin discussing the transition of the estate property and clock business to J. Rand's ownership.

I mailed the letter that afternoon after Mr. Beresford had signed it and added something in his own hand at the bottom before folding the letter, sealing it in the envelope, and then handing it to me to post.

Chapter Eight

As spring arrived, another shock rocked Pine Haven. The bodies of three boys, ages ranging from twelve to fourteen, were discovered in a field. These were boys that had gone missing from three different surrounding communities during the long winter. The bodies had been mutilated in a now familiar manner—throats torn out, torsos torn open, limbs gouged by deep scratches. A fresh wave of terror and suspicion washed across the community. Also, there was outrage that this kept happening and that the police had done nothing to further investigate the killings, or even assemble a group of skilled hunters to scour the hills, woods, and swampland to try to locate the beast or beasts and kill it or them.

The atmosphere in town changed dramatically with parents keeping their children indoors more, not allowing them to ride their bikes further than the end of the block, or as far as the parent could see them from their front porches or yards. Driving to the post office, it was like riding through a ghost town. If you did see a person outside, they were never alone. They traveled in pairs or small packs, their heads always turning this way and that as they kept a vigilant watch for anything unusual or threatening. My own anxiety had flared anew, but I knew that I was safe enough in the car and at Randolph Hall.

I felt conspicuous dashing alone up the marble front steps of the post office to send another letter to J. Rand who had not responded to the previous letter. I really hoped that he would answer this time. I wanted the rift between father and son to be healed before Mr. Beresford's cancer stole more of his vitality and energy away. Even if the rift wasn't completely mended, I desperately wanted the process to have at least been started so that Mr. Beresford could carry hope in his heart throughout his remaining days.

I hadn't even thought about what would happen when Mr. Beresford passed. I knew it would mean the end of my employment, but I stubbornly refused to dwell on that future point in time when I would have to make some life changing decisions of my own in regards to where I would go from here and what I would do.

"Good morning, Charlotte," greeted the man behind the counter, Mr. Czepiel. He had been a clerk at the post office ever since I was a little girl and would be sent by my mother to purchase stamps for the shop.

"Hi. I have an international letter to mail this morning."

"Trying to reach young Mr. Beresford again?"

I made a face. "He never answered the last letter."

"Bad blood between father and son can fester."

"I know, but they had been close until that terrible thing happened."

"Terrible things change people." He took the envelope from me, and then just stood looking at me. A terrible thing had happened to me. He was probably wondering if I had changed.

"I'm still me," I told him. "Only warier and more cautious when entering and exiting buildings these days."

"We're all more aware of the need for therapy and support systems being in place nowadays. Back then, nothing like that had ever happened in Pine Haven. We weren't prepared or equipped to handle a tragedy of that magnitude. J. Rand, he fell through the cracks."

"Yes. We're more educated about post-traumatic stress disorder nowadays. It is real, not imaginary as many people have thought. People's psyches do get damaged when they've seen or experienced something traumatic, and especially when they've experienced something horrific themselves. I have nightmares," I revealed.

"Do you?" I nodded. I had terrible nightmares; the wake up screaming kind. Not every night, but once every couple of months it would happen. There were no precipitating events as far as I could tell. I could have a perfectly ordinary, even boring day, and fall asleep after thinking about tasks to accomplish the following day, and a few hours later wake up screaming, heart pounding, staring into the darkness as if something evil was lurking in the corner. Once, I knocked the clock off the bedside table while wildly reaching for the lamp, the glass over the clock face shattering, my heart breaking at the senseless damage because, to me, the nightmares were very real, but when I'd calmed down, I felt humiliated and ashamed of my weakness.

Mr. Beresford had ordered a new glass disk to replace the broken one, assuring me that accidents happened, and then smiling gently at me, telling me that I was a very fortunate young lady to be employed by a clockmaker who could repair the damage to the precious little clock and not gouge her for the parts needed and the labor besides.

In truth, he had repaired the clock for me for free. In return, I had baked him a batch of hermits, his favorite cookies. We'd enjoyed coffee and hermits that evening in the library where Druce had built a fire, even though the late-May weather was mild. "I have quite a gem in you, my dear," he remarked, helping himself to a third cookie. His appetite had been off lately due to a medication change, so I was happy to see him actually enjoying something this evening.

"They say that people who truly enjoy their jobs and their employers are happier and more productive."

"You enjoy your job here then?"

"Yes, I do."

"I thought you might find it rather…tedious."

"No. I've found it much more interesting since you've allowed me to join you in the workshop to observe what you do." He had invited me into the shop about a month ago to watch him work on a clock he was making for a member of the royal family in England, a cousin or something like that. I had sat on a stool across the work table from him and he had explained what he was doing, shown me the tools he used, the parts he was putting into the clock. I had found it all fascinating.

"I thought I might be boring you to death in the workshop with all my technical jibber-jabber."

"No, not at all. I find it all rather interesting. I had no idea how a clock actually worked. The cheap wall clocks that run on batteries that you pick up at the big box stores are really so simplistic and far inferior to a hand-crafted clock that they now seem as primitive to me as a sand timer." He smiled at that. "I'm learning something new every time you let me observe you at work in the shop."

He nodded and smiled, obviously pleased that I was interested in his work. It occurred to me then that he must miss his son who had been the only other person who'd understood his work and had an appreciation for it.

It made me do what I did next, which was go up to my room after dinner that night and write a personal letter to J. Rand begging him to please come home, even for a few days, because his father desperately wanted to see him before it was too late, and wouldn't he himself live with regrets for the rest of his life, if he didn't at least make an attempt to repair the rift between his father and himself?

Well, I guess the letter worked, but I wasn't home when he showed up. Ripley invited me to go with her to New Hampshire, to Hampton Beach, for the long Memorial Day weekend, and Mr. Beresford had given me permission to take Friday off to go with her. J. Rand had evidently shown up unannounced at the house in the wee hours of Saturday morning, had slept in and just barely managed to join his father for dinner on Saturday night. They had adjourned to the study, according to gossip gleaned from Helen and Lorraine in the kitchen on Tuesday morning at breakfast, where they had shortly begun arguing. J. Rand had stalked out of the study and gone to his suite in the west wing and stayed there until Sunday afternoon before coming out and meeting with his father again briefly. And then he had departed before dinner, saying that he had a plane to catch.

I had totally missed his visit and regretted my not being there, but I hadn't known he was coming. He hadn't let anyone know in advance. I felt that, if I had been there, I might have been able to act as a buffer between father and son, both of them evidently still nursing raw wounds that they had rubbed salt into during this brief return of the prodigal son. I felt bad because on Tuesday Mr. Beresford was very subdued and dismissed me early, telling me that he just needed time alone.

I wrote a scathing letter to J. Rand and mailed it late Tuesday afternoon before I could think it all through, just reacting emotionally to how he had treated his father. Exiting the post office, a cruiser, with blue lights flashing and siren blaring, that had been speeding down Main Street stuttered to a squealing halt, and then backed up, the passenger side window lowering. "Charlotte! For God 'sake, get back to Randolph Hall and stay there! That beast has struck again! You shouldn't be on the streets alone!" And then he roared off, obviously responding to a call, but having recognized me by my red hair, I suppose.

I jumped into the waiting Bentley and Mr. Sanborn pulled away from the curb. "What's going on?" he asked, his eyes meeting mine in the rearview mirror.

"I guess the wolf has struck again," I replied. "That was Mom's new husband, Mike Emery. He stopped to tell me to lock myself in the house, more or less."

"That might not be such a bad idea," he replied.

"But I have a few more errands to run downtown," I pointed out.

"Then I'm going wherever you go because Mr. Beresford would skin me alive if I let anything bad happen to you, Miss Rumford. He thinks very highly of you."

So, I had an escort into the pharmacy where I had to pick up feminine supplies and shampoo, and then to the office supplies store to get a new printer cartridge, a new journal, and a package of pens. We then drove out to Clay Hill Road to a farm stand to buy peas and lettuce for Helen for dinner that night.

There were flashing blue lights just a few hundred feet down the road from the farm where we often bought produce for Helen. We thought there might have been a bad accident, but the farmer had shaken his head and grimly informed us that the road was closed because the bodies of two young people had been found discarded on the side of the road, just past the old machine shop, both of them mutilated, their throats torn out, their bellies torn open. Two females, he told us. "That's all I know about it right now. George found 'em not too long ago. Saw two different sneakers lying in the road and what looked like a pool of blood. Thought a couple of kids, maybe doubled up on a bike, had been hit and gone off the road. Stopped to look in the ravine and saw the bodies and came here to make the call. Had to call the ambulance as he was having bad chest pains, difficulty breathing. Probably gave him a heart attack seein' somethin' like that, poor George." He nodded toward a beat-up blue Ford pickup parked askew in the yard. "I'll have to see if he left the keys in it in a bit. Can't have his truck blockin' my driveway like that until he gets out of the hospital. His wife won't drive it. I'll have to get Betty to drive the car and follow me to George's place to return the truck, or get the spare keys. He never locks the place. Probably has the spare keys hanging on a peg near the back door, same as I do." He shrugged. "You best go on home, young lady, and stay there. Don't know what the hell this beast is that's killin' folk, but it's a nasty one, that's for damn sure."

We returned to Randolph Hall in absolute silence. Mr. Sanborn looked pale and grim. I felt queasy and thought I'd skip dinner, just going upstairs and lying down on my bed after taking one of my anti-anxiety tablets. The medication made me drowsy and I fell into a restless sleep, not waking up until Druce rapped on the sitting room door. I rolled over to check the time, and that's when I saw the envelope propped against the clock. I didn't recognize the handwriting, but grabbed it before going to answer the door. "Dinner will be on the table at seven o'clock. Mr. Beresford would like you to be present."

I felt dopey and wasn't hungry, but said, "All right."

"You're pale. Do you need a brandy or anything?" he asked, never very personable, but acutely aware of the undercurrents of mood running through the house.

I shook my head. "No." Glancing at the mantle clock, I saw I had a half hour. A quick hot shower without getting my hair wet would revive me and put some roses in my cheeks. "I'll take a quick shower, get dressed and be downstairs to walk with him to the dining room."

He nodded. "Very good, Miss Rumford." He turned away, but stopped and turned his head, regarding me for a long moment before saying, "Terrible business this is. It must be especially distressing for you. One of the young ladies was a former classmate of yours, Olivia Cusson." I nearly fell over, but he quickly grabbed me and steered me to a chair and had me put my head down. "I thought you might have heard their names from the farmer."

"No," I managed to say, feeling breathless and dizzy. "They'd only just been found."

"I'm sorry, Charlotte," he said, calling me by my first name for the first time since I'd started working there. "I will fetch you a small brandy. I would like you to drink it down. It will help." I nodded and he went off, returning shortly with a small snifter he placed in my hand. I bravely downed the drink, feeling a slow spreading of warmth through me afterwards. Somehow, it did make me feel less dizzy and sick. "Now, go and get ready for dinner, please. His visit with J. Rand did not go well. He needs your calming presence this evening. You're good medicine for him." I nodded and he left.

It was when I was rushing through the sitting room to make it downstairs in time for dinner that I saw the envelope, slightly crushed, lying on the chair Druce had steered me to. I must have tucked it down beside my thigh to take the brandy from him. I grabbed it and tossed it onto the mantle beside the clock before rushing downstairs.

I was shocked by how drawn Mr. Beresford looked, how frail he seemed. He clung to my arm as we walked from the study to the dining room. Druce was there to pull out his chair and help him sit down without falling. He then held my chair for me, giving me a brief nod, grateful that I had gotten the master of the house to the table.

"It did not go well with my son," he said, his voice low, full of disappointment and the pain of what he viewed as a failed attempt at reconciliation.

"I'm sorry," I murmured.

"He was distracted, angry."

"Angry with you?" I asked.

When he didn't answer right away, I raised my eyes and met his. He was regarding me with a distant look in his eyes, but then he shook his head. "No, I don't think he is as angry with me as he once was. He was angry about having to come home, angry that I'm ill, although I'm sure he realizes my illness had gotten beyond my control. No, he was angry about other things." I didn't know what to say about that. "I think he was angry that you had gone off with your friend for the holiday weekend. I think it disappointed him, that he wanted to see you for some reason and was angry that you weren't here."

"He most likely wanted to let me know he wasn't happy about the letters I'd sent him. I'm afraid I nagged him into coming to see you."

This drew a quick laugh from him. "It's been awhile since a female has nagged that one about anything, I'm sure."

"I just wanted him to come home and get this…started."

"Yes. I'm not going to scold you about writing separately to him. He mentioned that you had. He didn't seem particularly upset about that. I think your admonishing him did the trick rather than my begging him to come home. He is not angry with you like he is with me."

Druce brought in our soup plates, again giving me a look which more or less told me to see that the master ate his soup. I picked up my spoon as Druce headed back to the door to the butler's pantry from which he was serving our dinner as usual. "Helen has a way with her vegetable soup. These must be the peas Sanborn and I bought this afternoon. They looked so tender and sweet."

He stared down into his plate and, as I ate my soup, he slowly filled the bowl of his spoon and brought it to his mouth. He hesitated. Just when I thought the spoon would tumble from his hand, as it was trembling, he quickly opened his mouth and ate the spoonful of soup.

I chatted about how wet it had been in March and April and how dry it had been through May. I wondered what the summer would hold in store for us weather-wise. I told him that I had purchased two new journals and a package of disposable pens.

He said I should invest in a good fountain pen and skip the cheap pens. His eyes met mine as he leaned forward over his soup plate. "I pay you well enough that you can afford an expensive fountain pen and the cartridges needed to keep yourself writing busily for months to come."

"Yes, and I'm very grateful to you for that. I'll look into a fountain pen the next time I go to the office supply store."

"I have a nice fountain pen in the desk in my study. Allow me to pass that along to you. There are a few cartridges that I hope have not dried up. You'll undoubtedly have to put a new one in." He shook his head. "No, I will instruct Druce to replace the cartridge and clean the pen. Better that he get ink-stained hands rather than you, my dear."

The Clockmaker's Son

As we dined, he slowly let bits and pieces of his few brief meetings with J. Rand slip out. Rand had told him that he didn't want the estate or the old machine shop, that he could sell it all, that he had no interest in ever coming back to Pine Haven. That was during the first brief meeting. During the second meeting, he had relented a little and said that his father could leave him everything, if he was so inclined, but that he would only come home to find an agent to sell everything for him and then immediately return to Europe. Although this had lessened the blow of his not wanting anything from his father, it had still left Mr. Beresford feeling upset about his heir's indifference toward everything he had accomplished in his lifetime—especially all the clocks he had made for royalty, and the wealthy clients who sought out his craftsmanship. He had a veritable clock museum in a room on the second floor, a former bedroom that had library shelves lining the room, all of them filled with antique clocks—not cheap ones like one would find in ordinary antiques shops, but well-crafted, work-of-art clocks made by skilled craftsmen of bygone days for the wealthy and for royalty. J. Rand wanted none of it and that had wrenched his father's heart hard.

Speaking to me about it helped some. He ate an acceptable amount of his dinner in Druce's opinion, from his nod as he cleared our entre plates. I coaxed Mr. Beresford into coffee and a small piece of the lemon meringue pie Lorraine had made. After dessert, he'd excused me, telling me that he would ask Druce to escort him up to his room, draw him a nice hot bath. He would soak the stiffness from his joints, and then retire for the night.

I went upstairs to read. I put on my nightgown and climbed into bed, grabbing the book from the bedside table and reading for several hours. It was as I was putting the book back on the table at close to eleven o'clock that I remembered the crumpled envelope in the sitting room.

Flinging the covers aside, I padded barefoot out into the sitting room, retrieved the envelope, and brought it back to the bedroom where I sat on the edge of the bed and opened it. There was a single sheet of paper inside. The writing on the page looked hurried and was difficult to read, but more or less, in terse phrases, J. Rand had written that he wanted me to keep him advised of his father's state of health and to let him know immediately if his father took a turn for the worse and he should come home, otherwise, he didn't want to be bothered. He was busy. He'd scrawled, "*I can't trust that idiot Stroud to tell me anything straight. My father would be in the grave ten times over already according to his messages. I will come home if you tell me to. This is my private cell number. DO NOT give this number to anyone else. And DO NOT contact me unless it's a dire emergency.*" He'd scribbled *Julian* and then heavily crossed it out and written *J. Rand*, then drawn a line through that, started to write *Jul…* and then x'd out the 'ul' leaving only the initial *J*. Then he must have just folded the letter and stuffed it into the envelope in order to leave it in my room against the clock he had repaired for me years ago.

Even Julian Rand Beresford didn't know what to call himself anymore. That was interesting, and also a little sad.

Chapter Nine

A curious thing happened a few weeks later. I was leaving the post office after shipping a small clock to Texas when I ran into Mr. Gunther. He was standing on the steps scrolling through something on his phone as I came out the door. "Charlotte! Hello! I haven't seen you in a few years! How are you doing?"

"Hello, Mr. Gunther. I'm fine."

"Are you still living in Pine Haven? I thought you might have moved away after that bad business in the shop, and your mother marrying that police officer, Emery, was it?"

"No. I finished community college. I work for Mr. Beresford now as his personal assistant." I saw his eyes flick to the Bentley waiting at the curb.

"I see. That's interesting. Tell me, has anyone there had any word in regards to Rand? Does anyone know where he is? I thought I'd heard that he'd been in Pine Haven recently."

"Um, I'm not sure. I heard that he was home very briefly, but I was in New Hampshire with Ripley."

"Ah, yes. She's your best friend, if I recall. The two of you were thick as thieves all throughout high school." I nodded, not exactly remembering us as being thick as thieves, just best friends like any other pair of best friends. "So, you don't know for certain if he was home or not?" I shook my head, knowing that the Beresfords would not want me discussing their personal business with anyone, even a former teacher. "Too bad. I was hoping to meet up with him. We have some common interests. I was hoping to get his thoughts on a certain shared interest. Well, if you ever hear from him, would you let him know that I'd be interested in meeting with him when he comes back to town?"

"Yes. I can do that, if I hear from him. But he's more apt to contact his father than he is to contact me."

"Yes, of course. Well, if you'd kindly put the bug in Mr. Beresford's ear for me then?"

"I'll see what I can do."

"It's very nice to see you. You look well after all that you've been through. Your arm is healed?" His eyes lowered to my left arm which still bore the surgical scars from having to have a rod placed and a bone graft. "No lasting issues?"

"There's nerve damage in my arm. When I get tired or overuse my arm, I lose feeling in my hand. It goes numb." His eyes rose to meet mine again. "I manage all right. I just have to remember not to carry anything heavy for too long on my left side."

"I'm sorry to hear that. Well, good luck with your work. And remember, if you hear from Rand, let him know that I'd like to get together with him sometime."

"I'll do that. Bye, Mr. Gunther!" I dashed down the remaining steps and climbed into the car; Sanborn having gotten out and opened the door for me while I'd been talking.

As we headed back to Juniper Avenue, he glanced at me in the mirror. "That guy gives me the creeps," he said.

"He's just one of those guys who has always been rather full of himself."

"To the brim, if I say dare say so."

I turned my head and looked out the window, my thoughts leading me back to my high school days and the things that I'd heard about Mr. Gunther back then, even from Ripley who had gone to his home in the woods that one time. He'd given drugs to high school kids, had sex with under-aged girls, and provided alcohol to high school kids, among other things. I got a queasy feeling in my stomach thinking about what he had gotten away with, and was probably still getting away with to this day, since he was still one of the gym teachers at the high school as far as I knew. He appeared to be in great shape physically for a guy who must be in his forties by now. It made me uneasy to wonder what shared interest he could possibly have with Julian (I thought of him again as Julian because that was how he himself had started to sign his letter).

Back at the house, Druce informed me that Mr. Beresford would like the pleasure of my company in the workshop. I said I would join him as soon as I changed my clothes. The workshop was not a place to wear nicer clothes. I dashed upstairs to my suite, changing into jeans and a t-shirt.

The workshop was in the west wing on the first floor in the former ballroom. I liked this space because it made me think of Cinderella dancing with her prince, ladies in beautiful ball gowns, men in tie and tail, and musicians on the small stage at the far end, the rows of French doors open to admit the fragrances from the gardens they opened onto. I saw it as a romantic space, not a place of industry, which it now was.

I slipped into the room through one of the doors that opened onto the main corridor. I was vaguely aware that Julian had moved to a suite on the second floor in this wing after the incident that had changed his life. His mother had recently died. His two best friends had been slaughtered by a feral animal. He had been bitten, gouged, and nearly blinded. His father had been grieving. How lonely he must have been, secluding himself away in an unused portion of the sprawling mansion.

"Good morning, Miss Rumford," Mr. Beresford said, glancing up to make sure that it was indeed me who had entered his work space.

"Good morning, Mr. Beresford. I'm sorry I was delayed. I wanted to change my clothes."

"No need to apologize. Come and sit down here across from me, will you. I want to show you how to properly wind a clock."

I sat and thus began my continuing education in clock making. He seemed to find great personal comfort in instructing me. I had begun to realize that I was his substitute for the son who had left him a lonely man without family nearby. When he had hired me, he had, more or less, unofficially adopted me as his daughter. In front of Druce and the rest of the staff, and in front of Attorney Bean and Mr. Stroud, he treated me like he would a personal assistant, a hired member of staff. But here in the shop, he was more a fatherly figure, patiently teaching me the family craft. I began to understand that since Julian had stated that he would sell the business, his father was teaching me the skills that I would need to continue the clock making business when he himself was gone. I had no idea how he thought he could compress my education into the little time that he had left.

This realization placed me on a precipice with a vista that telescoped a terrifying distance ahead of me. He was essentially slowly dying even as he patiently instructed me each time we met here in the workshop. I felt an overwhelming despair at the thought that I would be a huge disappointment to him in the end because I would not be anywhere near trained enough to take over this special business. And then the more wrenching vision of his future for me rattled me deeply. Perhaps he thought his son would come home, find that I was a capable assistant in the shop, and Julian would decide to settle down, get married, to me of all people, and we would work together carrying on his father's esteemed trade.

It made me positively dizzy to contemplate a father so desperate that he would immerse himself in attempting to train a young woman with no mechanical or technical skill whatsoever in the highly skilled craft of clock making. I would be an even greater disappointment to him than Julian was. He was pinning his hopes of having his trade continue in the family on a not quite twenty-one year old girl and a twenty-four year old who wanted nothing to do with this house and this business. He had established his own home, his own business in Europe. The whole idea that I would be a colossal failure in the near future made me want to cry.

"Charlotte!" came Mr. Beresford's sharp voice. "Pay attention, please!"

"I'm sorry," I murmured, pulling my head out of the storm clouds that had been enveloping me, returning to the present.

He laid down his miniature screwdriver, reaching across the table to lay his hand atop my folded hands. "It's all right if you want to tell me that I'm a foolish man. I know well enough what I am. I appreciate you're coming here and humoring me."

My eyes met his across the work table. For several long moments, we just looked at one another, and then I said, "Do you mind if I move my stool around the table to sit beside you rather than across from you? I think I'd catch on more easily if I could see what you're doing better, not upside down and backwards."

He gave my hand a gentle squeeze. "Yes, of course. Bring your stool around and sit here beside me. I should have realized that was part of the problem." I moved my stool around, placing it beside his and then sitting down again. He moved the clock that he was working on over in front of me. "Here now, take the screwdriver and this implement that is magnetized so that it will hold the screw in place until you've got it started. You must have a steady hand for this."

I worked diligently and inserted three screws before my left hand began to tingle and tremble with fatigue. I set the implement down and shook my hand briskly. "Charlotte, I think we should look into some additional physical and occupational therapy for you. I don't think they did quite enough for you after your surgery."

So, that's how my lessons in clock making began in earnest, and my sessions with the physical therapist and an occupational therapist were initiated with the goal of my regaining more use of my left hand without so much fatigue. Mr. Beresford even sent me to a neurologist to see if there were any further procedures he could suggest that would rectify the nerve issues I had with that arm and hand.

I did have more surgery on my arm and wrist to remove scar tissue along the nerve paths. This occurred over the winter. I had two surgeries, and then more physical and occupational therapy. However, even as I recovered from the surgeries, I was meeting Mr. Beresford in the workshop and continuing my lessons.

Then, in February, he developed pneumonia and was hospitalized. His condition was grave. He was in ICU. Mr. Stroud and I were the only two allowed in for five minute visits every hour. Mr. Stroud sat scowling at me in the visitor's waiting room, nonverbally accusing me of something I had never done. Druce always made sure that the heat was on in the ballroom and I always made sure that he wore his heavy cardigan and utilized the lap robe while we were making a clock together.

His pneumonia was due to aspiration of stomach acid, acid reflux being a byproduct of his chemo and medication history. "Instead of sitting there glaring at me, you should be on the phone ordering him an adjustable bed so he doesn't aspirate again," I finally snapped at him before getting up and stalking out of the waiting room to go in search of the vending machines the nurse had said were just down the corridor.

It was while struggling to get the soda machine to take a crumpled dollar bill that Mr. Gunther strode past, stopped, and took three large steps backwards until he was even with the alcove I was in. "Charlotte! It is you. I would know that red hair of yours anywhere. Why are you here? Is your mother ill?"

"No, my mother is fine, as far as I know. Mr. Beresford's in ICU. I'm waiting to see him again before I head home."

"Is it the cancer?"

"No, he has pneumonia."

"Oh, dear. That can often be fatal to those already compromised by serious health issues. Has anyone contacted Rand? He might want to come home, if his father is at death's door."

"I don't think anyone has thought to contact him."

"You must know a way to reach him. Surely he hasn't cut all ties with the old man?"

Something was suddenly giving me a headache. "I'll send him a message when I get home," I murmured, rubbing my forehead.

"Are you feeling unwell, Charlotte?"

"No, it's just a stress headache. I'm trying to get a soda, but the stupid machine won't take this dollar bill and it's the last one I have."

He tutted, took out his wallet and thumbed through the bills inside, pulling out a crisp, new, one dollar bill. "Let's try this one, shall we?" He stepped past me, brushing against me before I could step back. My skin prickled. I frowned. "There we go. Now, what was it that you wanted?"

"Ginger ale."

He pressed the button and the bottle thumped down a chute inside the machine before thudding into the tray at the bottom. He snatched it, twisted the cap loose and then handed me the bottle. "There you go." He plucked the rumpled dollar bill from my hand, tucking it into his front pocket. "I think, if the old man is that sick, that Rand should be advised and urged to come home."

"I'll let Mr. Stroud know. He makes all the decisions when Mr. Beresford is unable to. I'm just an assistant."

He gave me a long appraising look and then smiled. "You under sell yourself. I think you've become much more than that to the elder Beresford. Take care, Charlotte." He walked off, greeting a young woman at the nurse's station just a few feet down the hallway.

I returned to the waiting room, dropping down into the chair I had recently been sitting in. "Do you think we should try reaching J. Rand?" I asked before sipping some of the prickly soda.

"What for? That boy is a plague on his father."

"Mr. Beresford is very sick. He could die."

"No one's said that death is imminent." He narrowed his eyes at me. "You may be his personal assistant, but don't make the mistake of taking the word personal to mean that you're allowed to involve yourself in Mr. Beresford's personal business."

His remark stung, but it also infuriated me. I wanted to retort that he was Mr. Beresford's business manager and that didn't imply that he had any business poking his nose into Mr. Beresford's personal business either. I was so annoyed that I took out my phone and texted Sanborn, asking him if he was still in the parking lot. He was over at the Big Dipper having a coffee, but said that if I was ready to go home that he could be there in less than ten minutes. I told him to come and get me, I was ready to go home. I was more than ready to go home.

I was so steamed up that I went right up to my room and sent Julian a text message informing him that his father was in ICU with pneumonia and his condition was grave. I then tossed my phone across the sitting room onto the loveseat, curled up in the wingchair I was sitting in, and cried for the man fighting for his life in the hospital.

I did not go down to dinner. Druce arrived at my door at seven o'clock bearing a tray. He gave me a long look before passing by me to place the tray on the table in the corner. "Mr. Beresford was disappointed that you did not join him for dinner this evening," he said, confusing me. "He's left to go and see his father."

It took me a few more moments to realize that he meant J. Rand was home. "Oh," I said.

"I told him you were feeling under the weather, that you've had additional surgery on your arm and have been worrying yourself sick about his father."

"Thank you, Druce. I had a terrible headache when I got home. I must have fallen asleep in the chair."

Susan Buffum

"Low blood sugar can cause a headache. Helen arranged a light supper on a plate for you, not the full five courses as usual. Go and eat. I'll come back and remove the tray in an hour. I suggest you retire early tonight. Food and rest will be the best medicine for you."

"Yes, thank you, Druce."

I ate most of what Helen had sent up—fish, rice pilaf, and green beans. Instead of dessert, she'd made a little fruit bowl for me comprised of grapes and apple slices. She'd also sent a small china pot of English breakfast tea. I drank all of that, realizing that part of my problem was dehydration, even though I'd had the soda at the hospital. I hadn't had nearly enough fluids or food.

Feeling somewhat better, I took a shower, pinning my hair up, but it still got a little wet. I towel dried it which brought out the natural soft curl. I left it loose, intending to let it air dry. I got into bed and then reached for my phone on the bedside table. It wasn't there.

Groaning, I got back out of bed, went out into the sitting room where I'd dropped my bag when I'd gotten home from the hospital and rummaged around inside it, growing more alarmed when I couldn't find my phone. Just as I was about to dump everything out of my bag onto the seat of the chair, a thought struck me. I turned and looked across the room, spotting my phone on the love seat where I had thrown it earlier.

Shaking my head, I went and retrieved it, flicking off the lights before returning to the bedroom. Druce had come and cleared away the dinner tray while I'd been in the shower. It didn't bother me that he had come into my room when I was in the bathroom. I always locked the bathroom door, but I seldom locked the sitting room door or my bedroom door. The house was secure. Caroline and Rose had suites on the second floor, as did Helen and Lorraine. This was the women's floor. The men had suites up on the third floor. Sanborn had the apartment above the carriage house. Druce, Ethan Sinclair, the handyman, and Kerry Noble, the gardener, all had suites upstairs from us. None of them had ever bothered us. I felt safe enough here.

Therefore, when a slight sound woke me from a dead sleep, I gasped, startled. I stretched my left hand out to reach for the flashlight on the bedside table and touched fabric. A scream started to rise up the back of my throat, but a voice said, "It's just me." I didn't know who 'just me' was. The low voice wasn't familiar to me. It was slightly raspy, as if the person was getting over a cold.

"What do you want?" I managed to ask.

"I didn't mean to wake you." I lay in the dark, my heart still thudding hard in my breast. If he hadn't meant to wake me then what was he doing in my room. The sound of him blowing air through his nose followed that sentence. "No, actually, I thought you might be awake. Stroud says you're worried about my father." My heart rate increased at the realization that this was Julian standing beside my bed.

"I am," I replied, my voice a little breathless with the whirlwind of emotion raging trough me. I wanted to jump out of bed and pound him to a pulp for being such a jerk to his father who loved him and always would. I wanted to hug him for somehow finding out his father was sick and coming home to see him. I wanted to throw myself into his arms and cry all the stress and worry within me onto his shoulder.

"They let me sit with him…for half an hour. I wasn't allowed to talk to him much, but…he knew I was there." He seemed to be having difficulty getting words out all of a sudden. "I just sat there and held his hand. His fever had spiked again. They thought he was going to pass."

"Did he?" I whispered, barely able to ask that question.

"No. The fever broke. He's sleeping, so I came here." I noticed that he didn't say he came home. He no

Susan Buffum

longer thought of this house as his home. "I thought you'd want to know."

"Yes. Thanks for coming to tell me."

I heard him move and thought he was leaving, but what he did was walk around to the far side of the bed. He sat down on the side of the bed, and then he startled me further by lying down beside me. "Cherry…" he said, and then he didn't say anything else. He didn't have to say anything. I could feel the emotions roiling inside of him. The bed fairly vibrated with the internal struggle going on within him.

"His cancer had slowed down. He'd been doing pretty well. I don't know what his being this sick will do to him. I'm glad you came home. How did you know he was so sick? Did Mr. Stroud contact you?"

"No. You're the only one who can directly contact me. I got your message when I was passing through customs at Logan Airport. I texted you back when I was finished at the car rental stand."

"Oh. I left my phone on the love seat and the battery died. It's on the charger. I just…I had a headache so I went to bed early."

"I thought you'd at least come down and have dinner with me." He moved his arm, raising it. I heard him run his fingers through his hair. "I thought you were pissed off at me when you didn't come down. I sent Druce up to ask you to come down, but he came back and said he thought you were crying, that you must be upset about my father. So he went to talk to Helen. He was worried about you, said you haven't been eating right."

"No."

"Are you pissed off at me?"

"Yes," I replied. I couldn't lie to him.

116

"Lots of people are. Here anyway. I didn't exactly leave them with a good last impression of me when I left Pine Haven."

"No, you didn't."

"I was fucked up, Cherry. I still am. I don't want to be here."

"Then why did you come?"

He was silent for a long time. He shifted and I thought he was going to get up, walk out, and never answer me. But, he settled back down. Finally, he said, "Because I'm not so fucked up that I don't know where my ability to build a clock comes from. I can only do what I do because of him parking my ass in the workshop and instructing me day in and day out." He blew out his breath. "I used to resent that with a passion. I hated him for years. He wanted me to be like him, to grow up and stay here in Pine Haven, take over the business, and never test my own limits, or explore my own capabilities. I never hated clock making. It's always fascinated me. It's magical. It's always been magical to me. To him, it's a job. To me, it's an art form." He shifted again, his arm brushing mine. My skin prickled. "Do you remember the day your mother brought you out to the shop with the broken clock? I was pissed off at my old man because I wanted to try my hand at building a tower clock and he'd said absolutely not. I'd drawn up the plans. I'd sketched pictures. I even had a damn blueprint drawn up. I was fuckin' fourteen years old and had this burning desire to build this amazing clock tower out of all that scrap metal left behind when the machine shop closed and all he said to me was 'absolutely not.' And then I walked out front and there was your gorgeous mother and little, freckle-faced, red-haired you looking like the most miserable kid on the face of the planet. I couldn't believe your mother made you pay for the broken clock. She made you pay the guy every cent you had, didn't she?"

"Yes."

"That pissed me off more than my father telling me I couldn't make the tower clock. And then he said he was too busy to fix the damn clock. Your face, when he said that, just crumpled. Jesus Christ, Cherry…you broke my heart. I didn't want to see you cry. So, I decided I'd fix the damn clock for you and I wouldn't charge you a red cent for it. I did it to piss him off, to piss your mother off, and to…I don't know."

"Show me you weren't such a horrible jerk after all?"

"No," he said. Then he kind of laughed. "I don't know. I thought it was cruel of her to make a little kid pay for what had to have been an accident. I couldn't picture sweet little you picking up a clock and deliberately dropping it. You were raised around antiques. You knew how to handle them. Accidents happen. The guy in that shop was an asshole for taking your money. Your mother could have handled that whole thing a lot better than she did. She's a dealer herself." I didn't say anything. It was still a little unnerving to me that he was in my room, that he was having this conversation with me. It was almost as if ten years hadn't passed, that he was fourteen and I was eleven again, that he was the Julian he had been before that camping trip. But, I knew he wasn't that boy anymore. I didn't know who this Julian Rand Beresford was.

He moved his arm again until it touched mine. Again I got that prickling sensation across my skin. It felt like static electricity. I thought it must be the kind of material his shirt was made of, his moving his arm across the covers I was lying beneath creating the static electricity, but then I realized that his forearm was bare. He was wearing a t-shirt or short-sleeved shirt. This was his bare arm against my bare arm. "He's trying to teach me how to make clocks," I blurted out. He was silent for nearly three minutes. I thought he might have fallen asleep, but then he sort of snorted and abruptly got up off the bed. Before he reached the door, I blurted out the other thing I had to tell him. "Julian, Mr. Gunther keeps asking me if you've come home."

He was back at the side of the bed in a heartbeat, had grabbed me around the throat and pulled me upright, shaking me. "What have you told him?" he growled. He literally *growled* at me.

"Nothing! I haven't told him anything!" I cried, suddenly terrified of him. He was angry. My skin was prickling like crazy where he was gripping me. "Julian, let go! You're scaring me!"

"Do not tell him a goddam thing about me, do you hear me?"

"Yes, I hear you! I won't!"

"And stay the fuck away from him, Charlotte. Just stay as fuckin' far away from him as you can."

"I will!"

"You'd better." He let go of me and I fell back against my pillow. "He's out of the woods," he said as he moved to the door. I thought he was talking about Mr. Gunther who lived in the woods out past the Renegade Club. It confused me. "I'm taking off. I have a meeting in Boston this morning. If he takes a turn for the worse, text me and I'll come back. But right now, I need to get the fuck out of here. I'm not ready for this yet."

"Julian," I said, but he was already gone.

Susan Buffum

Chapter Ten

Mr. Beresford slowly recovered. He was moved home and had a visiting nurse and home physical therapy. He was anxious to get back to the workshop, but was too weak to do so. He sent Mr. Stroud away and asked Druce to send me up with a book, any book of my choosing. He wanted me to read to him.

Therefore, every day I read for several hours and then he napped. In the afternoon, the nurse came, and then three afternoons a week the physical therapist came and got him out of bed. In the evening, Druce would give him his bath, and then I was summoned to read to him again for an hour. Then, he would tell me to stop and he would talk to me about his grandfather and his father who had passed the trade of clockmaker on to him.

As spring once again approached, he surprised me one night. "I had a dream when I was in the hospital. I dreamt that J. Rand came to visit me. It was such a vivid dream it warmed my heart. He sat beside the bed and said absolutely nothing, but he held my hand. I could feel him, the dream was so real."

Obviously no one had told him that his son had actually come here and sat with him one night when he was close to death. I didn't know if I should tell him that Julian had been here or not. "That must have been a nice dream."

"It was, Charlotte. It gave me hope that he and I can reconcile our differences before I leave this earth."

"I hope that's true, that you and he will repair what's broken between you."

"I failed him when he needed me most. I don't know how I can ever mend that wound in his heart."

"Sometimes we can't mend the wounds. Sometimes we have to acknowledge that they exist and cannot be repaired, but that bonds still exist that can't be broken. And then we have to find a way to move on and leave the past where it lies. Life is too short to haul so much emotional baggage around, adding more and more on top of it until it stops all forward movement dead in its tracks."

He sighed wearily, his eyes drifting closed for a few long moments before he murmured, "You are a very wise young woman. I'll say goodnight now, Charlotte. Will you please ask Druce to come up?"

"I will. Goodnight, Mr. Beresford."

"Goodnight, dear girl."

His recovery was slow and gradual, but finally, in early May, he was strong enough to go to the workshop and we resumed my lessons. They were briefer than in the past because he tired more easily now, but I was surprised by how much I had already learned. I viewed each lesson as a link being added to a chain of knowledge. I couldn't fabricate a clock case, but I knew quite a bit about the internal workings of a clock, what made it tick.

The Clockmaker's Son

On my twenty-second birthday in late May he summoned me to the workshop after lunch where he had a clock all in pieces spread out on the work table. "When you've finished assembling this clock, and it runs, we shall have cake and ice cream." He then left me alone in the workshop.

I nearly had a panic attack looking at all the pieces laid out on the table, the miniature tools lined up just so, the empty case of the clock awaiting the reassembled clockworks to be finished and inserted, and then the winding of the key with fingers crossed that it would begin ticking.

I felt an overwhelming urge to just sit there and burst into tears of uncertainty and despair. But, as I struggled to get control of my emotions, I began envisioning each link in the chain. He had taught me what to do. All I had to do was follow the steps. Assemble the chain, link by link.

Taking a breath, I looked over the parts spread out on the rubberized mat on the table so nothing would roll away. I studied them, and then found what I needed to forge link one. Link by link, I assembled the pieces and built the clockworks that was the heart of this mantle-size case clock. It took me several hours. I had to get up and pace the length of the room, stretch and work the knots from my shoulders. My left arm felt heavy with fatigue and the fingers of that hand tingled, but I kept going.

At twenty past three, I left the workshop carrying the clock. I knew I would find Mr. Beresford in either the study or the library. He was sitting in a wingchair reading in the library. He turned his head and watched me as I carried the clock to the table beside his chair and set it down. The heartbeat like tick-tocking was the only sound in the room. He watched the hands of the clock for three long minutes. I watched the hands of the clock, too, counting off the seconds in my head, feeling a burst of joy in my heart each time the hand advanced when it should. "Good job, Charlotte," he said. "Shall we go to the day room and have a little birthday party now?"

"Sounds good to me," I replied.

He smiled at me, nodded toward the clock and said, "And that sounds like music to my ears to me."

Druce cocked an eyebrow in obvious surprise when Mr. Beresford summoned him to the library. "She has reassembled the clock. Please return it to its place in the game room and then let Helen know that we'll be in the day room. It's time for some cake and ice cream in celebration of Charlotte's birthday."

I expected cake and ice cream. I didn't expect a bouquet of colorful balloons, streamers, a vase of beautiful pale purple and white roses, and a gift. He made me wait to open the gift until after we'd all had cake and ice cream. By all, I mean the entire household staff joined us in the day room. Mr. Stroud was noticeably absent, but he actually wasn't at the house every day. He did have his own office in Stockbridge and other clients besides my employer.

Finally, Mr. Beresford gave the nod and I opened my gift. My gift turned out to be a beautiful rosewood toolbox with a complete set of brand new miniature tools laid out in velvet slots inside. It was my very own clockmaker's tool set. "Congratulations, Charlotte. You've reached apprentice clockmaker status. You've earned your own set of tools."

Apprentice clockmaker! I was overwhelmed by his faith in me, that I could be a clockmaker. The tools were gorgeous! When I lifted one out to examine it more closely, I saw that on each handle there were tiny engraved violets and ivy leaves. I burst into tears, deeply touched that he'd had the tools custom made for me and then had had them personalized as well with my favorite flower and vine. "Thank you so much!" I managed to say, and then I got up, crossing the room, bent down, threw my arms around his neck and hugged him, kissing his gaunt cheek. "I can't begin to tell you how much this means to me." He was teaching me a trade. He believed in me. If his son had disappointed him, I was not going to follow suit. I was going to make him proud of me.

"Run upstairs. We're having company for dinner tonight in honor of it being your birthday."

He wouldn't tell me who he had invited. I thought it might be my mother and Mike, but didn't know why he'd invite them here. True, she was my mother, but since marrying the town cop and moving to Windsor, I really hadn't seen much of her and she hadn't contacted me either, except she had sent me a 'Happy Birthday' text with a cake emoji this morning. She had not sent a card or a gift or anything, just the message.

It struck me that the people in Randolph Hall were more a family to me than my own parents were. I seldom heard from Charlie either. He and my father had not sent me any birthday messages. Just my Mom had, and it was like she'd just sent the message to get it over and done with. It was disheartening that I didn't mean much to my own family. It made me wonder if I had ever meant anything to them. It had always been all about Charlie.

I was thinking about all this as I came downstairs in the only dress I owned that currently fit me. I had lost some weight again and was slimmer than I had ever been. Druce met me at the foot of the stairs. "I am to escort you directly to the dining room, Miss Rumford." And here he actually offered me his arm. This was unusual, but I slipped my hand under his crooked arm, laying my hand across his wrist, and he led me to the formal dining room. I noticed the prickling sensation, but didn't think much of it. I was excited to learn who our guests were.

There, seated at the table with Mr. Beresford were Ripley and a young man I recognized from dozens of facebook photos, Miles Worthy, her longtime beau. "Happy birthday, Charlotte!" they cried as I entered. Then, Ripley jumped up out of her chair and came to hug me. Tears of happiness were spilling down my cheeks, I was so surprised to see her. I knew she had graduated earlier this month, but her recent texts had been vague about what she was actually doing—working or taking a little time off before starting work. "Miles and I are visiting Mom and Dad before we head out west. Miles has a fantastic job lined up and they might have something there in another department for me. I wanted to see you again before we moved so far away. Why are you so skinny?"

"I've been swimming a lot and playing tennis." This was only partially true.

"Oh, Charlotte, don't go fading away! You're so pretty! Come on. Sit down. I hear Mr. Beresford has an amazing cook and the food in this house is delicious!"

"Both facts are very true," I said as she led me to the table. I paused to bend and kiss the cheek of the man who had arranged this awesome surprise for me. Then I sat down on his right hand side this evening. Ripley was in the chair I had occupied since coming to work here. I was in the chair Grace Beresford had sat in previously. It was a great honor to be allowed to sit in the mistress' place at the table tonight.

Druce, to his credit, did not even raise an eyebrow about the seating arrangements. He served us with the quiet dignity of a man who had served meals at this table for something like thirty years. I really didn't know how long he had been here or even if he had always served the meals. Maybe at one time, when Mrs. Beresford had still been alive, there had been more servants. Mr. Beresford had stated that he'd pared down the staff after her death.

I wasn't going to dwell on figuring it all out. This was my birthday dinner with my incredible employer and self-appointed instructor, and my best friend and...oh! It was as she lifted her water glass in her left hand that I noticed the diamond ring on her left ring finger. "Ripley! Is that an engagement ring?" She grinned and nodded. I threw my napkin down, jumped up, and ran around the table to hug her and kiss her cheek, and then I had to hug Miles and kiss his cheek and congratulate them both.

"Sit down and eat now. You can hug me again after we've eaten," Ripley said, grinning happily. I returned to my seat and we resumed eating the delicious seven course meal Helen and Lorraine had prepared—my birthday feast. It included all my favorite foods, and then there was another cake for dessert. The cake this afternoon had been marble. This cake was angel food, light and airy, the perfect finish for a huge dinner.

We adjourned to the informal parlor to visit and, there, Ripley got the proper hugs she deserved for graduating with honors and for her engagement. Mr. Beresford excused himself at nine-thirty. I hugged him and kissed his cheek, quietly thanking him for the best birthday I'd ever had. He'd smiled, patted my arm, wished me a goodnight, and then left. Druce, I noticed, was waiting in the hallway to assist him upstairs.

Ripley and Miles stayed until eleven-thirty. I walked them outside to their car, hugging and kissing them both again, my heart full of joy for them as they began their life together. I was glad she had found the right guy for her and everything was falling into place for them. I wished them both all the best, told them to come see me before they started their journey west next week. They said they would. I waved goodbye, went back inside, and closed the door. Druce was waiting to secure the house for the night. "Did you enjoy yourself tonight?"

"He is the most amazing man I've ever known. I did enjoy myself. My birthday was perfect. Goodnight, Druce."

"Goodnight, Miss Rumford." I was halfway up the stairs when he said, "He's quite proud of you for reassembling that damned clock. It hasn't worked in ten years. He's astounded that you brought it to him ticking."

"He's an excellent instructor," I replied. How else could I explain it? I'd just put the clock back together. I'd assumed it was a working clock and never thought for a moment that it was not.

It was an even better birthday than I had thought if I had impressed the clockmaker.

Chapter Eleven

And then the bottom fell out of my world. Three days before they were to leave for New Mexico, Ripley and Miles went out to dinner to celebrate the anniversary of the day they had met at college orientation in late spring, a few months before the start of freshman year. They did not return to the Forbes' house when expected. They'd only gone to Max's Grill and Tavern. Mr. Forbes, concerned, had driven out to Max's. There were still many cars in the lot. He found Miles' car near the rear of the lot. The restaurant was usually busy. If you arrived late, you had to park way out at the back of the lot and wait in line to get in. He got out to look into the car. While walking around it, he'd noticed scuffed gravel, and then he'd found Ripley's purse a few feet behind the car.

He'd called the police. It hadn't taken them long to find Ripley and Miles. They had been dragged only about thirty feet into the woods behind the car. They were both dead, their throats torn out, their bodies torn open, entrails strewn about.

I learned this from Chief Adams when he came to Randolph Hall at the request of Mrs. Forbes, who was unable to leave her own home to come and tell me herself, she was so distraught. "Charlotte," he said when I walked into the day room where he was waiting for me. "Come and sit down. I have something to tell you."

What he told me sent me over the edge, beyond grief and shock. I couldn't stop screaming. It brought back the horror of what I had seen in the shop, Chase's body torn open on the floor. My mind could not accept the thought of my best friend being killed in the same way. She'd been so lively, so happy, so beautiful and glowing just a few days ago. We were supposed to be going shopping this afternoon. Now, here was the Chief of Police telling me something I could not accept as fact, but at the same time, could not stop from filling me with a toxic brew of horror, revulsion, and shock so that I thought my heart would stop dead in my breast.

I did not remember the paramedics coming to the house. I remembered Chief Adams dabbing his eyes with his handkerchief as I continued to scream at him, accusing him of lying when I could plainly see that he had not, that he was deeply shaken and upset himself.

I suppose I was sedated because I had a dull nagging headache and a dry mouth when I opened my eyes to find myself in a treatment room, my wrists and ankles strapped to the bed rails. "What the hell?" I murmured trying to tug my right hand free. My nose itched. My eyes felt gritty. I wanted to scratch my nose and rub my eyes. "Hey!" I cried. "Hey!"

And then I dissolved into sobs so harsh, so intense that they made me curl upright and nearly vomit. My stomach was empty or else I would have been sick all over myself. And then I was shaking so hard the cot I was on rattled. That began to drive me crazy, that noise, like a trapped animal in a cage trying to get out. "Will you please unstrap me!" I shouted wildly.

A doctor came into the room and I fell back on the pillow. "Charlotte, let's not shout, all right? It disturbs the other patients."

"My nose itches. My eyes feel all crusty. Can't you just let me have one hand free?"

"Will you behave yourself?"

"I just want to scratch my nose and rub my eyes. Please!"

He freed my left hand. Gratefully, I took care of that nagging itch and rubbed the grittiness from my eyes. My lashes were still crusty from crying. I asked if someone could give me some damp paper towels so I could wash my face. He said he'd send a nurse in to assist me. Then he adjusted the IV flow, uncapped a syringe, and injected whatever was in it into the IV port. "What was that?" I asked, my voice already slurry.

"Just something to help you sleep. Close your eyes, Charlotte, and get some rest. It's been a long day."

I turned my head and tried to focus on the wall clock on the tiled wall, but the hand seemed watery, wavy, and wouldn't stay still long enough for me to figure out what time it was. Blessedly, oblivion swept me away once again.

I spent a total of fifteen days in the psych ward in a private facility in Pittsfield, having been transferred there from our small local hospital. Everyone had been afraid that I might harm myself with this even more personal loss. I suppose I did sort of lose my mind with grief and shock for a few days, but the medication they made me take, and twice daily counseling sessions during those fifteen days, balanced me, or at least made me become a functional human being again, although a deeply wounded one with a new tendency to lash out at people with an anger that was uncharacteristic for me.

I also had a roiling sense of frustration within me, frustration that these heinous mutilation murders had not been prevented or stopped because I knew in my soul that this was not the work of feral dogs or a wolf pack. This beast had slashed me close to the bone twice already by hurting Julian so badly he left Pine Haven and killing Chase. But this time it was very personal because Ripley and I had been best friends, as close as blood sisters, ever since pre-school when we'd met. This murder, because I refused to call it anything less, had rocked my world hard and twisted a simmering rage toward whatever creature was responsible for it into a roaring cyclone. I wanted to kill it. I wanted these senseless attacks on human beings and innocent animals stopped—the sooner the better.

I suppose you can say I fractured under the stress of this incomprehensible loss. To all appearances, I was Charlotte Rumford, personal assistant to, and apprentice to, clockmaker R. Hollis Beresford, living comfortably and safely in the mansion on Juniper Avenue. But, inside of me, there was this grief and rage fueled Charlotte plotting the death of the beast that had damaged her too much to ever be just plain Charlotte ever again.

When Sanborn came to take me back to Pine Haven, he brought me a raspberry iced tea. I sat in the back seat sipping the cold drink, not talking. I saw him watching me in the rearview mirror, trying to gauge my mood, my psychiatric status. Finally, I said, "I had a breakdown. That's all it was. My best friend and her fiancé were killed. I'm okay."

"I've known you for a few years, now, Charlotte. You've never been this quiet. You're not okay."

I shrugged. "I have a lot to think about right now."

"Are you thinking about leaving us?" he asked, his tone cautious. In his voice, I heard worry that I would flee Pine Haven in the wake of this more personal double tragedy, that I would abandon the man who had given me everything when my parents had given me nothing.

"No. How can I leave? Mr. Beresford isn't finished teaching me the trade." This made his mouth quirk in a quick smile as relief filled his eyes. "How is he?"

"Concerned about you, the same as the rest of us. Even Druce has been out of sorts with all this bad business."

I nodded and then went back to sipping my iced tea. As we neared Pine Haven, I asked, "Do you think it would be difficult for me to get an FID card and a license to carry a gun?"

"Well," he answered slowly.

"Are they going to count a mental breakdown from stress and grief against me? I don't have any history of psychiatric issues. The local police are well aware of what happened, that Ripley and I were like sisters. They know what happened to me in The Remains of Yesterday, when I found Chase dead on the floor like that and was injured. I'm not a psycho." But a little worm of worry was gnawing away inside of me that maybe I would become one in the near future, because I was going to hunt down this beast and kill it. I was going to free my town from its tyranny that had gone on for over a decade now and break the chain it had locked around my ankle to hold me here with these new murders.

"No, I don't think so. Everyone knows you here. They knew Ripley, too. Hell, even I used to see you girls riding your bikes around town, having ice cream at Lickity-Splitz. You're a good kid, a nice young lady."

"Can we stop at the police station so I can pick up applications?"

"No, not today. I'll run downtown later this week and pick them up for you. Mr. Beresford is anxious to see you. You need to give yourself a couple of days to regroup and get back into your regular routine. It's a little chaotic in the house right now."

"How so?" I asked, thinking that Mr. Stroud was there trying to convince Mr. Beresford to oust his crazy personal assistant.

"J. Rand has come home. He and his father have been arguing about the old machine shop. J. Rand wants to reopen it and use it for his own clock making business. He says he has orders he needs to finish. He's having materials shipped from Europe to Pine Haven. He needs the space the shop would provide. His clocks are massive. Mr. Beresford is concerned that J. Rand may have flashbacks, or whatever you want to call them, returning to the shop. They've been fighting bitterly since he showed up. He was also angry because he wanted to see you, but, of course, you had the no visitors order in place because of the involuntary admission. That set him off, too."

"Why would he want to see me?" I asked.

"I guess he was concerned about you, Miss Forbes having been so close to you all of your life. Remember, he lost his two best friends years ago. You two have that in common now, the loss of your best friends to this…whatever the hell it is that has been terrorizing Pine Haven."

This gave me something more to think about as we approached Juniper Avenue. What he'd said opened a window in my mind that gave me a better understanding of Julian Rand. Maybe he, too, felt as if he had been split into two persons. Maybe he had a side of him that wanted revenge on this beast that had brutally, savagely taken the lives of his two best friends and damaged him. The beast had also damaged me instead of killing me, which it could have easily done. I didn't understand why it had only thrown me half the length of the shop front and not torn out my throat and ripped my guts out like it had done to Chase. Maybe it had sated its bloodlust and appetite on her and I had just been a weak threat to it? I really didn't know, but that may have been what had happened. It had been satisfied by what it had done to Chase and I was just in its way as it had been leaving. Maybe, if I hadn't stopped for the coffee and had walked into the store a few minutes earlier when it had still been tearing at her, it might have been enraged by the intrusion and killed me, too.

At the house, the moment I walked through the door that was opened by Druce who had been watching for my arrival, I heard raised voices from the study. "It would be best if you go up to your room and freshen up. Lunch will be served at one o'clock in the informal dining room. Mr. Beresford is anxious to see you then."

"Is that J. Rand he's arguing with?"

"That young man will be the death of his father."

"He's lived on his own for some time. He has his own business. Maybe I can help Mr. Beresford understand that he can't change the stripes on this tiger, but he can tame it by allowing it the use of the old shop."

"He…"

"J. Rand has had over ten years to work through his grief and anger. I don't know why he's suddenly come back and is now willing to work from Pine Haven, but maybe he senses his father won't be with us much longer and he wants to repair what he can between them before it's too late."

"By fighting with him like this?"

"He's a grown man used to his independence. I'll talk to Mr. Beresford." He looked doubtful that I would have any influence on the bitter argument between father and son.

I went upstairs to my suite, where I found bouquets of lovely flowers in the sitting room to welcome me home. I also found a miniature clock tower, close to six feet tall, standing in the corner of the room. It looked like a castle tower and had a balcony. There were very detailed trees on either side of the tower.

Walking closer, I could see some slots here and there and that the double doors leading out onto the balcony had hinges, so I figured they must open. It was nearly noon, so I stood there watching the clock. At one minute of twelve, I heard the trill of a songbird and the soft whirring of a gear as a nest with a tiny feathered bluebird rose up out of the branch overhanging part of the balcony. Other songbirds appeared on several of the other tree branches. It wasn't loud. It was soft, sweet bird song, musical.

Then, at noon, the doors of the castle slowly opened and more gears whirred as a female figure with red hair, wearing a green gown, glided out onto the balcony, her very detailed head turning slowly side to side as she appeared to look from one trilling bird to the next, a smile on her face. Then her tiny hand rose, her arm extending, and another bird suddenly seemed to fly down from a branch and land on her hand. She brought her hand close to her face. The little red bird tilted slightly making it look as if it had kissed her cheek. And then her arm extended again and the bird flew back into the tree. The animation lasted for one full minute and was absolutely mesmerizing. I couldn't take my eyes off the clock. Therefore, when a hand reached past me, opened the glass clock face and began turning the hands ahead hour by hour until nearly twelve hours had been advanced, I jumped. "Now watch this," Julian said. I started to turn my head to look over my shoulder at him, but he said, "No. Keep your eyes on the clock."

I watched the clock. A light came on behind the doors and I could see the silhouette of the girl. She appeared to be brushing her hair, which was incomprehensible to me. How could a little mechanical figure do such a thing? And then she vanished, only to reappear a few seconds later. The double doors slowly opened and she stepped out onto the balcony in a lilac-colored, Juliette-style nightgown. Her head turned side to side as if she was looking for something. The birds remained hidden. A full moon had risen from behind the conical roof of the castle. Slender dark clouds seemed to be passing across the face of the moon. I realized that they must be on a slowly rotating wheel of some sort. And then the girl turned quickly to her right as a figure appeared to leap from the tree. It landed on the balcony and I began to tremble. It was a gray wolf with red eyes. I didn't want to see the wolf kill the girl and began to turn away, but again he stopped me. His voice was low as he said, "No, it's all right. Just watch."

The wolf started toward the girl, but abruptly appeared to drop down onto all fours like a dog. And then up arose a handsome young man in a royal blue coat with a fur collar. The girl rushed into his arms that opened to received her and they shared an embrace, and then a kiss. Behind the roof, the moon began to wane. The lovers parted. The prince seemed to kneel down, but when he rose again he was once more a wolf. The wolf held a forepaw out toward the girl. She extended her delicate little hand toward the paw, but they never quite touched before the moon set and the wolf turned, leapt back into the trees, and disappeared. The girl's jointed arms bent so that she appeared to cover her face with her hands for a moment before she turned and went back through the doors which slowly closed behind her. The light inside the room beyond went out and the mechanism controlling the figures went silent.

"Oh, my God," I breathed, not quite believing what I had just seen. It had been like a clockwork fairy tale. The action of the figures had been so smooth, so perfectly timed and coordinated. My mind was still working through how this could even be possible.

Julian reached around me to reset the clock. It was nearly one o'clock. I realized that he'd set the clock tower so it would operate close to my expected arrival time from Pittsfield.

I turned around. He was standing right behind me so I had to tilt my head back to look up at him. He was taller than I remembered him being. Of course, the last time he'd been home, he'd been in my room in the dark. I really hadn't gotten a sense of how tall he was. I didn't remember him towering over me like this in high school. "What's the matter?" he asked as I bent my head, looking down at his feet, thinking he was wearing boots with heels, but he had battered old work boots on his feet.

"When did you get this tall?"

He snorted. "The old man's had me on the rack while you've been on the psych ward." I flinched at that. "Been there, done that. The food sucked, but the night nurse was hot and had no qualms about providing patients her own brand of good medicine." My head slowly came up until my eyes met his. He had a sort of defiant look on his face. "At fourteen, if a hot babe wants to take you for a ride, you more or less just go along with it."

"She had sex with you on the psych ward?"

"Sure. The old man made sure I had a private room. I didn't have anything else to do at night. I couldn't sleep. She kept me occupied, my mind off…things."

"Julian!"

He laughed. "Jesus, Charlotte, I had you going there, didn't I?"

"You're such a jerk sometimes!"

"Only sometimes? I'll have to try harder." He stepped back, looking me up and down. "Why are you so damn scrawny? Didn't the old man's money buy you decent meals while you were away?"

"I've been a little stressed out."

He nodded vaguely, not looking at me anymore. He was looking around the room, and then he walked over to the mantle and took down the clock painted with violets and ivy. "Where'd you get this one?"

"From your father."

"Figures. He's got a soft spot for you, Carrot-top."

"Don't start that with me again," I said in a warning tone, wondering how much more time he would spend in my room before he was tired of me.

"So, what do you think of the clock? It's the sample size version of the real one that I'm currently building. Well, I'd be building it, if they'd fucking clear the shipping containers through customs and deliver the damn things. They're in Boston right now." He scowled. "And then there's the little problem of my father refusing to allow me to use the old machine shop as my studio. I need your help, Cherry." Ah, this was what the clock was all about. He was buttering me up because he needed an ally to intervene on his behalf.

"I want to get a gun. I want to learn how to shoot," I replied.

He cocked a brow at me, and then frowned. "What for? You going to shoot me the next time I sneak into your room in the dead of night?"

"Maybe."

He shook his head and then reached up with both hands, running his fingers through his dark blonde hair. It was long and shaggy. He needed a haircut. He needed a shave, although he was rather roguish looking as he was. His hair had darkened since he was that eighteen-year old boy flipping off Pine Haven as he'd walked away from his life here. Finally, he blew his breath out, dropped his hand, pulling the right side of his shirt up and aside to reveal a holstered pistol on his belt, concealed by his shirt tails. "Tell you what, you sweet talk my old man into letting me set up shop on Clay Hill Road and I'll teach you to shoot and buy you the gun besides. But, first, you need gun safety instruction. I don't need you shootin' my balls off playing tough girl, spinning your sweet, little, deadly weapon around on your index finger, showing off for me. Deal?"

I didn't think Mr. Sanborn was going to be an awful lot of help to me beyond procuring the needed applications. I already knew what I needed to say to Mr. Beresford to sway him toward his son's wishes. "Deal." I stuck out my hand.

He looked at my hand, and then, instead of shaking it, he took my hand in his and turned it this way and that way, examining it. He dropped my right hand and took my left hand in his. This time, he rotated my arm and tracked my surgical scars with his fingertip. Again, I had that prickly feeling that physical contact with him seemed to cause, but I didn't feel that sensation along the length of my scars. There was no feeling there. "I'll fuckin' kill that bastard," he muttered.

"What bastard would that be?" I asked.

When he raised his head, his eyes were narrowed behind the tinted lenses of his glasses. I could sense the anger burning in their depths. "The bastard that did this to you," he replied, his voice low and gruff. And then he dropped my arm and turned toward the door. "Come on, the old man expects us downstairs. It's already a few minutes past one." He stalked out of the sitting room. I had to jog to catch up to him, but he had long legs and was down the stairs before I was even halfway down.

Chapter Twelve

Lunch had been rather tense. I'd spent a lot of time trying to keep what little conversation there had been focused on general topics. But, still, as soon as he'd wolfed down the last bite of chocolate pudding from the bowl in front of him, Julian had leapt up from the table as if someone had lit a fire under his butt. "I've got shit to do," he'd said before he'd walked out of the small dining room.

"That boy is incredibly rude. I apologize."

"Do you feel up to going to the workshop with me? I've really missed working with clocks." His eyes met mine. "I've missed you, too."

"I suppose we can spend an hour or so in the shop, but then we have some business to catch up on in the study." Oh, right. I had almost forgotten that I was, first and foremost, his personal assistant, that I had been gone for just over two weeks.

"Maybe we should take care of that first," I said.

He waved that aside as he rose slowly from his seat. "Come along, my dear Miss Rumford. I've been working on a little beauty that I'd like to get your opinion on." He crooked his arm. I slipped my arm through his. My hand rested on his wrist and it shocked me how incredibly thin and frail that wrist felt beneath my hand. It made my heart skitter around behind my breastbone, and then that same heart was wrenched when he stumbled in the hallway and nearly fell. I grabbed him to steady him until he regained his balance and the façade he had constructed fell away. He had lost a lot of weight. He was bird-boned. A stiff breeze would tumble him across the yard.

He said nothing more to me until we were in the workshop and seated side by side on our stools. "I'm sorry I didn't have time to change before coming down for lunch," I apologized. He liked to keep the tradition of dressing better for meals, except for breakfast, which was as casual as you wanted it to be.

"The cancer has begun to spread again. I don't have anything left in me to fight it with, Charlotte, my love. My oncologist suggested hospice. I've refused. I'm not quite ready to throw in the towel and admit that cancer will defeat sheer willpower." I opened my mouth to say something, but he held up his hand. "Was J. Rand upstairs with you prior to lunch?"

"He set up a clock in my sitting room. He came upstairs to observe my reaction to it."

"The princess in the tower and the big bad wolf. Yes. He demonstrated the clock's mechanical function to me the day it arrived. Well, the day after would be more accurate, as he had to assemble it and get it working." I didn't say anything, just waited quietly to hear his opinion of the amazing clock. "I've seen the photos of the clock towers he's made. I have assembled a collection of real photographs of as many of them as my agent in Europe could locate. I have my own little scrapbook in the bottom drawer of my desk. I've looked at it often. It's one thing to see a photograph and imagine the movement, the mechanical marvel of the thing. But it is quite another thing to see a miniature version of such a clock, to watch the intricately articulated and timed movements of the figures. To fall under the spell of such an incredible work of art is something else again entirely. I had to watch the whole thing, both noon and midnight, several times apiece—the trilling birds emerging on the branches, the roses blooming on the trellis, the ivy swaying gently as she steps out through those doors onto the balcony at noon. My mind could not fathom how he had made all that wondrous movement happen."

I had not noticed the roses blooming on the trellis below the balcony, nor the green ivy leaves swaying. I had been too focused on the songbird and the princess. "I need to watch it again. I missed a lot of things."

"I watched midnight and noon arrive four times apiece. I thought he would become annoyed with me, but then I sensed something in him that I had not expected from a young man touted as being a master clockmaker throughout Europe. I sensed tension, apprehension. He was anxiously awaiting my opinion of his work. I realized, in that moment, that I had the power to crush my son and punish him for all the heartache he's given me the past nearly dozen years with just a single word. If I'd uttered 'junk', I honestly think that single word would have stabbed him clean through the heart and he'd have dropped dead to the floor." He stopped speaking as he struggled to gain control over his emotions. And then he continued. "I looked at him standing there looking so cocky, his arms folded, but from across the room, I could tell that he was as tense as a too tightly wound clock spring. I looked at him with the morning light coming through the window behind him, the light illuminating the lighter blonde highlights in his hair. He looked so much like

143

his mother that it had this powerful effect on me. The cage I'd locked my heart in to protect it from all the hurt he's caused me for all those years, it suddenly burst open and all the love I have ever felt for him returned and expanded. Love, combined with pride. I thought I would die of it, the simple joy of having my son home, of his showing me this marvelous creation of his.

"The towers he constructs, they're much larger than this sample sized clock tower. He told me the figures he makes range anywhere from three inches to twenty-four inches in height. They are three dimensional and fully articulated. They move in a way that simulates actual lifelike movements. He removed the wolf from the tree and together we disassembled it. The gears and levers are so minute, yet they all work together so meticulously. That my son could conceive such a thing and then sit down and fabricate all the myriad parts and build the clock is almost more than my mind can comprehend." He removed a handkerchief from his pocket, dabbing his eyes and cheeks. "I thought he was being a fool, wasting his time and talent creating these whimsical things. They weren't real clocks to me." He shook his head. "I was wrong, Charlotte. I was so utterly wrong about that! If there is a master clockmaker in this family, that clockmaker is my son, not me."

"You are *both* master clockmakers," I quietly stated. "You are *both* masters of your craft."

"I don't know what to do about him though. If I allow him to reopen the old clock shop, I fear the close proximity of it to the scene where his trauma occurred will affect him negatively."

"He's had over ten years to move on, to allow time for that wound to heal."

"How can anyone ever get over something like that?"

"It's not about getting over it. It's about focusing on the horizon and moving forward, getting on with life and not dwelling on the past. Maybe he's finally ready to do that."

"I don't know about that."

"Maybe he wants to spend some time with you before…before it's…" I choked up and couldn't say before it was too late.

He reached over and patted my hand. "What should I do, Charlotte? If I don't allow him to use the old shop, then he will leave me again, I'm sure. There is still so much anger inside of him. He's been venting that anger on me for the past two weeks. I'm tired. I don't want to fight with him, but it will kill me quicker if I make a wrong decision and my son suffers further psychological trauma due to my wrong decision."

"I think you know what you have to do, consequences be damned." His gaze drifted away toward the French doors leading out into the formal gardens beyond. His hand was still on my arm and I felt him trembling. "I'm here. He's flip and fresh, but there's been this sort of connection between us since he repaired the little clock for me when I was just a kid. He asked me to let him know when he needed to come home.

"Unfortunately, I was away when that need became evident, yet, here he is. There's a bond between the two of you that is stronger than either of you realize. He was damaged by what happened in the past. But, to keep him here for now, you need to let him test himself, let him gauge for himself just how much he's healed, how much further he has to go. Let him open the shop and work there. He obviously loves his work. He immerses himself in it. Maybe he needs to be in a familiar work environment in order to find the strength he needs to accept that he's losing you before he's ready for that loss. He needs to be able to pour his energy and anxieties into something.

"Wouldn't you rather have him building clocks in the shop where both of you were happy before that terrible camping trip, close to home rather than being far away from here in Europe? There are happy memories for him in that shop. Let him revisit those memories. They'll help him remember you when he's older, when perhaps he has a son of his own. He'll say, 'My father and I did this, my Dad and I did that. He taught me everything I know, and then I went on to teach myself all of this. I won't hold you back, son. I'll let you pursue your own passions, like my father allowed me to pursue mine.'"

He squeezed my arm. "Haven't I always said that you are a wise young lady? I must let him go to keep him close. I understand." He sighed. "I'm tired now, my dear."

"Do you want me to call for Druce?'

"Yes, please. I think I would like to lie down for a few hours. A nap will do me good. Meanwhile, if you would attend to some of the things in the study that I've left for you, that would be helpful. There are several folders and envelopes with your name on them on my desk. Take care of those things for me. I will see you this evening at dinner."

"I'll look forward to that. I've been dying for a decent, home-cooked dinner for two weeks."

"It's good to have you home, Charlotte."

I leaned over and softly kissed his gaunt cheek, then got up and went to summon Druce, using the intercom system, not wanting to leave him alone for even a moment. I then returned to my stool and stayed with him until Druce arrived with a wheelchair. I could tell Mr. Beresford was upset that Druce had brought the wheelchair in, that he wanted to exit the ballroom on his own power, but when he went to stand up, he nearly fell. "Damn it all!" he barked, humiliated by his weakness.

"Dad," I said, the word just slipping out. I had done a lot of thinking about fathers while confined and concluded that of all the men in my life, Julian's father had been more a father to me in the past couple of years than my own father had ever been. I would be proud to call him Dad. But, I could feel the color staining my face as Druce glared at me as he helped the frail, older man into the wheelchair, lowering the foot rests, making sure his feet were properly set on them before releasing the brakes. "I'm sorry," I said, my voice barely a whisper, I was so humiliated by the slip of my tongue.

"Charlotte, never apologize for paying a sick man a supreme compliment. God never blessed Grace and me with a daughter. I never had the pleasure of hearing a sweet young lady call me Dad. You honor me with that little slip of the tongue. It must mean that you have come to think of me as a father figure in your life. There is nothing wrong with that. Your own father was less than exemplary. I hope I have been a better father figure than he was for you."

"You have been," I acknowledged.

He nodded. "Now, if I could only hear my son tell me that I have not been the colossal failure I have felt I've been since that fateful summer, then I will leave this world a much happier man."

They left the ballroom. I looked at the clock he had on the table, a camel-back mantle clock with Roman numerals and hands embedded with real jewels. It wasn't anything I'd want on my mantle, but I was willing to bet the case was made with real gold-plated metal and that it was a real diamond inset above the numeral twelve.

I shook my head as I left the workshop, closing the doors behind me and then making my way to the study where I sat down behind the massive mahogany desk, not at the smaller, junior partner desk where I usually worked. Pulling the first folder toward me, I opened it and began going through the papers inside. Soon enough, I was back to doing the work that was familiar to me. And even though it was work for which I was paid, I couldn't help but feel that I was home, and that was a good feeling.

Chapter Thirteen

I was pacing back and forth in the dimly lit main floor hallways only a few nights later after having had a terrible nightmare. My heart was still racing. I felt jittery and anxious, but I didn't want to take anymore medication. I didn't like how dull and fuzzy-headed it made me feel, how slowed down I felt on antianxiety meds and antidepressants. I had stopped taking the antidepressants, but took the antianxiety med as needed.

I was outside the game room on the first floor of the east wing when the door creaked open, startling me badly. "Go upstairs, put jeans and a long-sleeved t-shirt on, and then meet me out front. I need to get the hell out of here for a couple of hours. Sounds like you need a change of scenery, too."

"What are you doing up?" I asked.

"Same as you. Go on. Don't wake the whole damn house up."

I went back upstairs and got dressed, brushing my hair back and gathering it into a ponytail. I grabbed only a little case with my ID in it and my house key, slipping it into my back pocket. I didn't want to be locked out.

Back downstairs, I saw that Julian had disarmed the alarm system. I could see him pacing out in the driveway. He had his cellphone out and was texting. I reactivated the alarm system so everyone in the house was protected, then slipped outside, closed, and secured the door. He glanced at me and then nodded toward his black pickup truck. He'd evidently bought it new off the lot when he'd gotten back because it was not a rental. I climbed into the passenger seat. He finished sending the message, stuffed the phone into his hip pocket, then got in behind the wheel, started the truck, and peeled out of the driveway. "I thought you didn't want to wake anyone up!"

He laughed. "That was for that fuckin' pompous ass butler of Dad's. It's always rubbed me wrong how he walks around with his nose in the air, looking down the length of it at us."

"Oh, he's not so bad. And he takes excellent care of your father."

He snorted at that. "You want something to drink?" I thought he meant he had a bottle in the truck somewhere and began to shake my head. "I mean coffee, iced coffee, iced tea, water?" I thought he was going to swing by an all-night convenience store, but soon enough he pulled into the drive thru of the Big Dipper. "Last chance," he said as he pulled up to the drive thru speaker.

"I want a medium iced mocha and I would kill for a glazed donut stick."

"Yeah, I bet you would—a long, glazed rod." He gave me a wink that nearly made me jump out of the truck, slam the door, and start stalking back to Juniper Avenue, but then he turned and ordered an iced dark roast with five sugars and just a splash of cream, my iced mocha, two glazed donuts sticks, and two glazed chocolate donut sticks.

He tossed the bag of donut sticks onto my lap, nestled the drinks into the cup holders in the center console, handed me the straws, and pulled away from the window. "Can you see all right at night with those dark glasses on?" I asked, worried that he really couldn't see where he was going.

"Yeah, of course I can," he snapped. "Give me a chocolate stick."

I wrapped one of the chocolate donut sticks in a folded napkin and handed it to him. He devoured it in three big bites. "You'd better slow down," I warned.

"I'm hungry."

"No, I mean there's a cruiser up ahead."

He eased up on the accelerator. "Good co-piloting, Cherry." I asked him if he wanted another donut. He asked if I was going to eat both of the regular donut sticks. I just wanted one, so he had the other, and then ate the other chocolate stick, but he did let me take a small bite, smirking as I leaned over and opened my mouth while he fed it to me.

"Don't be such a pig, okay?"

"I'm a guy. A girl opens her mouth like that and leans towards me, it gives me ideas."

"Keep your ideas to yourself."

"Christ, Charlotte, haven't you ever been laid? How old are you? A few years younger than me, right? You're like what? Twenty-one?"

"Twenty-two."

"And you haven't had a guy between your legs yet? What the hell's the matter with you?"

"Nothing's the matter with me!" I flared.

"Don't you want…"

"No!" I said too sharply. I made myself wince, and then I looked away. My heart was pounding. I did not want

151

to be having this conversation with him or with anyone else. I wasn't ready yet.

He was silent as he headed out toward Clay Hill Road. As he turned onto the road he asked, "So, who was it? A friend of Charlie's? A relative?" I shook my head. "Was it one time or did it go on for a while?"

"I don't want to talk about it."

"I told you about the nurse."

"She didn't force you! You wanted her to do it!"

"So, he fucked you and you didn't want him to do it. You do know that's rape, Cherry, don't you?" The sound that came rushing out of me as he stuck his finger deep into the raw wound inside of me made him fall silent. "Well, you might as well tell me," he finally said.

"I can't," I replied, barely able to get the word out. The name I would say would most likely cause him to veer over to the side of the road and shove me out into the brush. I did not relish the idea of being abandoned on this very rural road alone in the dead of night, especially with feral dogs or wolves running around.

He was quiet for the rest of the drive to the old clock shop. When he pulled around behind the building, my anxiety notched up ten more levels. "I'm parking back here because I don't want the cops seeing the truck." I started to reach for the door handle, not wanting to be confined in the truck with him anymore, but he stopped me. "Charlotte, hold on a minute." The sound of his voice stopped me. He had obviously been thinking about whom it could have been who had sexually assaulted me when I was younger and some dark dots had connected in his head. The underlying shock and anger in his tone told me that he knew and he was having trouble accepting the truth of it, but at the same time, he had already known years ago, although maybe not who the girl was. I doubt that would have been something he would have revealed, even to his best friends. "When did it start?" he asked, his voice low, terse.

"I was nine."

"So, he was, and I'm guessing here, twelve?" I didn't say anything. "And it stopped two years later. It stopped abruptly or else he would have kept right on abusing you, right?"

"Yes," I whispered.

"Why didn't you tell someone what was going on?"

"Because I really didn't even know how to tell anyone what he was doing to me! I didn't know! I just knew that he hurt me and told me that, if I ever told anyone, he'd get some older boys to take me down to the swamp and do the same things to me. He said it would hurt a hell of a lot worse and then they'd throw me in the swamp and drown me!"

"Fuck! Goddam him!" His anger exploded. He got out of the truck, cursing a blue streak, pacing, punching the truck while I sat there in the passenger seat crying and shaking. Suddenly, he yanked open the passenger door and pulled me out. I nearly fell, but managed to get my footing. He grabbed a flashlight from the glove compartment, slammed the door, and then hauled me along behind him as he stalked toward the woods.

"No!" I cried, thinking he was going to drag me into the woods, rape me, and then kill me.

"I'm not going to hurt you," he fairly snarled at me. "I'm just going to show you where the son of a bitch died."

"Julian!"

"It's all right. I've already been up there a dozen times."

"No, I don't want to see that place!"

But there was no stopping him. He was bigger and stronger than me. I stumbled and staggered along behind him, tripping over roots and rocks, branches lying across the path. He seemed to have some sort of preternatural night vision even with those dark glasses on. I was breathing hard by the time I saw the glimmer of starlight on water and realized that we were approaching the pond. He was just breathing normally.

"Let go of me!" I cried when we came into the small clearing. I shook my wrist loose of his grasp and rubbed it with my other hand. He'd been dragging me along by my left arm and my hand had gone numb.

"This is where he died." He walked over to a spot, turned his head to look at the pond, moved another foot over, and then stomped his booted foot on the ground, making an imprint. "Right here." He glanced at me and then walked a couple of feet away. "Austin was here." He stomped his foot again to mark that spot. "I was over here." He walked to where he had been sleeping. Now that the moon had come out from behind a charcoal cloud, I could make out the ring of stones still there in the center of the triangle the boys had laid their sleeping bags out in around it. Julian had been sleeping on the far side of the fire. Cody and Austin had been closer to the head of the trail. "I didn't hear anything. It killed Austin first. And then it went for Cody. It snarled. I think that's what woke me up. A growl or a snarl. It pulled Cody over onto his back and he sort of woke up and yelped. That's what woke me up more fully.

"I lifted my head and saw the damn thing tearing at him. I heard Cody gurgling on blood and sucking air, and then his body was bucking and that thing, it lifted its head and glared at me. Its eyes were red-orange, glowing. Shit! It scared the hell out of me. I couldn't move. I fuckin' peed myself, I was so scared. And then it started toward me. Austin was dead. So was Cody. I knew I was next and I had nothing to protect myself with. I scrambled out of my sleeping bag as it started ripping it open. I started running, but I didn't get far. It took a swipe at me, right across my back. I have the scars for every time it raked me with its claws, although they've faded. Then it grabbed me and bit me on the shoulder near the back of my neck. I'd cocked my head to the side to try to protect my neck. It bit my other shoulder. I think I passed out around then. I don't really know. I woke up in the cave. I was sore as all hell and bleeding. My brain felt like a frozen mass in my skull. I couldn't think. I just laid there and waited for it to come back to finish me off. I felt sick after a while. I most likely passed out again from shock and loss of blood, stress, and just plain fatigue. I don't honestly know how I got outside the cave. I was told I was found sitting on a rock just outside the entrance." He stopped talking and stood there watching me.

I looked at the three marks in the dirt, the stone ring full of the detritus of numerous autumns since that fateful summer. I turned my head and looked out across the pond, up the hill toward Big Pond. Two adolescent boys died here and the sole survivor was standing here in front of me, waiting for me to say something. "Do you own a gun?" I asked.

"Yeah, I do."

"Do you have it with you?"

"Yeah."

"Can I see it?"

"Are you going to shoot me?" he asked.

"No."

"Are you going to shoot yourself?"

"No."

Almost reluctantly, he pulled out his gun; a nine millimeter, fully automatic pistol, he told me it was as he handed it to me. "The safety's on. Go ahead and get a feel for it, and then I'll let you shoot it."

"I don't want to shoot it tonight. I want you to teach me how to shoot, but not at night. Not in the dark."

"You should know how to shoot in the dark. I've practiced night shooting lots of times."

"I agree, but first I need to know how to safely shoot a gun in daylight."

"Okay. Fine. When Sanborn gets around to bringing you the paperwork, fill it out. Enroll in a gun safety class. It's just a couple of sessions, a few hours. Get the certificate. We'll get the FID card for you and the license to carry. I honestly don't think your little breakdown will affect their decision. It didn't affect their decision to allow me to own and carry a gun."

"When did you start carrying?" I asked.

"When I was seventeen."

"Did your father know?"

"No. And I'm not telling him. Neither are you. And don't tell him you want to carry, all right? He thinks you're sweet and innocent." He came and took the gun from my hand. "You are sweet and innocent, but that innocence was tainted in the past by a fuckin' asshole who used to brag about his getting a piece of this girl and that girl whenever he wanted it. He never named names, but he'd drop clues, except he only referred to you as a girl who lived down the street. I thought he meant Hallie Wright. You know how she was, right?" I nodded. She was a flirt who liked boys way too much. "Christ, Cherry, if I'd had any idea that he meant you, I would have killed him myself. He knew I thought you were cute but way too young for me. He knew because I told him that when I was twelve years old." I squeezed my eyes shut as I turned away from him. His telling his best friend he thought I was cute had probably made that best friend want to do what he did to me, so he could smugly tell Julian all about what he'd done, without revealing who he'd done it to, evil little bastard.

Suddenly, I spun around and slapped him across the face so hard his glasses went flying, his head snapping around. He cursed and grabbed me by both wrists as I started to swing back around, intending to slap him again, even harder, if I could do it. "You must have known what he was doing to me! You had to have figured it out!" I spat at him.

"I didn't figure it out. And most of the time Austin and I thought he was just full of shit, making stuff up to make us jealous, or make us think he had something that we didn't have, some sort of sexual prowess that had eluded us. I was still pretty damn naive about sex when I was twelve. If you want to know the absolute truth, I hadn't even seen a totally naked girl at that age. That didn't happen until your brother took the three of us to Mr. Gunther's one Saturday afternoon and he had some stupid porno movie playing in the basement playroom. Holy shit, Charlotte…by the time we left that night, we'd all been laid to the point of being sore and I spent the next three months worried sick that I'd caught something from one of those girls from the Renegade Club that he had there who were more than willing to initiate teenaged boys. Then my mom died and I thought it had something to do with what I'd done, that she had found out and the shock of it had killed her." He tugged my wrists and I stumbled a step closer to him. He had his head bent and I thought it was because he was ashamed of himself. He was. I could tell that much, but there was something else going on.

"Will you look at me?" I asked.

"No, I can't."

"We're both so messed up it's not funny."

"Tell me about it." He let go of my wrists. "Where did my glasses go?"

"Can't you see without them?"

"I can see just fine," he replied. "I just don't know where they flew off to."

"Over there." I nodded toward where they'd landed.

"Can you get them for me? Make sure they're not broken." I went and retrieved them for him, holding them up

Susan Buffum

toward the moon which was again exposed and bright. The tinted lenses did not look broken, so I turned to hand them back to him. He raised his head and I caught a glint of red-orange where his eyes should be. "I'm going to look at you, Cherry. Don't be scared." It sounded like some sort of a warning, but I didn't understand why he'd said it like that.

He raised his head and I yelped, fighting the urge to back away from him. His eyes were what were glowing that red-orange color. "What's the matter with your eyes?" I cried. "Were they damaged when you were attacked?'

"Yeah, it's from the attack. It..." He started to say something, but stopped dead, his head turning. He tilted his head back slightly. Although I couldn't hear him sniffing, I could see his nostrils flaring. "Give me my glasses." When I didn't move, he snatched them out of my hand and put them on. "Come on, time to go."

"What's wrong? Are there ghosts up here?" I asked nervously. He was scaring me.

"Yeah, ghosts and monsters. Stay close." I heard a low sound, a grunt or a snort. It didn't come from him. Instinctively, I moved closer to him. He put his arm around me, moving me in front of him, and urging me to move. I heard a branch crack sharply behind us. "Run, Charlotte! Here, take the keys! If I'm not right behind you, get in the damn truck and get the fuck away from here! Don't stop! Go straight home!"

He shoved me and I ran, something growling behind us. I really couldn't even see a trail, just an occasional pale ribbon. I realized that he must have marked the trail again because the old bits of ribbon would have rotted away by now. I tripped and stumbled headlong, but regained my balance and leapt over a rock, skidded through leaves and debris. I knew which direction to go in, down. I was breathing hard when I burst through the tree line to find myself in the back of the machine shop. "Julian!" I

158

screamed, but he wasn't right behind me. I knew what he'd said, but I hesitated until I heard ungodly howls. I knew he had the gun. I knew he was familiar with the woods, had grown up exploring them. He'd be okay. At least, I hoped he would.

The howls and snarling, growling and grunting sounded too close for comfort, although a quick glance over my shoulder showed me nothing but the dark tree line. I nearly dropped the keys, but managed to get the driver's door open. I climbed in, pulled the door shut, locked it, and jammed the key into the ignition. I didn't want to leave him, but the way he'd told me to get out of there, and with what I'd seen and heard, I was too scared to disobey him.

I quickly adjusted the seat, started the truck, threw it into reverse, then into drive, and flew out of the parking lot. I didn't care if fifty cruisers chased me up that dark country road, through the quiet downtown, and all the way to Juniper Avenue. I ran lights and never slowed down.

I arrived at the mansion, leaving the truck in front of the door, letting myself in after summoning up the courage to get out, shaking like a leaf trying to open the door, nearly forgetting the security code and waking up the household, but I got the door secured and the alarm reset before I ran up to my room.

I peeled off my dirty clothes, leaving them in a heap on the bathroom floor. My face and hands were scratched. I washed quickly, pulled on my nightgown, and then climbed into bed, pulling the covers up around me until I was cocooned inside them, shaking, scared, trying to make sense of everything.

If I hadn't been able to sleep before, I had only made the problem worse by slipping out of the house with Julian. We'd shared terrible secrets in those woods and now I had a feeling that we had not been alone there. Ghosts? Maybe.

But, I think he was more right than I was. There were monsters there as well.

I gnawed my lower lip raw and bloody worrying about him, thinking that whatever had been there had surely killed him. If he was dead, then his father would surely die, too, unable to withstand the shock of his son's death. Waves of guilt crashed over me as I thought I'd killed both Beresford men, the two men who meant the world to me. I didn't know how I was ever going to live with myself, if that was the case.

Chapter Fourteen

I did not sleep a wink. I was wrung out, bleary-eyed when I made my way down to the kitchen at six-thirty, a half hour earlier than my normal breakfast time of seven o'clock. Helen glanced at me as I came into the room. She was stirring the batter for a quick bread, but when she took a second look at me, she set the bowl aside, wiped her hands on her apron, and then opened her arms. I hesitated for one heartbeat, then rushed into her arms and let her smother me in a motherly hug. "Oh, sweetie!" she murmured. "I don't even have to ask what sort of night you've had. It's written all over you as if a fiend tagged you in the dark." She stroked my tangled ponytail, pulling bits of torn leaves and twigs from it. "Were you outdoors?" I nodded. "Well, sometimes a house can feel too confining. I know just the thing for you. Tea. I'm going to make you a nice, hot cup of tea."

"I should go comb my hair," I murmured.

"No. You go sit down right over there at that table. I'll have your tea ready in just a few minutes. You're staying where I can keep an eye on you for now." She gave me one last squeeze before turning me and giving me a little push toward the table. I walked across the kitchen and fell into a chair, propping my elbows on the table, holding my head in my hands.

My stomach was in a knot. All the adrenalin last night had made me nauseous on top of the donuts and iced mocha. Plus, I was worried sick about Julian. Had I left him there to get torn to pieces by whatever beast roamed that hillside? I had basically abandoned him to his demon, the same demon that happened to be my demon. I was weak. I was a total failure.

Someone came into the kitchen. I glanced up and saw that it was the handyman, Ethan Sinclair. He was a few years older than Julian and had been the handyman here at Randolph Hall since graduating from high school. "You look like hell," he said as he helped himself to a cup of coffee from the urn on the counter.

"I had a bad night."

"J. Rand must have, too. He left his truck parked at a crazy angle right outside the front door. Druce'll be pissy about that," he said, lowering his voice and looking around as if the butler would suddenly appear and be angry with him.

"Oh, that was me. I should go move it."

"You? What were you doing driving Rand's truck around last night?"

I gave a little shrug. "I couldn't sleep. We went for donuts."

He laughed. "You guys went for donuts, eh? And he let you drive?" I nodded. "Where'd you leave him? At the Big Dipper? Do I need to go get him?"

"I didn't leave him anywhere."

He snorted air through his nose, letting me know that he knew that I was lying. "He's always up at five o'clock. He comes out and walks around, does some stretches, and runs. I usually see him shooting some hoops over by the tennis court when I walk over for breakfast. There's neither hide nor hair of him this morning."

Helen brought my tea and then went back to her batter. "I left him at the clock shop," I said, my voice low.

"Why? Did he get fresh with you?"

"No." I shook my head. "He wanted to show me what his plans are for the shop. And then, because he couldn't sleep last night either, he told me he wanted to stay and move some stuff around. He's expecting his shipping containers to be delivered, so he needs to make room for the materials they contain. I guess he needed to burn off some energy. He gave me the keys, told me to go home." I stared down into the cup. "Guess I was tired when I got home."

"Guess so. You got the keys on you?" I shook my head, told him they were on the mantle in my sitting room. "I'll run up and grab them, move the truck out by the carriage house, and be back before Druce pitches a fit about it." At my nod that he could go get the keys from my suite, he stood up and left the kitchen.

I was eating an English muffin with orange marmalade that Helen had prepared for me when he returned. She was making bacon and scrambled eggs for the staff. He set the keys on the table, and then took my phone from his pocket and set that down beside the keys. He went to refill his coffee cup after telling me that my phone had been buzzing when he retrieved the keys.

I slid the phone over closer, swiped the screen, and saw that I had a number of text messages. I tapped the icon to open them. There were three messages, all from Julian. I was relieved to know that he was alive. He had to be alive to send me messages. I opened the first message. *Am in the shop, safe enough here for now. You get home all right?* I winced. He must have started texting me earlier this morning and I had left my phone in the sitting room when I'd emptied my pockets. Dumb! Thoughtless and stupid! The second message read, *Are you mad at me? Or…are you afraid of me?* I wasn't mad at him. I didn't know if I was afraid of him or not. I didn't quite understand what his glowing, weird eyes meant. Was it a medical condition? Was it because of some injury to his eyes that he'd suffered when he'd been attacked? Had he been given new lenses? Corneas? I didn't know anything about that stuff. He'd been wearing darkly tinted glasses since the camping incident. The third message simply said, *Hey, I'm stranded here. At least send Sanborn or Ethan to come get me. I'm not walking my ass home.* This was the message Ethan had heard coming through. He'd sent it only a few minutes ago.

I grimaced. As Ethan sat down, I stood up. "I have to go pick him up," I said. I glanced at the clock. I had gotten up early. I'd had something to eat. I could run out to Clay Hill Road, pick up Julian, and be back by eight o'clock to start my day. I still had a lot of work to do. "I'll be back."

"Charlotte, you look like you crawled through the jungle last night. I have a better idea. Why don't you go upstairs? Take a nice hot shower or have a long soak in the tub and get yourself cleaned up. I'll go get J. Rand."

He was right. Mr. Beresford would be alarmed to see me looking like this. I nodded, grabbed my phone, and sent Julian a text. I wrote, *Sorry, wasn't thinking straight. I'm okay. Not mad. Ethan's coming to get you. I'm a mess.* I sent the text before realizing that he might think the 'I'm a mess' meant that I was an emotional mess. I started to write another text, but then deleted it. I was a mess. That was only stating the truth, on many levels.

I excused myself, went up to my suite, and started the shower. I stood for several long moments just staring at my hollow-eyed reflection in the mirror, and then I blinked and focused. No, I would not be that girl, that weak girl who just allowed some monster to kill people, especially people she loved. "Wherever you are, you're living on borrowed time, buddy," I muttered as I turned away from the fierce-eyed girl in the mirror and stepped into the shower. I was a little afraid of her, of the part of me that had had enough of this.

I was back downstairs just before eight o'clock, slipping quietly into the study and sitting down at my desk in the corner. I dove right into the work I needed to catch up on, half listening to the sounds of the house, people walking around, low voices. At eight thirty, Druce quietly cleared his throat from the doorway. "Yes?" I asked, half turning in my chair.

"Mr. Beresford would like to see you in his suite."

"Yes, of course. I'll go right up. How is he feeling this morning?"

"Mr. Beresford the elder, is feeling as well as can be expected. I was speaking of the younger Mr. Beresford." I frowned. "J. Rand would like you to meet him in his sitting room."

"I don't even know where his sitting room is."

"His suite is in the west wing." Well, I knew that much, but if it was anything like the east wing it was more or less a long, broad hallway with many closed doors off of it. "His is the only occupied suite in that wing. I'm sure you'll find him."

"Does Mr. Beresford, the father, need me? I work for him, not J. Rand therefore, if he needs me, I should go to him first."

"It might brighten his day if you popped in to say good morning and hello."

I got up and walked to the door, slipping past Druce and into the reception hall. As I passed him, I accidentally brushed against his arm and got a static shock. "Ow," I said because it smarted it was so strong. I looked down at my left arm, and then at his arm. He was standing on the marble tiled floor in the reception hall. I had crossed the oriental carpet in the study and then a section of polished wood floor. It puzzled me that either one of us would have built up so much static electricity that I'd have given him a shock like that, but I shrugged it off and ran up the broad staircase to the second floor main hall off of which Mr. Beresford's suite was.

He was sitting in his recliner in the sitting room, a blanket over his lap. He had on his satin smoking jacket with the velvet collar. "There you are!" he said, smiling as I knocked on the door frame. The door was ajar. "Come in, Charlotte."

"Good morning. How are you feeling today?"

"So-so," he replied, making a rocking motion with his thin, right hand. "I miss our time together in the study and the workshop."

"So do I."

"How are you managing with everything I left for you to do?"

"I've gotten through one folder and have started tackling the second one this morning. I should be completely caught up by the end of the week, unless something urgent comes in that I need to take care of."

"Mr. Stroud is coming at ten-thirty this morning. We have a meeting with J. Rand. It's time that he and I begin discussing the estate and other properties that I own. We'll see how this goes. He has not been very receptive to discussing his inheritance when I've attempted to start this discussion previously."

"I think he's like any other young man. He doesn't want to think about his father dying."

"Maybe so, but he can't deny what he sees. I'm declining, Charlotte. Faster than I thought I would."

"You've rallied before." He was shaking his head, giving me a resigned look. "Well, I can continue to be optimistic, can't I?"

"Yes, of course you can. You can be whatever you want to be. You cheer me up. Who knows? Your positive energy may send this terrible disease back into remission after all. One can always hope."

"There you go. Hope. Sometimes it's all we have to hang onto."

"Ah, here's Druce, come to shave me and comb my hair so I look less like a dying man and more like a desperately ill man to try to fool Mr. Stroud and my own son. Run along now, Charlotte. It would please me if you'd join me for lunch at one o'clock, if I'm still awake and above ground."

"Will we be eating lunch here in your sitting room?" I asked.

"Yes. I don't feel up to being jostled around trying to get to the main floor."

"Then I'll see you a little before one o'clock."

"Just come straight here. Druce has already informed Helen and Lorraine that you and I will be enjoying a private luncheon here in my sitting room." He gave me a smile meant to be charming and warm, but it alarmed me somewhat as I noticed that he had lost a canine tooth between the last time I had seen him and now.

I managed a smile in return before slipping out of his sitting room and making my way to the sturdy door to the west wing. I cracked it open and slipped into the dusty hallway beyond. There was a nearly floor to ceiling window with a fan light above it at the far end, the same as at the end of the second story east wing hallway. There were occasional nook-like spaces between rooms with a window looking out toward the front lawn or the rear gardens. These areas and the window at the end of the hallway were the only source of illumination without flipping the switches up to light a row of hanging lights along the length of the hallway.

I began walking down the carpeted corridor. All the doors were closed. It was absolutely silent. However, as I neared the end, I heard a sudden burst of foreign language with more familiar curse words mixed in. It was Julian's voice and he sounded pissed off, furious. Something shattered, making me jump. The thought crossed my mind that I should just turn around, go back downstairs, and not obey his summons. He was in no mood to be civil.

I started to turn away when a door was wrenched open. "Get the fuck in here!" he snapped at me. "What the hell took you so long?"

"I had to see your father first. He's my employer. I'm working," I replied as I slipped past him into his sitting room. Again, I got that static shock sensation as my left arm brushed against his because he'd moved his arm to swing the door shut as I was passing him. "What is with that?" I muttered, rubbing my arm, frowning deeply.

"What's with what?"

"This house is full of static electricity this morning. I keep getting shocks."

"Maybe they're nerve shots, not static shocks. Isn't that your bad arm? Don't you have nerve damage in that arm?" He came toward me and I took a step backwards because he looked pissed. "Stand still!" he barked. I stopped, but my body went rigid as he drew nearer. "Jesus, what's the matter with you this morning? You are scared of me, aren't you?"

"You look like you want to hit me."

He stopped about a foot away from me, his expression altering. He cocked his head slightly to one side, and then he did something I didn't expect, he reached up and very slowly lowered his glasses until he had exposed his eyes just above the top rims. I jumped. This morning I could see his irises were the same color as they had always been—all the warm colors of autumn blended together. "I don't want to hit you. I just want to look at you and make sure you're all right." I couldn't tear my eyes off his. His pupils were normal looking, round. The drapes were drawn across the windows. It was dim in the room.

"Maybe you should look at me in natural light," I said. Walking over to the nearest window, I whipped the drapes open. As I turned back toward him, he was settling his glasses back on his face, his eyes shielded once more from my view. "No. You had the guts to show me something last night by moonlight. Have the guts to show me again this morning by daylight." I walked right up to him and this time he was the one taking steps backwards as I kept going until he stopped.

"All right, gutsy girl. Go ahead, remove my glasses and take a good long look at what that fuckin' thing did to me." It was a challenge, but there was an underling apprehension in his tone. He was afraid I would run screaming from the room.

I took the last step so that I was right there in front of him. My eyes fell on his glasses. I could just make out his eyes behind the darkly tinted lenses. They looked normal enough. Slowly, I raised both hands and then gently lifted his glasses up, slipping them off and just holding them in one hand as I looked into his eyes by daylight. His irises remained that gorgeous color, the same as his father's eyes, but his formerly rounded pupils were contracting and narrowing in the sunlight streaming through the window, even though the light didn't directly reach this place where we were standing. "How did it do this to you? Did it scratch your eyes and damage the pupils somehow?"

"No," he said tersely.

I searched his eyes, watching his pupils widen and contract, fascinated by the strangeness of them, although I had seen cat's eyes do this, and lizards. It was more than a little unsettling to see it in person. It was like some kind of special effects were at play. The thought crossed my mind that maybe it was some sort of contact lenses that he wore, but, then, why would he need the dark glasses?

A slight frown must have creased my brow because he reached for his glasses, but I moved my arm around behind me so he couldn't reach them easily. "Wait." I raised my left hand and touched his jaw with just my fingertips. I got that prickling sensation just by touching him, both of us just standing stock still, our eyes locked. "I want to know how this happened to you, how this is even possible."

"I can't," he said, shaking his head slightly. "Cherry, it would send you right back to the psych ward. Trust me on that."

Like the gears inside a clock, my brain was ticking and clicking, gears meshing and advancing, but instead of seconds and minutes coming and going, images and thoughts were forming and shifting. "They've told me again and again that it wasn't real," I said quietly. "But, I saw it. I know what I saw. Everyone has tried to convince me that it was a feral dog that jumped up to tear aside the curtain in the shop. But, it never jumped. It walked. It didn't have a human gait. It walked upright and swiped the curtain aside. It looked back at me over its shoulder. Its eyes met mine. We looked at one another, and then it was gone."

"Charlotte…"

"No, Julian. I'm totally fine."

"No, you're not."

"I want you to show me."

"Show you what?"

I stepped sideways and set his dark glasses on the mantle. "It did something to you, didn't it? It made you the same as what it is? Am I right? You're some kind of a wolfman creature? Is that why you really left Pine Haven and don't like coming back?" I hammered him with questions until he finally raised his hands in resignation and surrendered.

"You want to see what I am? I'll show you, but you'd better not fuckin' scream the house down. If it cracks your psyche, I'm never going to be able to forgive myself, you know." He grabbed me and steered me to the couch. "You'd better sit down. I'm going to go stand behind the wing chair. I have to strip off my clothes. I am not going to stand here naked in front of you. You'll see enough and, I promise you, I won't come out from behind the chair. I won't come near you. You just stay here, I'll stay over there. You trust me, don't you?"

"It was in the woods last night, wasn't it?" He crossed the room, tugging off his t-shirt, dropping it on the seat of the chair. He was lean, all muscle, not an ounce of fat on him. I saw faded scars on his back. "How did it know you'd taken me up there?"

"I don't know." He shrugged then shook his head. "I think it's following you." He was behind the chair now, unfastening his jeans. He glanced at me and then bent over, tugging them and his boxer briefs off, dropping them onto the chair. He was already barefoot, so I knew he was now totally naked, half hidden behind the chair. Some little visceral thrill rippled through my abdomen and pelvis, but my heart was pounding. "Are you absolutely sure this is what you want me to do?" I nodded, my teeth clenched. "Charlotte, I have to say this again. Do. Not. Scream." I shook my head, my jaw locked to keep myself from doing that. "All right. I have honestly never stood in front of a mirror and watched this happen. I don't know exactly what you're going to see. I can see you and hear you the same as always, well, no, more acutely. If you do scream, you're going to make me snarl because it's going to hurt my ears. And then I'm going to have to leap across the room and shut you the hell up whichever way I can and you won't like that." I nodded. "I shouldn't…"

"Just do it, Julian! Just go ahead, do it, and get it over with!"

He suddenly laughed. "You sound like a girl who's just letting a guy have his way with her, who can't wait until it's over and done with. It wouldn't be like that, you know, not with me anyway." I was just about to jump up, run across the room, and slap his grinning face when, suddenly, he began to sort of stretch and writhe. He grimaced and seemed to grow even taller, his shoulders broadening, his arms lengthening. His face changed dramatically and, although it seemed to go on forever, I think the process of transforming actually took less than a minute.

I thought I could handle it. I thought I would be able to handle seeing him like that, since I knew it was him and was fairly certain that he would never hurt me, but it triggered a fear center within my brain that I hadn't quite dealt with. He looked like the beast I had seen, the one that had killed Chase. And in that location in my brain, that beast he had become was identical to the one that had killed my best friend just a few weeks ago. My heart was hammering. I could hear it, could hear the roar of blood rushing through my veins because of it. It filled my ears. I went to stand up and run out of the room, but the world tilted and the carpet abruptly met my face. I heard the wind rush out of my lungs, and then everything went silent and dark.

Chapter Fifteen

I woke up lying on a strange bed. The room was dim, the drapes drawn. "I'll give you credit, Cherry. You didn't scream. You just passed out." I turned my head and found him sitting hunched forward in a chair in the corner of the room, elbows on his knees, hands loosely clasped between his thighs. He looked like himself and had put his clothes back on, thank God. "Hindsight is always twenty-twenty, so they say. I don't think you were as ready to see that as you thought you were."

I was silent for a few minutes while my brain shook off the fog of shock and the sluggish remnants of unconsciousness. "Will you answer one question for me? Absolutely honestly?" I finally asked.

"Yeah."

"Have you ever killed a human being?"

"No."

"But you've killed other things? Animals?"

"Yeah."

"Is it some compulsion you have to do that?"

"Yeah, every now and then. You know what they say about the full moon." He raised his head. He had not put his glasses back on. "I fight it for as long as I can, but when I do that, I'm no better than the son of a bitch that made me this way. There's like this bloodlust that comes over me. If I fight it for too long, then the end result is that I'm as brutal as that asshole is. If I satisfy the urge a little here and a little there, I still kill animals, but I don't go ripping them apart while their hearts are still beating." A sound rose up out of me at the thought of Chase and Ripley having still been alive when he'd torn them open and ripped their guts out. "Damn it! I'm sorry. I'm just steppin' in shit here left and right and tracking it straight across your heart."

I had managed to get the urge to vomit under control, but I still felt sick. However, it was more heartsick than the 'I'm going to puke' kind of sick. My mind was free-wheeling and I knew I'd lose it if I didn't distract myself somehow. "Julian," I said, and then I shifted to the far edge of the bed. "Come and lie down beside me for a few minutes."

"You want me to lie down with you? Isn't that kind of risky, inviting a wolf into the same bed with you?"

"Yes, I suppose so."

"No, that's just playing with fire."

"I don't have anyone else," I said. The pool of lonesomeness in which I bobbed aimlessly around in on a daily basis was rapidly spreading out in a flood all around me from every leak in my damaged being. "Please." I wasn't going to beg him to hold me. I saw the indecision and reluctance written on his face and turned onto my side, my back to him so he wouldn't see how close I was to totally losing it, to just letting go and allowing it to swallow me whole.

A few moments later, I felt the bed tilt as he climbed onto it and lay down behind me. "I haven't let anyone get close to me since this happened," he said, his voice quiet. "I've gotten physical relief where I can, but I can't let anyone get that close to me. I can't allow myself to have that kind of relationship with anyone, not even you. You understand that, don't you?"

"Yes," I whispered.

"I like you, Charlotte. I always have."

"Don't say anything else, okay? Please, don't say it. Not right now." My voice cracked, but I had to get one more thing out. "Cody stole what I would have given to you, if you'd asked me. Not when I was eleven. When I was older. But you were gone by then. You walked out of my life. I haven't been able to let anyone touch me. I think I'd let you. You're the only one. So, isn't it ironic that the one man I would give myself to is a wolf who doesn't want me?" I started to roll off the edge of the bed so I could get up and leave, but he shifted, turning on his side, throwing his arm over my hip and pulling me back against his body. "Julian...don't..."

"Did you hear me say that I didn't want you?" he asked, his voice a low growl. "Damn it, Cherry...I'm not even sure you're in your right mind right now. I just showed you something totally mind-blowing. It made you faint. It upset you, obviously. I'm just trying to figure out where you are in your head right now. I'm trying to figure the same thing out for myself. I knew it was a huge mistake coming home." I tried to move away from him, but he tightened his arm around me. "No! Hold still. You and I have to start hashing this out between us."

"You have a meeting with your father and Mr. Stroud this morning."

"I can't stand that smug bastard! He can wait."

"But your father can't wait. You should go."

"My father is fine. He'll wait. This, right here, is more important than anything that arrogant ass, so-called business manager has to say. He thinks he's better than me. He has this resentment toward me that he harbors, as if my leaving the country after graduation was a personal offense against him, an insult."

"Everyone is very protective of your father."

"I get that. I just don't get why my going off to make a name for myself away from my famous father pissed everyone off so much."

"I think it was the in-your-face way that you did it that stung them."

"I was struggling every day with what I'd become. I couldn't control myself back then like I can now. I've learned a lot since then. I've learned self-discipline and self-control. I totally lacked that at eighteen." I didn't say anything. He was quiet for a few minutes and then he hauled himself up onto his elbow and leaned over my shoulder. "Are you crying?" I nodded. Tears were still trickling from my eyes. "Oh, Cherry…" He shifted me, turning me toward him so that he could look down into my teary eyes. "I don't want to hurt you. Big bad wolf that I am, I have this big soft spot in my heart for you. Always have, always will. But…" He saw the skin around my eyes begin to contract as fresh tears flooded my eyes. "Fuck it all," he said. And then he bent his head and began softly kissing the tears from my face. My heart was aching. His lips against my cheeks felt warm and sweet. I had to close my eyes. I was trying not to cry. He very softly kissed my closed eyelids, and then the bridge of my nose. He lightly kissed the tip of my nose. "You're so damn pretty," he murmured. And then his lips touched mine. The ache in my heart expanded until I thought I might implode. My lips parted as a wail of despair began to form in my breast, but it never made it out. He began kissing me and his kisses turned the wail of despair inside out, they turned it into a moan of longing. "Open your eyes," he said quietly, his lips still lightly against mine. "Look at me." I opened my eyes. They met his. His pupils looked almost normal, but they seemed to be pulsing. When they pulsed, they narrowed. The pulses seemed to match his heartbeat. It was hypnotic to watch. "You're right. I have to go meet with my father and Stroud. So, I just want to tell you that you need to think about this. I need to think about this." He brushed a stray lock of hair off my cheek where it was stuck to my damp skin. "I don't trust easily. Basically, what I've just done here is place my trust in you. I've placed my life in your hands. If you say one thing about my being a lycanthrope to anyone, especially with all these damn killings going on, I'm a dead man. I'm not going to simply be arrested, Charlotte. I'm going to be hunted down and shot dead. You know that, don't you?"

"Yes," I whispered, my eyes having fallen to his lips that I desperately wanted against mine again. "I swear to you, Julian, I will never tell anyone your secret. I don't want you dead. But, I do want the whatever it was that made you this way dead."

"Lycanthrope. Werewolf. Son of a bitch, bastard, heartless evil fucker…whatever you want to call it, I want it dead, too. If I can kill it, there's a chance I might get my life back." My eyes shifted from his lips back up to meet his eyes. "I'm still gathering information on that, but I've seen a few things in old texts that more or less imply that, if you kill the beast that made you, once it's dead, it holds no power over you anymore and you will revert back to your former self. Maybe not instantly, but over time."

"Will you still teach me how to shoot?"

"Yeah, but if you ever aim a gun at a werewolf, you'd better make damn sure it's not me you've got that thing pointed at." The corners of my mouth twitched. That caught his attention. He ducked his head, capturing my mouth with his and giving me a real kiss, a deep kiss. It made my heart race, took my breath away. "Think about that, too, whether you really want this kind of relationship with me right now." He gave me one last, lingering, tender kiss before turning and rolling off the bed, getting to his feet. "I need to piss and then get over to Dad's suite before he sends the penguin man up here to drag me there by my ear like a naughty boy."

It made me smile that he thought Druce looked like a penguin, too. I got up off his bed and came around it. "I have to go back to work."

"After this meeting, I'm going out to the shop. I have some more work to do there. And just maybe the shipping containers will finally be delivered this afternoon. I am so damn behind on this current project that I'm surprised they haven't canceled the order."

"Will you be home for dinner?" He shook his head as he headed for the bathroom. "Be careful, okay?"

"I will be. You, too. Don't go out anywhere alone. Text me if you do go anywhere. Like I said, I think it's watching you."

That sent a shudder through me as I walked through the sitting room. I slipped out of his room, making my way back down the hallway to the massive door, opening it, and slipping into the main house. I saw Druce coming from Mr. Beresford's room, a dark scowl on his face. He saw me near the door to the west wing. "J. Rand is coming. He had a phone call that's delayed him." It was a plausible lie. "I'll be downstairs in the study."

I went back to work, diligently applying myself to the tasks I needed to accomplish. While working, I heard Mr. Stroud leave close to twelve-thirty. I was having lunch at one o'clock upstairs, so I finished up the letter that I was typing, printed it, and put it into a folder so Mr. Beresford could sign it.

At a few minutes to one, I ran to my suite to freshen up, and then made my way to his suite. He was sitting at the table in his sitting room, our trays having already been delivered. "I'm sorry. I lost track of time."

"Everyone seems to be running late today," he replied. "Come and sit down, Charlotte. You must be famished."

"I've typed the letter to the Garden Club Chairwoman. I have it here for your signature."

"Ah, yes. She's been after me to allow the ladies to come and take some clippings from a number of Grace's vintage rose bushes. I've been foolishly denying the club the clippings for too long. If Grace was still with me, I'm sure she'd have shared her beautiful rose bushes with all of the ladies before now. It's time to share them before I'm gone and J. Rand has them all dug up and burned to make way for a concrete platform to construct one of his clock towers on behind the house."

"I don't think he would ruin a garden to raise a clock tower," I replied.

"Oh, he has a head full of crazy notions, I'm sure." He waved his hand dismissively. "It'll all be his to do with as he wishes after I'm gone. I made him see that I will have it no other way. I don't want to know what he'll do with his inheritance. That's his business. I will be beyond caring before it is officially in his hands."

"Mr. Beresford," I said quietly. "Please eat your soup. You're getting yourself into a state. That's not good for you."

He nodded as he picked up his soup spoon. "Yes, my dear girl, you're quite right. I can't let him push me over the edge into my grave before I'm ready to go."

"He doesn't want to do that, you know."

"I wish I could believe you."

"He just wants to build his clock towers. That makes him happy. Don't you want your son to be happy?"

"Of course I want him to be happy. It would make me happy to see him settle down, get married, start his own family. I would love to see him teach his own son how to make a clock. Whatever kind of clock he sees fit to make." He set his spoon down. "His ordeal changed him. Now I fear that it may never happen. He doesn't let people get close to him." His eyes rose from his soup plate to meet mine. He looked somewhat confused. "Did you leave the house with him last night?"

"Yes," I answered honestly. "I had a nightmare and couldn't get back to sleep. I went downstairs to pace where I wouldn't be disturbing anyone. He was sitting in the game room. He was having a bad night himself. He thought taking a drive might help both of us relax. We went for coffee and donuts."

"Caffeine is hardly conducive to sleep."

"I wasn't going to be able to fall back to sleep anyway. And, apparently, neither was he. We just drove around for a while."

"He didn't come home, but you did."

Someone had told him that. It had to have been Druce. He had found out after all. "No, he didn't. He drove to the shop, told me he was going to do some more cleaning up. He gave me the keys and told me to drive the truck home, that someone could come and get him in the morning."

"He was rather foolish, allowing you to drive home alone in the early hours of the morning."

"I guess neither one of us was thinking that it might be dangerous."

"There's a monster in Pine Haven, Charlotte. For quite a few years now it's struck close to a number of families in this town. But it has struck close to you, in particular, twice. I told him that he's not to leave you alone, if you go out together again in the future."

"I don't think that will be a problem. He said he's expecting the shipping containers today. Once they arrive and he gets them unloaded, he's going to be busy at the shop working on that clock order that's been delayed by his coming here." I gently tapped the bowl of my spoon against the rim of my soup plate. "Please eat a little more of your soup for me."

He looked down at his plate. I could tell that he had no appetite, but he did pick up his spoon again and took another couple of bites to please me. I was even more worried now about his state of health than I had been previously.

That night, I was the only one in the dining room. Mr. Beresford had retired to his bedroom, was only taking a nutritional shake for dinner. He'd told Druce that his stomach was upset. It felt strange to be alone at the table, but I had a lot to think about, so that's what I was doing— eating and thinking.

I jumped when Druce appeared beside me to remove my plate. "The younger Mr. Beresford has just arrived home. He'll be joining you shortly," he informed me.

Julian arrived as Druce was setting my dessert and coffee cup in front of me. He dropped down into the chair across from me with a weary sigh. "The damn fork lift was never delivered. I unloaded some stuff, but the rest of it is just too damn heavy for me to lug inside." Druce had gone back into the pantry. Now, he returned with a tray containing the entire meal. He started laying it out before Julian, who looked at the food and then began reordering the plates and bowls to his liking before digging into the fruit cup.

"Will you be needing anything else at the moment, sir?" Druce inquired.

"Yeah, can you see if Helen and Lorraine have a pretty girl in the pantry willing to jump into the sack with me later on tonight? That might satisfy my appetite more than dinner will." Druce's nose went up into the air as he spun on his heel and stalked off through the butler's door. Across the table, Julian winked at me and then resumed eating. "That'll teach him for asking me stupid questions when I'm eating."

"You're in a mood." He shrugged. "So, is everything here now?"

"Just about. The forklift, like I said, is missing. Hopefully it'll get delivered tomorrow. I spent a little time getting my office set up. I could use a good secretary, receptionist, order taker, organizer type person to keep me on track. Know anyone who might fill those shoes?"

"No."

"No personal assistants, administrative assistants come to mind? What, did you graduate the one and only of your kind in your class?"

"I didn't take names and numbers in case someone asked me one day in the future if I knew anyone looking for work. Sorry. Post the job online."

"No. I'd rather steal you from my father. How much is he paying you? I'll give you twice that much." My eyes widened. He shook his head. "Skip it. I'll just wing it for now."

"I'm not going to leave your father to work for you. If he starts feeling better, I want him to teach me some more about clock making."

He shrugged and continued eating. I stayed until he was done. We left the table together, walking to the reception hall. "What are you doing tonight?" he asked me as we climbed the staircase to the second floor.

"I'm reading."

"What are you reading?"

"Jane Austen. *Pride and Prejudice.*"

"Is it any good?"

"I guess."

We'd reached the top of the stairs. He stopped. I started toward the doorway to the east wing. "Charlotte, are we good?"

I had my hand on the doorknob, but I turned to look at him over my shoulder. He looked anxious, worried, and nervous. I'd heard a little of that in the way he'd asked that question. "Yes, we are."

"Did Ethan get the forms from the police station?"

"I haven't seen him today. Not since breakfast anyway."

"Find a gun safety class and enroll in it. The sooner the better."

I nodded, said goodnight, and then slipped around the door into the east wing hallway, closing the door behind me and walking to my sitting room door, letting myself inside. It was as I was undressing, getting ready to climb into bed to continue reading about Elizabeth and Mr. Darcy, that a thought struck me. He had been alone at the shop most of the day. I wondered if he had seen or heard something to make him think that the werewolf that was killing people in and around Pine Haven had been nearby again, watching him.

Instead of the book, I grabbed my phone and used the internet connection on it to look up gun safety classes. There was one at the Elks Lodge that was starting next week. I filled out the online application and sent it. I would be notified by email if my application was accepted. It hadn't asked me if I'd ever been confined involuntarily to a psychiatric ward. I figured that if they didn't ask, I wasn't going to volunteer that information. Maybe it didn't matter if you were crazy or not. Maybe it was a HIPAA violation, asking one's medical and psychiatric history. Whatever. I'd just wait to see if I was accepted for enrollment in this class.

If not, I would look for another. Maybe I'd have to call my stepfather and ask him, although I'm sure my mother would freak out about her lunatic daughter wanting to learn how to shoot a gun.

That accomplished, I leaned over, set the phone on the bedside table, picked up my clock and gently wound it before switching off the bedside light and lying back to stare into the near darkness, my mind still buzzing.

I finally turned onto my side and closed my eyes, but that only brought the image of Julian in his wolf form into my mind. It occurred to me, that in the dark, I wasn't sure if I could tell him from another lycanthrope. The resemblance to the one I had seen, the one that had killed Chase, was too close.

Chapter Sixteen

I didn't make it into that gun safety class, but was told I'd be welcome to take the next one. I could accept that two month delay. Meanwhile, Ethan had gotten me the forms I needed to compete and return to the police department, so I did that. Julian had also, apparently, done this. He had been licensed when he was a teenager, had a few guns in the house, but needed to get a current FID card and license to carry a firearm. He even signed up for the gun safety class I was taking, and to my surprise, so did Ethan.

I didn't talk to Mr. Beresford about this because I thought it would upset him, that his personal assistant wanted to learn how to shoot so she could kill a werewolf. It wasn't really a conversation I wanted to have with a man whose son was a werewolf. I was certain he wasn't aware of that fact, but I just didn't want to run the risk of accidentally blurting it out while trying to explain my need to carry a gun for my own safety.

Mr. Beresford had a little rally toward the end of summer. We were able to go outside and sit on the patio under an awning to enjoy the fresh air, the scent of roses wafting from the garden. Mrs. Hastings from the Garden Club had come with several other ladies to take clippings from Mrs. Beresford's lovely roses under the supervision of Kerry, who did not want the overall symmetry of the garden destroyed by a pack of women with pruning shears and flat baskets running wild along the meandering paths cutting off rose bush canes willy-nilly. But, they had all been thoughtful, long time gardeners. While elated to finally be able to take the clippings, they had been careful and considerate of the late Grace Randolph Beresford's rose bushes.

Julian spent much of his time at the shop finishing the clock tower which was in three sections that would be shipped and then assembled at its final destination in late September. He was seldom home in time for dinner. I was often tinkering in the ballroom workshop when I'd receive a text message from him asking me to come to the informal dining room to keep him company while he ate. Most of the time he was sweaty and grungy from working long hours in the hot shop. Often he had cuts and abrasions on his hands and forearms. The worst ones I insisted he let me treat with antibacterial ointment, dressings, and bandages. He muttered about needing to redesign some of his lift and pulley systems so pieces that he was welding and working on didn't slip. But, some of the cuts looked like deep animal scratches and gouges. I suppressed the shudders that threatened to run through me as I cleaned his wounds. It worried me that he was more active as a werewolf/predator than he'd led me to believe, but that was a conversation I wasn't anxious to initiate with him.

We did attend the gun safety class together with Ethan. All of us passed. On a crisp, early October Saturday morning, the three of us went gun shopping in Pittsfield. Ethan wanted a high-power rifle. Julian had his nine millimeter and wanted something similar for me. But, he also wanted a large caliber pistol. The man behind the counter examined our identification cards carefully before we signed paperwork for the guns. There was a forty-eight hour wait period before we could come back to pick up our purchases. Since Sunday was a non-business day, that meant we could pick up our guns on Tuesday. Julian said that he would drive back to Pittsfield to get them since I had to work and Ethan was busy preparing the grounds for the coming winter.

On Thursday of that week, Julian still hadn't had time to run to Pittsfield to pick up the guns, so Ethan and I were going that afternoon. I had some packages to ship from the post office, small clocks Mr. Beresford and I had made for clients and finally finished. Once again, I ran into Mr. Gunther on the front steps of the post office as I came out of the building. "Charlotte! We meet again!"

"Hello, Mr. Gunther," I replied, cringing inside because, although he was a handsome man, he was just plain sleazy.

"You're still working for Beresford?" I nodded. "Do you like your job?"

"Yes, I do."

He nodded. "You're a lovely young lady. Are you seeing anyone?"

"Not at the moment." It was the truth. I just didn't want him to know that I never saw anyone.

"I'd like to have dinner with you. When are you free?"

"Um…"

"I have something to tell you that you might find rather interesting." He gave a small shrug. "So, J. Rand has opened the old clock shop. I saw him bringing some cartons

187

inside when I was on my way home a few weeks ago. He builds clock towers, doesn't he?"

"Yes. Amazing ones." He'd left the sample-sized clock tower in my sitting room. At least twice a week I went out into the dark sitting room just before midnight to watch the magical clock. Where I had originally thought that the prince had been hiding and knocked out the wolf to the delight of the princess who kissed him for his bravery, I know realized that she came out of her tower room to meet the wolf who transformed into the prince who received that kiss from his one true love, and then he transformed back into a wolf and fled before she returned to her room. Julian had been telling me something when he'd placed that miniature clock tower in my suite. He'd been giving me a hint of what he'd still been too fearful of telling me then.

"I'll be in touch. Let's not wait too long before we have that dinner though." I nodded. "Mr. Beresford is well?"

"As well as can be expected."

"Is he on hospice yet?"

"No. He refuses. I suppose it will be inevitable, but he's a strong-willed man, if truth be told. He's not ready to give up the fight."

"Yes. And the apple did not fall far from the tree, did it?" I didn't quite know what he meant by that. "J. Rand. He's quite strong himself. He saw two of his best friends die. He suffered injuries that changed his life. Yet, he finished high school and then flew off to Europe at age eighteen to make a name for himself as a different sort of clockmaker. You know people are leery of him, don't you? They're uncomfortable about his return to Pine Haven. That creature that prowls our quaint town has been more active since his return. Have you noticed that?" He didn't give me a chance to respond. "Of course you have. It killed your dearest friend and her fiancé. People think there's a connection there—his return and the increase in the mutilation killings."

"But animals and people were killed when he was in Europe for eight or so years. Why would his coming back here have any correlation to the increase in killings? He's busy building clocks. He's home at night."

"Is he, Charlotte? Or does he come home for dinner, go up to his room, and then...?"

"That's a ridiculous idea!" I flared.

"Is it?" he queried, giving me a long look. And then he smiled. "Well, let's get together over dinner soon and have a conversation. I think you will find it to be quite enlightening." He moved past me on the steps. "Have a lovely day, Charlotte."

I walked down the remaining steps feeling as if I had just rolled in hog slop. I wanted to go home and take a long, hot shower. "Wasn't that the high school gym teacher fellow?" Sanborn asked.

"Yes."

"He always seems to be here when you have packages to ship."

"He's like a bad penny."

"Are there any other errands to run before I take you home?"

I almost said no, but then said, "Yes. Can you drive me out to the clock shop? I need to talk to Julian for a few minutes."

His eyes met mine in the mirror, but he didn't say anything, just shifted the car into gear and pulled away from the curb, making the loop around the town green and heading back up Main Street to the intersection that would take us to Clay Hill Road.

Julian's truck was in the lot, but the front door was locked. I rapped on the door, but there was no response. While Sanborn waited in the car, probably playing a game on his phone, I hiked around the building. The loading dock door was unlocked, so I slipped inside into a receiving bay area. I could hear clanging farther inside the shop, so I walked to the door with the window with chicken wire embedded between the panes of glass and peered inside. The window was dirty, but I could see a fairly large portion of the shop area.

There were racks running vertically and horizontally from floor to ceiling along both side walls and old, sturdy, wooden tables down the center of the space with hanging shop light fixtures above. There were gaps between the tables and one open space. I saw a shower of sparks and realized that Julian was welding something. I waited until there was a pause in the sprays of bright sparks before banging loudly on the door.

A shadowy form wavered on the far wall of racks as he slowly came up the aisle toward the rear of the shop to investigate the noise I'd made. He had a heavy apron on, had raised the face shield of the welding mask. He frowned when he saw me, but came and unlocked the door. "What the fuck are you doing here?" he demanded.

"I needed to see you."

"I told you to text me if you needed to talk to me."

"I don't want to text you about this."

"Did you come out here alone?"

"No, of course not. Sanborn drove me."

"So, where is he?"

"Out front in the car."

He looked annoyed, but let me inside, closing and locking the door behind me. "Come on." He lifted off the mask as he led me down the aisle, leaving it on one of the tables that we passed by. The shop smelled of old machine oil, grease, old wood, raw metal, hot metal, and hot, dusty light fixtures.

He opened a door that led to a hallway off of which were a bathroom that had a shower facility, an office where he obviously conducted his business from, and then a front area with a counter. There was an old desk behind the counter, shoved up against the wall. This is where customers could come in to place orders or pick up orders. It was where my mother had brought me when we'd come to see Mr. Beresford about the little clock.

He told me to wait at the counter and then he went to the door, looked through the window, then opened the door and shouted for Sanborn to come inside. The driver was surprised at being summoned inside; however, he climbed out of the car and came in. Julian closed and secured the door again. "You," he said, pointing to Sanborn, "sit there." He indicated the vintage office chair with its tatty arms, the stuffing leaking out of rips in the leather that was at the scarred desk. "You," he said, grabbing my arm, "come with me." He led me to his office, pushing me inside, following me in, and then slamming the door shut. "What the fuck is so goddam important that you made Sanborn drive you out here like this?"

"I've been invited out to dinner." He had his dark glasses on, but I could tell that his eyes had narrowed as he focused his gaze on me. "I was told there's something interesting that I need to hear."

"Told by whom?" he asked, his voice pitched low.

"Mr. Gunther." I thought he was going to kill me, he came at me so fast, grabbing me and shoving me up against the chipped plaster wall, his hand around my throat, his face so close to mine I could feel the heat of his breath coming from his nose. He was breathing hard, fast, his nostrils flaring. It was almost as if he was sniffing me, trying to pick up the scent of the man on me, but Mr. Gunther hadn't touched me.

"You listen to me, and you listen to me very carefully, Charlotte Rumford. I forbid you to go anywhere with that man. Stay away from him. He's corrupted enough young women in this town. I'll be damned if he corrupts you, too. He has nothing to say to you. Nothing! I'll fuckin' kill him if he so much as lays a finger on you, do you hear me?" He was snarling at me, he was so enraged.

"Julian Rand Beresford, you'd better get you hand off my throat right now or my knee is going to connect hard with your groin," I replied.

He, apparently, was willing to risk that because he did not let go, only leaned into me harder, his face so close to mine that he was blurry in my vision. "You're mine," he growled.

"We haven't established that yet," I pointed out. "You don't let anyone close to you. You told me so yourself. And I've never been one to let people get close to me either."

"Fuck you, Charlotte!"

He was furious. He literally shoved me toward the door so that I crashed into it, rattling it hard in its frame. "Charlotte?" called Sanborn from the front counter area. "Are you all right?"

"Go home and stay there," he growled at me. "Go!"

He didn't come any closer to me. I grasped the door knob and twisted it, but before I pulled the door open I turned back to him and said, "Don't you dare ever treat me like this again," in as cold and deadly a tone as I could muster. And then I flung the door open so hard that it crashed against the wall. I was pretty sure the door knob left a decent size dent in the old plaster, but the glass remained intact. He did not follow me out of his office, but stayed where he was. "Sanborn! Let's go!" I said briskly as I entered the reception area, making him jump up out of the chair that creaked in protest.

He was on my heels as I unlocked the front entrance door and strode outside. A charcoal gray luxury sedan was just pulling slowly away from the side of the road in front of the shop. The driver must have stopped to respond to a text message or to send one. I really didn't pay too much attention to that as I opened the rear door and climbed into the car.

I certainly did notice the rabbit, the torn up, dead bunny, on the seat that I normally sat in, the rear passenger side seat. I'd gotten in on the driver's side rear, too steamed up to hike around the car. I screamed as if there was an agitated rattlesnake in the car and jumped back out, still screaming.

Julian came running out of the shop. "What the hell's the matter with you?" he shouted.

"Jesus Christ!" Sanborn cried, having glanced into the car to see what had upset me so much. "Someone killed a rabbit and put it in the car while we were inside."

The language that erupted out of Julian turned the air dark blue. He was instantly alert, his face fierce as he scanned the entire area. "Did you see anything? Was there anyone around when you came out here?" he demanded. I was incapable of speaking. I just turned, walked over to the far side of the lot where I vomited into the weeds. I was shaking, shaken.

"There was a gray sedan that pulled away as we came out," Sanborn replied, having seen the vehicle also.

"Did you see the driver? Did you get a look at him?"

"No. I think it was a man. That's the impression I got. I really didn't pay too much attention to it. Cars stop at the side of the road all the time these days. People with their damn phones."

Julian went back inside to get something to clean up the carnage on the back seat. When he had the dead rabbit removed and had laid a shop towel over the bloodstain, he said, "Take her home. She has medication. Tell Druce to make sure she takes something to help her calm down or you'll be driving her right back to the psych facility." He slammed the passenger side rear door shut. "Charlotte! Get your ass over here! Get in the fucking car! You're riding in the front passenger seat! Move!"

I came and got into the car. He was holding the door, waiting for me to pull my other leg in. I looked up at him and my face crumpled, but I still managed to say what I needed to say. I said, "Fuck you, Julian," as I grabbed the door handle, brought my leg inside the car, and slammed the door. He barely got his fingers off the door jamb in time before it closed. I turned my face away, unable to look at him any longer.

Sanborn climbed in behind the wheel and started the car. "Well, I guess you told him," he said quietly as he backed up, turned the car, and headed out of the lot. "There was no need for him to talk to you like that, inside the shop or out."

"I don't want to talk about him. I just want to go home." I didn't say another word until we got home. Druce met me at the front door, having seen the car approaching. "I'm sorry, but I don't feel well. I'm going upstairs to lie down. Please extend my regrets to Mr. Beresford, but I cannot join him for lunch. Also, I'm unable to work this afternoon." I continued across the reception hall and up the stairs. Let Druce get what information he could from Sanborn who would be out at the carriage house attempting to get the bloodstains out of the back seat fabric.

I took two anti-anxiety tablets, put on my nightgown, drew the drapes, and crawled into bed. My mind was filled with crazy thoughts as I tried to comprehend why this had even happened. But the thing that fought the medication's effects the hardest was the pain in my heart. It was too deep, too raw a wound. I got out of bed, stumbled to the bathroom, and swallowed a third tablet.

That did the trick. I went out and stayed out.

Chapter Seventeen

"Charlotte, wake up!" I didn't want to. "Charlotte! Damn it all, wake up!" It was Julian. Some part of my brain was trying to formulate a biting response, but only my fist obeyed as I swung at him as hard as I could, connecting with his jaw with a jolt that hurt my whole arm. "Jesus Christ! I'll hold her, you try to get some coffee into her. She must have come damn fuckin' close to overdosing."

"Hell of an arm on her when she's still pretty much out of it," another male voice responded. It was Druce. "Here, Miss Rumford, have some coffee. Be careful, it's hot." Julian had somehow hauled me upright and wedged himself behind me. "Come on, young lady. This is urgent."

I mumbled something about leaving me the hell alone, but Julian shook me hard and some hot coffee spilled down the front of my nightgown, scalding me. "Come on, Charlotte, cooperate! My father is dying. He wants to see you, but I'll be damned if he sees you like this! Wake up!

Snap out of it! Drink the damn coffee and then we're going to get you properly dressed and to his room before it's too fuckin' late!"

"He's not!" I cried, trying to hit him again.

"Miss Rumford, stop this. Please listen to me. Mr. Beresford is in critical condition. He's not expected to see morning. His wish is to see you before he draws his last breath. *Do not disappoint the man who has been better than a father to you!*" he said sharply, pressing the rim of the cup against my mouth. His angry tone, the words he had just spoken, penetrated the dense fog filling my head. I sipped the coffee, but still couldn't keep my eyes open. Every time I began to drift off, J. Rand shook me hard and Druce plied me with more hot coffee. Finally, the caffeine began to work its way into my bloodstream.

When I could hold myself upright, they turned me sideways, sitting me up on the edge of the bed. Druce began going through my dresser drawers. He tossed a bra and panties onto the foot of the bed. Julian snatched them up as Druce disappeared into my walk-in closet. Julian got my feet into my panties and pulled them up to my thighs. "Lift up."

"I can do this." But I couldn't. I had to slump over his left shoulder while he lifted me up high enough so he could get my panties on. While he had me over his shoulder, he bunched my nightgown up to my hips, then sat me back down on the bed and then tugged the nightgown off over my head. He studied the bra, realizing that it had front hook closures, got it right side up and onto me, bringing the cups over my breasts, his knuckles grazing my skin as he fiddled with the tiny hooks. "I'm better at undoing these damn things then doing them up," he muttered. I slapped him upside the head and he pinched the inside of my left breast hard enough to hurt. "Stop hitting me," he said, his voice low, angry.

"This should do," Druce said, returning to the bedroom with a purple blouse and black slacks.

Together they finished dressing me, tucking my shirt in, finding a belt and buckling it. Druce went into the bathroom, located my hairbrush and brought it to Julian. I was now on a chair in the sitting room. Druce went back into my bedroom in search of shoes because I was barefoot. Julian began brushing my hair which was all snarled. As Druce knelt to slip my shoes on, Julian went to find an elastic for my hair. Druce stopped him from pulling my hair back severely, telling him that his father wanted to see the lovely girl he'd taken into his home and under his wing, not the personal assistant who handled his affairs in the study.

They got me to Mr. Beresford's suite. The doctor looked quizzically at me. Julian shook his head, steering me into the bedroom. "Dad, Charlotte's here," he said. "I've brought her like you asked me to."

"Yes. Charlotte," he murmured, his heavy eyes opening to bright slits. "There's my girl. So pretty."

It jolted me more than the caffeine had to see him so ashen pale, so near death's door. I felt a stab of guilt at not being there for him, for not noticing his sudden decline. It snapped me wide awake. I shook off Julian's hands and walked, just a little unsteadily, to the side of the bed. I sat on the edge like I had done often enough in the past when he was going through a bad spell, lifting his thin hand, holding it in mine. "I'm sorry," I whispered. I was sorry for being such a disappointment to him in his final days.

"I need to hear you say it," he murmured.

"What do you need me to say?" I asked. His eyes opened more and he gazed at me with such a look of love that it wrenched my heart hard. I felt unworthy of his affection for me. But, I knew what he wanted and I could do that. It would not be a lie. It would be the God's honest truth and he would know it. I leaned toward him, my eyes steadily holding his gaze. "I love you, Dad," I said quietly but clearly. "I love you so much. Thank you for everything you've done for me."

"No, thank you, my dear," he whispered. His eyes shifted to Julian who was standing just behind me. "Son, our differences…"

"Don't worry about it, Dad. We're good."

"Take care of her, will you?" Julian hesitated and then said that he would. "Take care of yourself."

"I will," he replied as he placed his hand on my shoulder and gave it a gentle squeeze. "I'll do what you've asked me to do." I felt him shrug. "For what it's worth, I'd have done it eventually anyway."

"Can you say it for me?" his father asked.

I felt a tremor go through Julian but, to his immense credit, he said it aloud. "Yeah, I can. I'm sorry, Dad. I love you."

"My children…" he murmured, a smile at the corners of his mouth as his eyes drifted closed. "Grace…" was the last word that passed his lips as the breath left his body for the last time.

I leaned close and kissed his sunken cheek and then I tried to stand up, except my legs wouldn't support me. Julian caught me, but he immediately passed me along to Druce. "Take her back to her room and put her back to bed. I want to sit with my father for a little while."

"Shall I telephone Winslow and Waterman's?" I recognized the name of the funeral home downtown.

"Yeah, but tell them not to rush right over. I want to be alone with him for a bit."

"Very good, sir." He easily lifted me in his arms, my head lolling backwards. I was suddenly as limp as a ragdoll.

Somehow, I was put back to bed. I wasn't going to dwell on the how of it. I'd been put back into my nightgown. When I woke up, the sun was up, streaming through a gap between the drapes in a stripe across the foot of the bed. I turned my head to squint at the drapes, wishing them to close completely. I had a dull headache. My mouth was dry. I felt lethargic, sluggish, although I was aware that I had just woken up.

When I turned my head to see the clock, I noticed Julian sitting slumped in the wingchair, his head bent forward. I thought he was asleep, so let my eyes move to the clock. The hands informed me that it was after twelve-thirty. "Helen's bringing you something to eat." His voice was as dull as my mind felt.

"What are you doing here?" I asked, remembering that I was thoroughly pissed off at him. There were other things floating about in the pea soup fog in my skull. The image of his hands fumbling with my bra emerged and I made a sound at the sudden sensory memory of his knuckles grazing my bare skin. It confused me. And then I remembered Druce kneeling down, putting black flats on my feet as if I was Cinderella and he was Prince Charming. "You need to go," I said.

"Yeah, I know. I have funeral arrangements to make. I just wanted to make sure that you were going to wake up and that I didn't have to plan two funerals." The word 'funeral' struck a chord in me that twanged my heart hard. I tried to sit up as a great sob erupted out of me, but I couldn't move.

"No! No, no! No!" I sobbed.

"Charlotte....don't," he said quietly, his voice raw with emotion.

"That was real?" I cried.

"Yeah." He slowly rose from the chair, looking as if he didn't have the strength or energy to reach the door.

"Wait!" He hunched his shoulders. "Julian...wait!" I was still trying to clear my head. "Just...wait."

"I want to get this over with. I want to get all of this over and done with." He walked out of the room.

I lay in bed crying, feeling as if my world had just been torn out from underneath my feet and I was falling down a deep hole with nothing to grasp onto. "Julian!" I cried, wanting him to come back. I needed something or someone to hold me here. "Julian!" Panic ripped through me, jumpstarting my aching heart. I flung the covers aside and swung my legs over the side of the bed, sitting up and then getting out of bed. I walked three steps before I just dropped hard to the floor. That didn't stop me. I started crawling toward the door. "Julian! Come back! Please, come back!" I made it to the doorway between the bedroom and sitting room before I collapsed into a sobbing heap. "I need you," I said. "I need…you." But he was gone.

It was Druce who scooped me up and put me back into my bed, propping me up. He washed my face, made me blow my nose. And then Helen laid a tray across my lap. "You had best eat now, Charlotte," she murmured. "We, all of us, must bear up under this burden of sorrow that has fallen upon us."

I had no appetite, but she cajoled me and when that didn't work, she fed me as if I was a baby. As the food she managed to get into my mouth began to be digested, I started to feel less sluggish and weak. She went downstairs taking away the partially eaten lunch tray and then returned with a milkshake that she'd made for me. I could taste banana and raspberries. It was cold and thick. I ate part of it with a spoon, and then sipped what remained. Afterwards, I felt full, slightly bloated even. "You'd best use the bathroom and then climb right back into bed, although a shower would do you some good. You've been indisposed for several days now."

"Days?" I didn't know how that could be.

I had a seat in my shower, so she stayed and helped me, making sure I didn't fall and hurt myself. Then she unsnarled my hair, used the blow dryer to mostly dry it, and then plaited it loosely before putting me into a clean nightgown. Caroline had come and changed the bed linens. I was put back to bed, told that my dinner would be brought up on a tray, but I was expected to get out of bed and eat at the table in my sitting room.

I napped for the remainder of the afternoon. Druce woke me, telling me that he'd brought my tray up. He fetched my robe from the closet, helped me into it. I tied it around me, stuffed my feet into slippers and walked out into the sitting room. He had most of the lights on. I squinted, but sat down. He removed the domed cover from the dish. "I'll return in half an hour to clear."

"Is J. Rand home?" I asked.

"Yes, but he left instructions not to be disturbed." He hesitated and then said, "It has been a difficult day for him." I knew the loss of his father was rough on him, but from the way Druce was looking at me, I knew my own behavior had done nothing to help matters.

"I'm sorry. I lost track of the number of tablets I took."

"I would hope that this will not happen again."

"No, it won't. I'm going to throw the rest of it out. I don't want to be making a mistake like that again."

"Perhaps I can take the vial. Should you need a tablet, it will be available."

I shrugged. "If you want to do that, fine. It's in the medicine cabinet."

He went to fetch the medication and took it with him. I really didn't think that I wanted to take any more of it anyway. I needed to remain clear-headed. I was more than likely going to be fired after the funeral service. Julian wouldn't want me around anymore. I was too volatile, too messed up. He had enough on his plate to deal with.

I sighed, pushing food around on my plate. I hadn't done anything but lie in bed, so I really wasn't hungry. However, I made myself eat half of everything on the plate. I drank the milk, I ate the brownie. Then, I went to brush my teeth and, afterwards, I crawled right back into bed. I heard Druce come in and clear the tray. He also turned off the lights in the sitting room. I fell asleep in the silent house and slept straight through until dawn.

Chapter Eighteen

The wake was held on Tuesday evening. I attended it along with the household staff. Julian, in his dark suit and dark glasses looked like a hip Secret Service agent standing there stiffly shaking hands with the mourners who filed through, many of them friends of his mother's from the Garden Club. They nodded to us, the staff, but didn't approach us. I dabbed at my eyes which leaked tears. I couldn't look at the clockmaker in his casket. It was true; he had been more a father to me than my own long gone from my life father had been. I wasn't close with my stepfather for obvious reasons. He'd wanted to date me and then he'd married my mother. That, to me, was a little weird. I seldom saw them. Therefore, I was caught off guard when they entered the viewing room.

They paid their respects to Mr. Beresford and then shook hands with Julian. Officer Emery was speaking quietly to him as my mother made her way over to where I was sitting. "Charlotte, I'm so sorry. Have you made any plans yet?"

"No, not yet."

"Mike and I have a room if you need a place to stay and regroup while you look for a new job."

"Thanks, but I've saved some money. I'll probably go someplace else, not stay here."

"Yes, maybe that would be better for you, to move on. There isn't much left here for you anymore."

"Thanks for coming, Mom."

"J. Rand doesn't look much different than he did in high school. A little older. Still the rebel."

"Why do you say that? He came home to be with his father at the end of his life. He basically moved his business here. He works hard."

"The long hair, the dark glasses. Mike's heard that he hangs out at the Renegade Club." That was news to me. "That boy is trouble, Charlotte. The sooner you move out of that house, the better."

'That boy' was in his mid-twenties and had been on his own since he was eighteen earning a living making mechanical clock towers. I didn't feel compelled to point that fact out to her, not at a funeral anyway.

Officer Emery came over, nodded to me, and then steered my mother to a couple of chairs across the room. They sat and chatted with some people who remembered my mother from The Remains of Yesterday. I watched them for a few minutes. Mom was talking about her shop in Windsor.

When I turned back, I saw that Mr. Gunther had arrived. As he crossed the floor space while approaching Julian, some change in the atmosphere of the room reached me. My skin was practically crawling. It was tingling and prickling. Julian was tense. I could see the rigidness in him. He shook hands with his former gym teacher, but I could tell he was not happy to see the man. Mr. Gunther said something to him and I saw a muscle twitch along the ridge of Julian's clenched jaw. He turned his head slightly and all but glared at me. And then the man approached me. I thought for sure Julian was going to whip out his nine millimeter and shoot him dead right in front of everyone gathered to mourn R. Hollis Beresford. I thought he would grind his teeth down to bare nerve and root. He was absolutely livid.

"Charlotte, so sorry for your loss. The man was so good to you." I murmured something, probably thanking him for coming. My mind was buzzing there was so much tension sparking around me. Mr. Gunther seemed cool and calm. Julian was seething. I honestly thought violence would erupt. "I'd still like to have dinner with you. I'll be in touch." He moved on and I lost track of him.

On Wednesday afternoon the funeral took place with a reception following at The Castle, a restaurant in Windsor that had been built in the thirties to resemble a stone castle. It had been a favorite dining out spot for Mr. and Mrs. Beresford, the place they had gone each year to celebrate their anniversary.

That evening I went home with the rest of the staff. In the kitchen, we had a toast to the man who had been our employer, and then I made my way upstairs. I wasn't tired, so I put on my nightgown and sat in the sitting room reading.

The tower clock in the corner startled me when it began moving. I hadn't come out to watch it for a couple of weeks now. I'd almost forgotten it was there.

Setting the book aside, I got up, crossed the room and stood in front of the clock watching it—all the marvelous and magical little mechanical movements. The princess came out and the wolf leapt onto the balcony from behind the tree. He disappeared below the railing and then reappeared as a prince. The miniature metal roses, painted red, bloomed. The green-painted metal ivy vines gently swayed. The moon moved in the background. The prince and the princess kissed and then he once again changed into a wolf, leaping off the balcony and she retreated into her room. I leaned closer, peering through the still open doors, and gasped. Her room, I saw, was decorated with tiny violets painted on the walls, purple curtains. I had never before thought to look inside the room that she disappeared into. This was an unexpected revelation.

The clock struck the twelfth chime and the light went out in the princess' chamber. The roses folded shut reverting to buds, the ivy stopped swaying. I leaned closer and then around the side of the clock, searching for the wolf, but he apparently slid into a wide slot within the metal tree where he was hidden from view. I tried to open the doors but they wouldn't budge. I didn't want to force them to open and end up breaking them.

I examined the entire clock. It was heavy, so I wasn't able to pull it away from the corner in which it stood. I wanted to look at the backside of it. But that would have to wait for another day, for when I could get someone to pull it away from the wall for me.

It was almost twelve-thirty when I finally stood up, switched off the lights, and retreated to my bedroom. I slipped into bed, leaned over, picked up my little clock and wound it. After putting it back down, I switched off the bedside lamp and lay in the dark trying to come up with a plan.

I didn't have any idea how soon Julian would be kicking me out of the house. I was a non-essential employee, his father's personal assistance. He had no use for me. If he planned on staying here in Pine Haven, the rest of the household staff would probably be kept on. I didn't think that he was all that fond of Druce, but I couldn't see him firing him. Finally, I sighed deeply, turned on my side, closed my eyes, and waited for sleep to come.

Over the next few days, I cleaned up loose ends in the study, leaving what I accomplished on top of the desk for Mr. Stroud to deal with. Then I went to the ball room and began straightening up. There was an unfinished clock on the table. Feeling sad, I sat down and uncovered it. This was the last clock we had been working on together. It was nearly finished.

Absently, I opened my rosewood tool box and got out my tools. Then I began the final assembly work. I checked everything over when I was done and then screwed the back of the case onto the clock. Taking a deep breath, I gave the key a gentle turn. Turning the clock to face me, I watched the second hand begin to move.

R. Hollis Beresford had signed the clock, attached the brass plate to the base. It was, for all intents and purposes, a completed clock, an order filled. It had always been my job to pack and ship the clocks he made to order, so I packed it up safely in an inner box, and then snugged that box into the outer box. I printed the packing slip and then the shipping label. The clock had been paid for in full. I knew he would want me to ship it out. He was a man of good business. He had never disappointed a customer and I didn't want to disappoint this one, a prince in Norway. This clock was a wedding gift for his future wife.

I put away my tools and then carried the parcel and my tool box to the study. I left the parcel on my desk there before taking my tool box upstairs. He had given the tool box to me. It was mine. I was going to take it with me. I probably wouldn't be able to find a job as a clockmaker, but I wanted to keep my tools. They meant something to me.

I had lunch in the staff dining room where I asked Sanborn if he would drive me to the post office to ship one last package. He replied that Julian was meeting with each staff member this afternoon and he wasn't sure when he would be free. He said he could drive me tomorrow morning. I nodded. There had been no message for me that I was to meet with Julian.

After lunch, I went upstairs, gathered up all my laundry and washed it. While it was washing, I pulled out the suitcase I had moved in with and dusted it off. Then I began emptying the dresser drawers. I grabbed my duffle bag and stuffed my underwear and socks into it. I really didn't own much in the way of clothing. I'd mixed and matched a number of basic pieces for work and then had my regular clothes for my off time.

I made a mental note to ask Sanborn to take me to the big box store in Windsor so I could get another bag for my toiletries. Again, I wasn't one to fuss much with my appearance, but I had soap, shampoo, lip gloss, deodorant, and feminine supplies to pack from the bathroom.

When I was finished, I dropped down into the wingchair in the bedroom and just stared at the wall across the room. This had been my home for close to three years. I had felt like I belonged here, but that feeling had been sheared away with the death of the man who had taken me in. I was a balloon adrift amid the walls. When I walked out the door, I was at the mercy of the wind as to where I would go from here.

I had to make myself go downstairs to dinner in the staff hall. Everyone was chatting about being asked to stay on. Julian was staying here for a while, at least until the will was settled. He had inherited everything. There were a few minor bequests for staff. I knew there wouldn't be anything in the will for me. I was just an outsider hired to assist him.

Feeling sad and like a damper on their little celebration of continued employment, I excused myself and went back upstairs. It was too dark to go outside now. I curled up on the loveseat in the sitting room and tried again to think what to do, where to go. It was as I was thinking things through that it struck me that I needed to buy a car. I couldn't go anywhere unless I traveled by bus or cab. Grimacing, I saw my savings account rapidly dwindle. Even small, economical cars were expensive to a girl suddenly jobless and being cast out into the world on her own. But, I'd be damned if I went to Windsor and took my mother up on that offer of a room. I could not live with them.

Again, the clock startled me by whirring to life. I sat up and watched it. Lucky princess, I thought. She had a roof over her head. Her prince, even though he was a werewolf, came and kissed her every night. Feeling a wave of sadness and despair crash against my heart, feeling overwhelmed and defeated by life, I got up and turned out the lights, went into the bedroom and closed the door before the clock had completed its run cycle.

Sanborn drove me to the post office. As had happened numerous times before, Mr. Gunther was on the front steps waiting for me when I came out. It was downright eerie how he always seemed to be there, as if he was stalking me. Maybe Julian had been right about that, that there was someone watching me. This seemed more than a coincidence to me now that I was thinking about things in a new way. "Charlotte! We meet again. I didn't think you'd be down here shipping any more packages now that the old man is gone."

"There was one last clock to ship."

"You're a dedicated employee. He was lucky to have you. Now, what about dinner tonight?"

"I really can't make it tonight. I have some things to do. I'll be leaving Pine Haven soon."

"Leaving? Rand is not keeping you on?" He seemed taken aback by this news. "I can't help but say that I'm surprised to hear that."

"He doesn't need me."

"I see. Well, are you sure about tonight? I could pick you up at six. We could go into Stockbridge, to the Red Lion Inn for dinner. It's very nice there. I'm sure you'll like it."

It sounded tempting, but I had set my agenda and wanted to stick to it. "I really can't. Not tonight."

"Then how about tomorrow night? I'd really like to talk to you before you leave Pine Haven."

"All right. Fine."

"Six-thirty?" I nodded. "I will pick you up tomorrow night then."

I nodded and then walked down the remaining steps to where Sanborn was waiting with the door open. He was driving me to the super store, and then to the closest car dealership on our return trip, which was most likely the Toyota or Subaru dealership. I didn't really know because I had never been in the market for a car before.

While in the store, I received a text from Julian asking me to meet him later this morning. I texted him back that I was buying a car and would not be home until later. He texted back that he had a meeting and then dinner tonight to discuss some business. Then he asked me to have dinner with him tomorrow night. I texted back that I had a previous dinner engagement at that time, sorry. He did not text back for several minutes and then it was just, *Who with?* I texted back that it was none of his business and then shoved my phone in my pocket because I was in the checkout line.

I didn't look at my phone again until after I'd written a check for the full amount for a new Toyota Corolla. I got a great deal, at least I was fairly certain that I had. They had treated me like a queen at the dealership. I guess they didn't have too many young women my age come in and pay the whole amount for a new car. I hadn't intended to do that, but then I'd realized that I didn't have a mailing address. I didn't have any address. Shortly, I would be homeless, a drifter in a shiny new sedan. I'd also had to pay the full, outrageous amount for my car insurance. The Beresford house was the address I had to use, but I knew someone at the house would collect my mail and forward it to me wherever I ended up.

I arrived back at Randolph Hall with substantially less money than I had left with in my checking account. I put my things in my room, grabbed a warmer jacket, and then went outside to walk around in the garden. Kerry and Ethan had buttoned up all the flowerbeds and mulched the roses. The fountains had been turned off and drained, winterized. A few leaves had drifted onto the brick paths. They made a crisp, crackling sound as I walked.

I sat on a bench for a while to try to plan my immediate future, but it was kind of chilly and raw. Soon enough, I grew cold, stood up, and headed back inside. I returned to my room and just paced back and forth, trying to drive the wild horses of random thoughts into the paddock of my brain, but they were unwilling to gallop through the gate.

I went downstairs, ate dinner alone in the kitchen, which caused Helen to give me an odd look as she carried bowls and platters into the staff dining room. I wasn't all that hungry. I rinsed my own dishes, loading them into the dishwasher, and then headed for the main staircase. Julian was just coming in with a breathtakingly gorgeous young woman who was laughing. She stopped laughing when she saw me, giving me a quizzical look. "Who is that?" she asked him.

"My father's personal assistant," he replied.

"I thought your father was dead."

"He is."

"Then why is she still here?" she asked.

I didn't wait for his explanation. I didn't wait for him to say that I was on my way out the door soon enough. I dashed upstairs and was surprised to hear them on the stairs as I opened the door to the east hall. Why was he bringing her upstairs? Hadn't he told me he was taking a client to dinner? I glanced back over my shoulder to see him leading her to the west wing hall doorway. She glanced over her shoulder at the same time, looking back at me. Her smile was smug as he led her through the now open door. I turned and continued through the east wing door, going to my room and staying there.

Tomorrow night I was having dinner with Mr. Gunther. I didn't like him. He oozed sleaze. I knew I shouldn't have even been talking to him. Julian had forbidden me to. But, what did anything matter anymore? I had a werewolf pursuing me that wanted to kill me. Maybe I shouldn't have wasted all my money on a new car and car insurance. My mother could have used that money for my funeral. However, there was enough left in my bank account to cover a cremation and urn, and still have enough left over for her and Mike to take a few nice trips someplace. Maybe they could dump my sorry, ashy remains somewhere during their travels and be rid of me forever.

I opened my bag and took out the gun that I carried. If he got out of line, I at least had some sort of defense. I thumbed the safety on and off for a few moments. Ethan was supposed to be taking me to the sportsman's club to do some target practice. I didn't even really know how to use the gun. I could more or less aim and shoot, but I really had no skill with it.

Disgusted, I stuffed it back in my bag and then hurled my bag across the room. It struck the clock and fell on the floor in front of it. I got up, went into my bedroom, and slammed the door. Maybe it was time for me to leave. If Julian was going to be bringing girls home with him, then I couldn't stay here. Already a piece of my heart had broken away and fallen into the abyss. Every time he brought a girl to the house another piece of my heart would be torn away and lost. It would kill me.

I went to bed and just lay there staring at the ceiling. Maybe being dead would be a blessing. Chase was dead. My rapist and tormentor, Cody Underwood, was dead. Austin was dead. Ripley and Miles were dead. The random thought that I had never actually lived drifted through my mind.

Rolling onto my side, I buried my face in my pillow and cried myself to sleep. I was the walking dead— that's all there was to it. Let the damn beast come and tear my guts out while my heart still beat. My heart was broken anyway. What did it matter? What did any of this really matter? When it finally tore my throat out, I would follow the rest of its victims into oblivion.

Susan Buffum

Chapter Nineteen

Julian did not go to work the next morning. I went down to breakfast and there was a message waiting for me asking me to meet him at nine o'clock in the study. It was seven o'clock. I quietly ate my breakfast, just a cinnamon raisin toast and a cup of tea, then returned upstairs, carrying my bags downstairs, one at a time. I loaded them into my car that was parked in one of the formerly empty carports. As I was heading back to the house for the last bag, Sanborn fell into step beside me. "Taking a little vacation?" he asked, having seen me stow one of the duffle bags in the trunk.

"No. I'm leaving. I thought everyone knew that."

"Leaving? Where to? Did you find a place of your own? Is something wrong?"

I looked at him and then shook my head. "Everything is wrong," I replied as I stepped inside the back hallway. Before he could ask me anything more, I turned and ran up the back servant's staircase. I had seldom used this staircase but it was a quicker route back to my suite. I didn't want to talk to him or anyone else right now. I would grab my last bag and just leave. I'd find a place to hang out somewhere. I could leave a message at the school for Mr. Gunther, telling him that I would meet him at the Red Lion Inn in Stockbridge at six-thirty. I would book a room there for the night, and then take off in the morning. I needed to run some errands in town, like go to the bank to get some money for traveling, swing by the market for some water and snacks to have in the car.

I was making my dismal little mental list as I entered the sitting room, but stopped dead when I saw Julian pacing the room. He looked pissed. I didn't want to fight with him. I was done fighting. I was ready to sink to the bottom of the lake and be done with it. "I'm not meeting with you this morning or ever again," I told him as I reached for the last duffle bag sitting on the floor beside the chair.

"Sanborn told me Gunther was at the post office again when you went there. You're having dinner with him tonight, aren't you?"

"Where I go, whomever I see, that's really none of your business."

"Let me ask you this then. What sort of a gravestone do you want? You don't have anyone else who gives a fuck about you, so I suppose it'll be up to me to pick it out."

"White marble with a clock face engraved on it with the hands set at midnight. That's the hour I came into this world." I made a dismissive gesture with my hand. "No, don't even bother putting yourself out, Julian. If there's anything left of me, burn it and just dump the ashes in the woods behind the shop. That'll be more convenient for you. I wouldn't want to be too much trouble for you." I turned toward the door.

"Hold on, Charlotte. Let me just tell you something before you go. It's not going to be very pleasant having your guts torn out, watching that beast devour them before his big paw reaches through the gaping, raw wound in your belly and up under your sternum to yank your still beating heart out. He'll eat that too, and then he'll tear your throat out just for the fun of it. That's what's going to happen to you tonight."

Despite the jolt I felt from his vivid description, I said, "I don't care anymore."

"Wait. Now let me tell you what's going to happen to me before you go. He's not going to kill you in Stockbridge. He's going to kill you at the shop. Not in the woods. No, he's going to kill you and leave you where I'm going to find you tomorrow morning."

"Why would he do that?"

"Because he knows it will push me over the edge. If it doesn't kill me, seeing you dead, torn all apart like that, and believe me, he will most likely rape you first because he knows exactly how I feel about you, it'll push me right over the edge. He'll desecrate you just to fling it in my face, that I am weaker than he is since I refuse to take what I want from you because I can't do that to you. He's never restrained himself. He doesn't have a shred of decency left in him. Every goddam second of my life, I fight to keep what decency I have left in me intact. Every fuckin' second, Charlotte. I'm getting tired. He's wearing me down.

"When I was in Europe, I was far enough away from his influence over me. But here, I'm practically living in his side yard when I'm trying to work at the shop." I refused to turn and look at him. "This is what's going to happen if you walk out that door; if you walk away. You'll die a violent, ugly, brutal death. He'll make you suffer to torment me, but when he finally kills you, it'll be all over for you in a few seconds. You'll be free. But, you'll have condemned me to a living hell because I really am going to lose it. And when I do lose it, I'm going to be much, much worse than he is. I've held the beast in me back for over a decade. It's just going to rush through me like a volcanic eruption because I'll have nothing left to live for anymore. I'll have no love in my heart because you'll have taken that with you, whether you know it or not

"Charlotte, I chained my heart to yours a long time ago. I made you my anchor in this world. When you're gone, your death will break that chain and you'll have helped unleash a monster more violent and brutal than he is on all of Pine Haven and all of the surrounding communities. Innocent people are going to die, unless I kill myself, or..." He came up behind me, reaching around, taking my right hand and placing his nine millimeter pistol in it, closing my fingers around it. He flicked the safety off. "...you can just turn around and kill me now. You can save Pine Haven and all the surrounding communities from a raging beast who won't give a fuck anymore because the one and only person he has ever loved has been torn to pieces and left on his doorstep in bloody, gory shreds." He stepped back. "Die a heroine, Charlotte. Turn around and shoot me through the heart. I know you haven't had the training you need, but I think, at this range, you really can't miss."

"Did he make you watch him kill Cody and Austin?"

"What do you think?"

"Were you honest with me when you told me that you'd never killed a human being?"

"Yes."

"Mr. Gunther *is* the werewolf who did this to you? He killed Chase and Ripley?"

"Lycanthrope. And, yes, he is."

I bent my head, feeling a great fatigue and despair wash over my shoulders. "I'm broken, Julian," I said quietly. "You have to know that."

"I do know that. But, I think I can hold you together, maybe even put you back together, if you'd let me."

"I don't know. I'm in too many pieces. He's already torn me apart psychologically."

"I can see that. You're ready to take the easy way out of this. To be honest with you, so am I. All you have to do is turn around and shoot me. It'll be over and done with. I can't kill anyone if I'm dead. There are specially made silver bullets in my gun, Charlotte. That's the only kind of bullet that will stop a lycanthrope dead. The clip is full of them. Don't hold your finger on the trigger. Just shoot and let go. You're going to need the rest of those bullets to stop Gunther."

"I can't shoot you, Julian," I said. It was the truth. If I killed him, I would not survive that. I would just curl up and die beside his body. "Can I ask you something not related to what we're talking about right now?"

"Yeah, I suppose so."

"Who was that girl?"

"What girl?"

"Don't play stupid with me. The one you took to your suite last night."

He shook his head. "Her? Don't worry about her."

"I worry about everything. I worry about everyone."

He sighed. "Her name is Allyson Gray. She's an interior designer. I told you that I had a meeting. She was who I was meeting with. I want a larger suite in the west wing revamped and redecorated. I actually want to combine two suites into one larger one. I took her upstairs because she needed to see the spaces I want to renovate and make into one sort of luxury suite, I guess you'd call it. She and I toured the rooms and I told her what I wanted. She tossed out a few ideas that she had after seeing the spaces. Now she's working on a blueprint. Does that satisfy your need to know everything so you don't feel compelled to worry about it?" I nodded, ashamed of myself for having assumed he was bringing girls home to satisfy his needs now that his father was gone and he ruled the roost. Of course he would want a nicer suite of rooms now, especially if he was going to stay here for a while. "Do you suppose we can sit down and finish our conversation now or do you think we're both too damn fucked up to try to work these things out between us so that neither one of us necessarily has to die?"

I turned around, handing him back his pistol and then walking past him to drop down at one end of the love seat. "Better put the safety back on," I told him as he went to tuck the gun into the waistband at his lower back.

"Thanks. I don't want to go blowin' my own ass off." It was such a ridiculous statement that it made me laugh, not wildly, just a little, but it was a sign of progress to him.

"Can't we just go kill Gunther at the Red Lion Inn and be done with this already? I can try to find his number and call him, tell him to meet me there, that I've left Randolph Hall and taken a room there and will meet him in the dining room. We can eat and then I can suggest that we take a walk. You can be waiting someplace nearby and just take him down."

He raised his arms, running his long fingers through his hair, and then squeezing his head, frowning as if he had a headache. "I am going to make things a helluva lot worse right now. I don't need you freaking out on me, okay?"

"Don't go telling me that you're also a vampire or something even worse than a werewolf."

"No, don't be silly." He was silent for a few minutes, and then he dropped his hands, removing his glasses as he did so. He folded the stems and then tucked them into the breast pocket of his natural denim work shirt. "I would be a complete and total idiot if I believed that I'm the only one of my kind that he's made." He hesitated, allowing that remark to sink in. When it did, he must have seen my eyes widen in realization of the implication of what he had just said. He held up his hand to halt the words ready to tumble from my tongue. "Lucky for us, I'm just a partial moron. I'm not the only lycanthrope in town. He's made others. I'm just the most troublesome one, the one he wants to eliminate because he can't control me. I bolted from Pine Haven. I became an independent. He must have thought that, when I came back, I'd just buckle under the raw force of his influence on me, but I didn't. And I'm trying like hell not to, believe me. So, what he's trying to do now is fuck with me. He's focusing on you. Maybe he's aware of my feelings for you. I'm not exactly sure, but I think that's true. Maybe he can read me like an open book. Or maybe there's someone supplying him information." He shook his head. "Although I haven't made how I feel about you common knowledge."

"No, you haven't. Not even to me." He opened his mouth to respond to that, but I shook my head. "That's neither here nor there at the moment."

"I disagree. It needs to be here or there. It's impor…"

"Hold on! Just stop! What I want to say is that you've always treated me differently than you've treated everyone else. People pick up on that. They notice stuff like that. Badass J. Rand, the bad boy rebel, who doesn't give a crap about what people think about him, actually does care about what Charlotte Rumford thinks about him."

"Yeah, I hear you."

"And I have always had this sweet spot for you, so maybe those same observant people have noticed that and have connected the dots, linked those two facts."

"That's a reasonable assumption." He crossed the room to drop down onto the other cushion of the love seat. "Damn it all, Cherry," he said, and then he tilted his head back and closed his eyes.

He looked stressed, worried, and tired. He was the personification of exactly how I felt. My heart melted in that moment, the ice chocks holding it still falling away, allowing that fist-sized muscle situated behind my sternum to flex and beat again.

Without over thinking it, I moved, getting up, turning around, and then climbing onto his lap, straddling his thighs and hips, facing him. He opened his eyes, not all the way, just slitted them as I leaned forward, watching me as I captured his lips with mine and kissed him. He let me give him a dozen sweet little kisses before he moved his right hand up behind my head, pulling me back to him. He began kissing me—hard, hungry kisses. Fierce kisses. Possessive kisses accompanied by little growly sounds low in his throat that quickened my heartbeat. His left hand moved to cup my butt, pulling me closer, right up against his crotch, letting me know what my kisses had done to him. I shifted my pelvis against him, making him draw in an unsteady breath. I felt it then, a rush of power—in me, not him. I had power over the wolf in him! I had power over the man he was, as well.

Something was thrumming through his bloodstream—and it began to thrum through mine as he deepened his kisses. "Charlotte," he managed to get out in a low, rough voice.

"He never stole what's always been yours," I whispered in his ear, meaning Cody, not Gunther. "If you want it, take it before it's too late."

It startled me how strong he was, because he just stood right up with my hundred and five pounds wrapped around him with seemingly no effort, carrying me into the bedroom, kicking the door shut behind us. "Cherry... I'm having a little trouble controlling my...urges."

"Julian, to be totally honest with you, so am I." His eyes, those incredible eyes with the oval pupils, met mine.

In the space of a half dozen heartbeats, I was naked, on the bed, and he was over me, kissing me seemingly everywhere, licking me in certain places, tasting me, savoring me. He raised his head and said, "You can touch me, you know. Wherever you'd like."

I let go of the bedding that I'd been gripping as if expecting to be thrown off the bed if I didn't hold on tight. I laid my hand on his lean hip. He growled low in his throat and moved my hand to where he wanted me to touch him, folding my fingers around his erection, moving my hand up and down the length of it, showing me, teaching me how he wanted me to touch him and give him pleasure.

When we were both to the point where we couldn't stop, he moved my hand low on his erection and helped me guide him to where a hunger for him had roared to life in me. He guided me, but let me put him into position. He did not force himself on me. He gave me control of this first time being with him. I moved my hips, taking him into my body a little at a time, the feel of a man in me a new sensation, surprising, and completely different from what I had experienced as a much younger girl when Cody had been rather brutal with me. "You can let go now. I've got this." I moved my hand back to his hip, my fingertips pressing hard into his butt as he pushed the last few inches into me. I had arched my back, pushing myself up hard against him. He smiled, and then he kissed my throat. "Does it feel good?"

"Oh, my God…yes!"

"Don't move. Just stay still for a minute. I'm wound pretty tight at the moment." He ducked his head, focusing his attention on my breasts. I wasn't a big girl. I only had a little something there that fit his hand perfectly, but he seemed to be thoroughly enjoying himself. His pleasure increased my pleasure and I found I needed to move my hips. I needed to feel him moving inside me. "You want it that bad?" he murmured.

"Yes, I do."

"Yeah, me too, Cherry. I've been waiting for this for a long time. You ready?" I nodded. "Hold on tight. If I get too rough for you, slap me upside the head, all right?" He did get rough, but not so rough that I couldn't tolerate it. It was exciting and wildly arousing.

I didn't know how much time had passed, so was surprised when I turned my head and noticed the clock. It was past lunch time! "I'm surprised Druce hasn't come looking for us!" I said.

Julian sort of chuckled. "He probably did. Maybe he thought I was killing you, the way you were screaming, and slunk away to let the others know that I'll be in jail before sundown." I elbowed him and then snuggled against him. He had his arm around me. I had *not* been screaming, not loudly anyway. "We need to talk a little business right now," he said.

"Do you always conduct business in bed?"

"Only with my *personal* assistant." I tilted my head so I could see his face. He raised his head and looked at me. "If you want the job, it's yours."

"If I don't accept, it I'll be unemployed *and* homeless."

"I'd rent you this suite fairly cheap. If you paid me in sex, you would live like a queen, trust me."

I pinched his ribs. "So, I'd basically stay on as your personal assistant and do the same sort of work for you that I did for your father?"

"Yeah. You want to discuss a raise?"

"No. My salary is fine. But we can discuss benefits and perks if you'd like."

"Yeah, however, we might get carried away picking and choosing the benefits and perks we like best."

"I wouldn't mind."

He ruffled my hair. "Glad to hear that. But, you and I have some planning to do. You're going to dinner with Gunther this evening."

I startled at that and began to protest, "But, I thought you said he was going to kill me tonight and shred me alive at the clock shop, leave my eventually dead body there for you to find in the morning!"

"I think that's his plan."

"You *think*?" I pushed myself away from him and sat up, turning around and glaring at him. "Julian, that's unacceptable! You'd risk my life like that to do what? What exactly are *you* going to be doing?"

"I'm going to be at the clock shop. Sanborn will drop me off. Ethan, meanwhile will follow you in your brand new Toyota which is going to be hidden in the carriage house out of sight so that when Gunther picks you up, it's not visible. Ethan will know where you're going."

"Okay, so what if he changes plans and takes me someplace else, and then rapes me and kills me at that location?"

"I'm counting on his incredible arrogance and belief that he is invincible to be in full force tonight. He's actually torturing me by taking you some distance away from me where I can't regain control of the situation easily. He's going to wine and dine you, get you to relax. Meanwhile, I'll be here in Pine Haven in an agony of anxiety and self-doubt, second guessing myself, worried sick that I've made a whole bunch of serious mistakes trying to outguess him."

"Um, what if that's true? What if this all goes terribly, fatally wrong?"

"If he dumps your dead body on the loading dock behind the shop, then I'm just going to come out and shoot myself. Well, I'll do that immediately after I've shot him dead."

"This plan has more holes in it than Swiss cheese," I muttered.

He sighed. "Yeah, you're right. Do you have a better idea?"

"I might, but you probably won't like it."

"Okay, so what's your plan?"

"I could pretend that I'm totally enthralled by him. He is a narcissist after all. He gets off on seducing young girls. He obviously likes sex. I can suggest that he show me his house. It's a place that I've heard a lot about when growing up, but I've never actually been there. I'm sure he'd be happy to take me out there."

"Charlotte," he said, a warning in his tone.

"No, listen to me. He probably feels safest in his own slimy lair. Think about all the stuff that's gone on there. No one has ever bothered him. He's got this smug sense of security there, right?"

"I suppose you're right about that."

"Let me get him there. He won't be expecting you to be there. He'll be thinking that he has me where he wants me and all to himself. He'll be thinking about the fun that he can have with me in his lair where no one will hear me scream. He'll be thinking that he's going to get away with murder... again."

"And he'll be dead wrong." He pulled me back down and held me close again. "Let me think about this for an hour or so."

I sighed. "You know what?"

"Mm, what?"

"We really need more time. We need to plan this better. We need to fine tune it all before we do anything."

He exhaled deeply, sounding frustrated. "Yeah. I have to agree with you on that."

I twisted around, hauling myself up on top of him. "Julian?" His eyes met mine. I could easily lose myself in his amazing eyes, regardless of those weird pupils. We just looked into one another's eyes for a long time, him slowly reaching up, brushing my hair back away from my face, tucking it behind my ears. Then he pulled my face down to his and kissed me very tenderly. "We need more time because we're only going to have one shot at getting it right."

"Yeah, I know."

"What are we going to do then? About tonight. We're nowhere near ready enough to do what we need to do to put an end to this once and for all."

"Do you know how to contact him?" he asked.

"No." But then I shrugged. "I could call the school and leave a message."

"I doubt they would take kindly to jotting down personal messages as if they're his social secretaries."

"Well, do you have any better ideas?"

"I could lock you in the dungeon."

"Is there a dungeon here?"

"I don't know. I've never gone looking for one." He moved his hands down to cover my breasts. They fit into the cupped palms of his hands perfectly, as if he had molded me from clay to meet his specifications. He was aroused. I shifted until he was between my legs. "I think I'm recalling some business I need to take care of out of town," he said. "I'll need to take my newly hired personal assistant with me." He let me position him and lower myself onto him, his eyes never leaving mine. "We'll be gone for a few days. You can leave a message for him with Druce. When he arrives, Druce can hand him the envelope with your regrets at being unavailable this evening."

"Where will we actually be going?"

"You tell me. Where would you like to go?"

"I don't know. I've never really been anywhere."

"Okay then…we'll just jump in the truck and drive until we need to find a place to get a room."

"We might want to eat first, so we don't pass out from hunger. We've already missed lunch."

"Point taken." He pulled me down and kissed me very sweetly, letting me make love to him. And then, he rolled me over onto my back and took over. We lost another forty minutes.

This time, he got up and went to turn on the shower, came back, and hauled me off the bed. He led me into the bathroom, pushed me into the shower, and then followed me in. We couldn't keep our hands off one another, but eventually managed to wash one another from head to toe. I wrapped myself in a large bath sheet before stepping out into my bedroom where I gasped loudly. He came up behind me. "What's wrong?"

"Look!" I pointed at the bed.

"What about it?"

"Julian, someone came in here and made up the bed while we were in the shower!"

He pushed past me, went to the bed, and flipped the comforter and blanket down. The wry smirk he gave me over his shoulder made me flush scarlet. "Clean sheets," he said, even though that's what I'd suspected. Caroline or Rose had slipped in, stripped the bed of the linens bearing all the evidence of our lovemaking, and made up the bed with fresh linens. "Guess the cat's out of the bag in regards to this development in our relationship."

"Do you think they'll know it was you?"

He cocked a brow at me. "Are you in the habit of entertaining men in your bed? Is there something you want to share with me?"

"No! Put your clothes on!"

He flipped the covers back up and then grabbed his clothes that were neatly folded on top of the dresser beside his 9mm and began dressing. I hadn't noticed the folded clothing. Mine were beside his. "You already packed your stuff, didn't you?"

"Um, yes. Just about everything I own."

"That'll save some time. I'll have Sanborn move your luggage into my truck. It shouldn't take me long to pack a few things. You get dressed and go write a nice letter of regret. Let him down gently. He'll know it's my doing. He won't blame you. Leave it open ended. Say that you'll be happy to dine with him another time." I nodded. "We're leaving by four o'clock at the latest." He walked to the closed door to the sitting room and then looked back at me over his shoulder. "Although you look fine in a bath towel, you'd better put your clothes on before you come downstairs." And then he was gone, my new employer. My boyfriend. My lycanthrope lover. My last remaining friend in this crazy world.

I didn't know what the immediate future would bring, but after a few unexpectedly intimate hours with Julian Rand Beresford, I was feeling a whole lot better about life, even with the threat of a horrendous death hanging over my head like a dark pall. A little glimmer of hope had poked its nose through that pall. I was going to be damn sure I grabbed that elusive glimmer and pulled it toward me with every ounce of strength and determination that I had.

As it turned out, I really didn't want to die after all.

Susan Buffum

Chapter Twenty

We ended up in Mystic, Connecticut. It was fall, all the kids back in school, the majority of tourists having returned home to resume their normal everyday lives. We arrived late, so it was already too dark to really see anything.

We got a suite in a hotel. I'd been a little anxious, thinking that he might change his mind about me now that he had gotten what he'd wanted from me, but he evidently wanted more because he ordered room service meals for us that we ate at the table in the sitting room of the suite. It wasn't horrible food. It was actually pretty good. He'd gotten me the scrod, mashed potatoes, and peas. He had a New York Strip steak with mushrooms, a baked potato, and peas. We both had salad. It surprised me that he'd ordered milk for both of us. I thought he'd drink a beer with his dinner. We both had New York style cheesecake for dessert. I'd wanted mine with cherries. He'd ordered his with blueberries. They delivered a carafe of coffee and we both drank coffee while watching the weather report for the next few days.

At nine-thirty, he put all the plates, glasses, flatware, cups and saucers on the cart in the hallway outside the door, hung the *do not disturb* sign on the doorknob, and shut the door, bolting it for the night. Then he came across the room, bent, took my hands in his, and pulled me up off the couch and into his arms. "I'm not used to being with someone like this," he said. "If I brought a girl to my room in a hotel, I sent her away after a few hours and spent the rest of the night alone."

"Maybe you should have gotten me a separate room."

He shook his head. "No, I want you with me. I kind of like it."

"Kind of like what? Define what 'what' is. The sex? The company? The novelty of it all, at least until it wears off?"

"Charlotte, why are you so negative? Has life soured you this much, made you a sour Cherry?" He drew me closer. "What can I do for you to sweeten you up again?"

"I don't know," I replied. I had no idea.

He gave me a sly smile and then said, "I have a few ideas. Let's go into the bedroom. We'll be more comfortable there."

His ideas involved showing me things that he'd learned in France. It was more than obvious to me that he had been a diligent student of these techniques. I really couldn't dwell on who his instructors might have been; he was taking me to places I had never even imagined existed. He took me on an erotic journey that left me a quivering jelly girl on the bed, and then he climbed onto the bed and proceeded to make love to me some more. I thought there would be nothing left to me but a husk of a girl by the time he was finished with me, but I found the complete opposite to be true. I was filled up with a rare happiness that left me almost giddy.

Afterwards, he propped himself up on some pillows and then turned on the TV, finding a black and white movie to watch. I snuggled against him. "I have trouble sleeping the first night in a strange bed," he told me.

"You're not tired after all that vigorous activity?" I was silly-happy, but drowsy.

"Nope." He pulled me closer after putting the remote control on the bedside table. "Are you all right? I didn't hurt you?"

"No. I'm good. I'm fine."

"Are you, by any chance, happy?"

"I am," I acknowledged.

"Good, then you can close your eyes and go to sleep, if you want to. I'll be fine just lying here holding you."

I turned a little more toward him, my left arm moving across his flat, hard belly. The outside of my arm brushed against him. I was surprised that he was aroused. But, the other thing that I noticed was that my skin was tingling and prickling whenever I touched him or he touched me. "Julian? Do you give off some sort of static-like energy?"

"I don't know. Why do you ask?"

"Because when we touch one another, there's this sort of static-like charge feeling. A crackling sensation across my skin. It's prickly and, sometimes, like a static electric shock."

"I don't notice it."

"But, I do. And it's not just with you. When I brushed against Mr. Gunther, I got the same feeling from him. So, maybe it has to do with both of you being werewolves."

"Lycanthropes," he corrected. "When you say werewolves, it makes it sound like I've been cast in a bad

233

horror movie." He slid his right hand under the covers, taking my left hand and moving it onto his erection. I got the message and took him in my fist. He let go of my hand.

"But, I don't know why it would happen with other people."

"What other people?" He sounded a little distracted by what I was doing to him.

"Well, it's happened a few times with Druce."

"Druce? Are you shittin' me?" he asked. "Why would…" And then he stopped. "Oh, fuck!" He said it so loud that I jumped. He put his hand back down on top of mine. "No, sorry…don't stop. I was just…" He flipped the covers aside. "Cherry…go down on me."

"What?"

"Take me in your mouth and make love to me like that. Like I did with you." My mind suddenly went black and cold and my hand stopped. He slowly covered himself, removed my hand, and turned toward me, pulling me closer and holding me. "It's all right, Cherry. It's okay. You don't have to do that. I just needed to know if he'd made you do that when you were little. Now I know. I won't ask again."

Although my brain was still in a dark place, I found myself saying, "But…if it's what you want… if it makes you happy…I just need…"

"Shh! No. Really, it's all right. We're new to this relationship business. What we do together is fine, right?"

"No…um…I mean, yes, but if you…"

"Let's give it some more time, okay? Let's just establish some boundaries for now and worry about moving them here and there later on."

We made love one more time, the regular way, and then he turned off the TV and we settled down to sleep.

The next day we visited the aquarium, took a scenic drive, had pizza in the village of Mystic, did a little shopping and more sightseeing, and then had dinner out before returning to the hotel. Our suite had a Jacuzzi tub, so Julian ran a bath and we lit a couple of pillar candles we'd bought in the village and enjoyed a leisurely and romantic soak in the tub. It was a different kind of experience for both of us, just quietly cuddling in the tub, kissing a little, not really even talking. Just bonding, I suppose you'd call it, as a couple.

Afterwards, we climbed into bed and watched another old black and white movie on TV. And then we turned off the TV and made love, slow and easy. It was really nice. He was very good with me, always picking up on any unspoken signals, whether I was aware of having given them or not.

I was still awake, happily thinking about our new relationship as lovers when my cellphone rang. He was asleep, but woke up when I moved, leaning over to grab my phone off the bedside table on my side. I frowned when I saw Mitchell Adams was the caller, glanced over my shoulder at Julian who had his eyes open but hadn't moved. He was just awake because of the phone ringing. "Hello?" I said quietly, my heart already pounding. It was never a good thing when the chief of police called you on his personal cellphone, especially close to one o'clock in the morning.

"Charlotte, it's Mitch. Honey, I hate to disturb you. Druce said that you and J. Rand are on a little trip. I tried his cell, but it went straight to voice mail." Julian's phone was dead, currently out in the sitting room charging. "I don't know where you are, but..."

"What's the matter?" I asked. He did not sound like himself.

"Let me ask you this first. Are you far away from home?"

"No, we're in Connecticut, down on the coast. What's wrong? Are you at Randolph Hall?" This caught Julian's attention. He leaned up and I turned the phone a bit so he could hear, although I suspected that he had better hearing than the normal guy his age.

"We had a call from the house about a break-in, several of the occupants being attacked."

"Oh, no," I said, barely able to get the words out.

"Give me the phone," Julian said, taking it from my hand.

"It's Rand. What the hell's happened?"

I couldn't hear, but I knew it had to be bad because Julian went rigid and I could sense the fury radiating off of him. I slipped out of bed, turning on the bedside light. I quickly dressed and then just started packing our things. He was watching me, still talking on the phone. I didn't like what I was hearing and went into the bathroom, closing the door.

I was suddenly cold and shivering. He'd said something about Windsor that had indicated to me that something bad had also happened there. Windsor was where my mother and Mike Emery lived. My stomach was in a hard knot and it hurt. There was a roaring in my ears, so loud that I didn't even hear Julian come into the bathroom. I only became aware that he was in the room when he crouched down in front of me and laid his hand on my shoulder.

I flinched and he moved his hand immediately, but I grabbed his arm and gripped him so hard that it must have been painful for him, but I needed to hold onto him that tightly because I knew that what he was going to tell me would tear me off the face of the earth otherwise. He'd told me that I was his anchor in this world. Well, he was mine. I had no one else. I just hadn't realized, until this moment, how true that had become.

"Charlotte, we have to go home. Three members of my household staff are dead." I squeezed my eyes shut tightly, scrunched my shoulders up to my ears. "Kerry, Caroline, and…" He hesitated. He knew the third person he had to name was the one that would tip me into the abyss. I think he was actually afraid that he wouldn't be able to pull me back. "Cherry..." he said. "Do you have any of your medication with you?" I shook my head. Druce had my medication under lock and key somewhere in the house because I was obviously a danger to myself with it at times, had nearly overdosed. I'd been fairly sure that it had been an accidental overdose, but still, little worms of doubt had also made me think that maybe I really didn't want to be here anymore. "There were...in Windsor...he heard it over the radio while he was at our house...two people killed there." He shook me a little because he could tell he was losing me as the world telescoped into the distance leaving me perched on a flat, black plain of nothingness. "Charlotte, hey! Pull it together, okay? Pull it together for me! I can't lose you right now! Goddam it, Cherry! Look at me!" He shook me harder, and then grabbed my jaw with his free hand, tilting my head back, squeezing my jaw so hard I thought he might crush it.

"Ow! Stop it!" I said through teeth clenched together because I couldn't even move my jaw. My eyes met his and I saw that flash of red-orange in their depths again. He was struggling to control the beast in him. I found myself tuning into him. His skin seemed to be crawling, rippling over muscle layer and bones. He was on the verge of transforming and that frightened me. I did not want to be alone in the bathroom with a werewolf who was absolutely devastated and thoroughly enraged by further losses. He'd just lost his father and now someone had broken into his home and killed...No! Not someone! Something! And that's when the comprehension of what had happened slammed me hard. It knocked the breath out of me, made me feel as if someone had reached into me and wrenched my insides around and then tried to pull them out through my chest. "No!" I cried, struggling to get additional words out, but he still had ahold of my jaw.

Susan Buffum

"It also killed Helen at our house. In Windsor, another werewolf must have killed your mother and Mike." I could tell he was struggling to hold it together himself. "Evidently Mike's service revolver was found on the floor of the bedroom where they were attacked. He'd gotten off two shots. One bullet was found embedded in the wall across the room. They couldn't find where the second one had gone and think he might have hit whatever attacked and killed him. There was blood everywhere, but there was also a blood trail leading to the balcony door that it left through. There was blood on the balcony and down on the grass underneath it. He'd got off a decent shot and he'd wounded it." His eyes returned to mine. "Can I let go of your jaw now? Or are you going to scream and wake up the whole damn hotel?"

I nodded. He let go of me and a flood of words tumbled out of my mouth. "He did this to punish me! He did it to get back at you for taking me away! Oh, my God, Julian! We ran off and left them all behind to be murdered in their beds! What does that make us? How could we have been so stupid and selfish?"

"He's far more out of control than I'd thought," he replied as his phone chimed to let him know he had a message. He'd gotten dressed prior to coming into the bathroom to deal with me and stuffed his now charged phone that he'd turned back on into his hip pocket. He stood up to get it out, swiped the screen, and tapped to open the message.

"Who is it from? Not him, is it?" He shook his head, still reading. "What does it say?"

"It's Ethan," he replied. "He says Rose was injured and was taken to the hospital. Lorraine is at the hospital being treated for shock. Druce is with him and Sanborn at the house. The police are still there, the state police are just arriving. We need to get home." I nodded, agreeing with him. "The police in Windsor are being advised that you're with me and that we're coming home." I nodded again. "I'm going to have to do what I need to do, Cherry, you know that, don't you? It'll probably get me killed. If it does, then you need to do whatever you can possibly do to stop this."

"Why does he hate you so much?" I asked as I stood up. He was gathering our toiletries to pack. I hadn't gotten that far yet. I grabbed the pillar candles from the tub ledge, following him out into the room and stuffing them into one of my duffle bags.

"Because he can't control me." He zipped the toiletries bag closed. "Everything packed?" I made a quick circuit of the room and then nodded as I put on my barn jacket. He grabbed the heavier bags. I grabbed the duffle bags and toiletries bag and we left the room, taking the elevator down to the main floor.

The night desk clerk was somewhat startled to find us in front of him. We'd woken him up. "Is there a problem with the room?" he asked, worried that the hotel's reputation might be at risk.

"No. There's been a death in the family. We need to go home," Julian replied in a terse, somber voice. It was the truth, but there was so much more besides that going on.

"I'm sorry, sir." He printed out a paper that Julian scrawled his signature on. His credit card had J.R. Beres as his name. It occurred to me that his money was in Europe, all his credit cards were European issued versions of our American cards. But money was money in the world of business, although it gave me something to think about after he'd stowed the bags in the truck and pulled out of the parking lot, heading toward the highway. I wondered how much money J.R. Beres had in the bank. He was in the process of inheriting an acre of money from his father's estate. I'd heard a rumor about a large house on Lake Winnipesauke in New Hampshire. I vaguely remembered my mother talking about Mrs. Beresford having had a summer home on a lake and the wonderful gardens she'd had there. I wondered what state those gardens were in at this present time. I couldn't imagine that the lake house and grounds had been neglected since her death. Someone must have been taking care of that property, although I didn't think anyone had been to that house since Mrs. Beresford had died.

"So, who do you think killed my mother and Mike?" I asked.

"I'm not sure yet. If he's pissed at me, he'd have killed my staff to show me how displeased he is with me. And he'd have sent someone he *can* control to Windsor to kill your mother and her husband, to show you that he's not to be messed with."

"So, what am I supposed to do now? Have dinner with him and let him kill me?"

"Dinner is not happening. He's just going to grab you whenever the first opportunity arises and…Damn it all!" he said, clearly upset. "I can't let that happen to you." His knuckles were white on the wheel. "Charlotte…" His voice cracked like a teenager's. That's when I knew in my heart how he really felt about me. He hadn't been able to say it yet and maybe he never would be able to. I didn't know, but he didn't have to actually say it. "Cherry…"

"I'm going to kill him," I said. "Leave this to me."

"No, I…"

"Julian, he's pushed me so far over the edge now that I'm no longer on the plane where the rest of the world resides. Maybe I was in free fall for a little while, but you know what? He's just had my mother killed. Maybe she and I haven't exactly gotten along recently, but she's still my mother. He killed my mother's best friend, and then he killed my best friend. But when it's family, it's as personal as it can get. He wants me dead because he thinks it will destroy you. Well, guess what? I'm not going to give him another shot at doing that. He's a walking dead wolfman, he just doesn't know it yet."

"You haven't even been trained to shoot a gun yet," he pointed out.

"Right, and that makes me even deadlier because I don't know what the hell I'm doing." I turned my head and looked at him. "And now, I'm a psycho bitch besides."

"Are you?" He looked a little worried about that.

"Oh, I will be when I lay eyes on him again."

"Charlotte, you're going to get yourself killed. I can't allow that."

"No, you need to stay the hell away from me because he can sense you. He'd know if you were nearby. It has to be just him and me. You understand that, don't you?" Through the shock of so much loss, my thoughts were now coming crystal clear. "You said that if he's dead then you have a chance at getting your own life back to normal, right?"

"Yeah, according to the stuff I've found and read. But I don't know how accurate all that is. It's old stuff with a lot of legend woven through it. I don't know anyone who's actually survived what amounts to gross disobedience of the alpha wolf."

"That's why you can't be involved in this," I said. He was silent as he got on the highway to head west toward the next highway we needed to take north in order to continue our homeward journey.

I leaned back in the seat and closed my eyes. My body and brain felt as if they were vibrating. Julian was absolutely silent. I didn't think he was happy. In fact, I knew he wasn't. He was still shocked by the deaths that we were more or less responsible for. He was thoroughly enraged with Gunther. He was also deeply worried about his crazy girlfriend with the death wish, but in all honesty, I really had no desire to die. I liked what had developed between him and me. I hadn't had any hope of it ever getting as far as it had, but now that it had, I didn't want to lose that.

"Ethan's a hunter," he suddenly said. "I'm not sending you out to kill Gunther alone."

"Won't he sense him nearby?"

"Not necessarily." He was now tapping his fingers on the steering wheel, thinking. I could almost hear the cogs and gears turning in his brain. "Austin, Cody, and I built a lot of stuff in those woods when we were kids. That's where you're going to take him down, Cherry, in the woods where he created me." He turned his head to glance at me before returning his eyes to the dark road ahead. "Those woods have been my territory since I was a kid. My father bought the shop for himself with the hope that, when I grew up, I'd work there with him.

"But, he bought the property on the hillside behind the shop for me. That was my playground. Those were my woods to explore and conquer. You know your way to Turkey Pond and the site where he did this to me. Yeah, he killed your fuckin' little bastard tormentor there and did you a huge favor, but he probably doesn't know that history. I didn't even know the truth of it. However, I think he had an inkling that Julian Rand Beresford had a sweet spot for pretty and sweet little Charlotte Rumford. I don't think he had any idea that I was going to bolt after graduation. Do you know why I chose that day to disappear?" I shook my head. "Because he was sitting on stage playing the part of the beloved gym teacher, basking in that aura of popularity. The kids loved him because they could get away with anything and everything at his sleaze-shack in the swamp. The teachers liked him because he was charismatic, except for Mrs. Claxton. She hated his guts, didn't she?" I nodded. "I chose graduation day because he was stuck on stage. My last name starts with a B, so I was near the front of the long list of students getting their diplomas. He couldn't just get up and run off stage to chase me down.

"Also, I was rather volatile. He was used to that, of sensing that hot mess of emotion in me. He probably figured it was all because I'd been arguing with my father the night before about working with him in the shop. He expected me to just graduate and then jump right into the business with my father. It was tearing me apart inside to fight with Dad about it, knowing that I was going to blow his whole world to smithereens the next day, but I had to create the chaos to cover my real intent." He sighed. "Knowing how he is now, I'm surprised he didn't kill my father."

"Maybe he left him alive thinking that you'd eventually come home and he'd pounce on you then and punish you for leaving."

"Yeah, maybe. He wasn't this powerful back then either, I don't think. It was more like a game to him. Now it's something else entirely."

"So, what does Ethan being a hunter have to do with anything?"

"I'm going to ask him to sit in a perch with a sniper rifle with a night scope on it as your back-up."

"Oh." I thought about that and then frowned. "What if he hauls me out of range?"

"He won't be the only one backing you up. While he's occupied with you, I'll be at his house with Chief Adams opening up the can of worms that Gunther's been sitting on for well over a decade. I have an acute sense of smell. I'll mark the places where he's buried a number of bodies back near the swampland. I'll start doing that this morning. He'll be at the school acting as if nothing unusual has happened."

"But, won't he know you're up to something?"

"I don't think so. He senses me when my emotions are riled. He can't pinpoint my exact location unless he's close enough to sense me against his nasty hide. He'll just sense that I'm not in a good place and, believe me, tracking down and marking the location of dead bodies is not going to be any picnic in the park for me. I'll be plenty riled up. Plus, I'm going to have a lot of trouble trying to stop myself from thinking about you."

I was quiet again as I thought all of this through, working out some things in my head as he drove. There weren't any other cars on the road. We seemed to be traveling in a dark world devoid of human life. It was as if we had passed into an alternate reality. "Julian?"

"Mm?"

"There's something I want to tell you. I should probably tell you now. There might not be another chance."

"No, don't. Not right now. You'll know when."

"Do you know what I want to tell you?" I asked.

"Yeah, I think I do. But, if I hear you say that right now, it's going to totally mess me up." I turned my head away, gnawing at my bottom lip, thinking that maybe he didn't feel the same way about me and he wasn't ready to disappoint me, at least not while flying along at eighty miles per hour on a dark highway in the dead of night. "It would mess me up in a good way," he amended when I remained silent. "I need to stay messed up in a bad way right now."

"Yeah, I suppose so," I said quietly.

"You understand what I'm saying, don't you?"

"Yeah, I do." He was right. I had to lock these kinds of feelings away in my heart and concentrate on the darker, more violent and angry feelings still swirling around inside of me. "You're right. You're absolutely right."

Chapter Twenty-One

The house was still in a state of chaos when we pulled up. The state police were up on the second floor in the east wing where Caroline and Helen had been killed. More police were up on the third floor in the east wing where Kerry had been torn apart. Chief Adams was still on the scene, having taken a command position in the study, so Julian and I went there as soon as we were allowed inside by the officer stationed at the door.

"Hey, kids," the chief said, leaning back in the chair I'd become so used to seeing Mr. Beresford seated in. He used both hands to scrub at his face. He looked pale and haggard, tired.

"Is it all right if I go to the kitchen? Has anyone made any coffee or anything for you?"

"Sweetheart, I don't think anyone's been in the kitchen yet. If you could brew a pot of coffee, that would be

245

wonderful. It's been a long night and it's not over by a long shot yet."

I nodded and slipped out to do that. I was familiar enough with the kitchen to be able to make coffee and maybe poke around to see if there was anything I could offer the officers working here. Another officer stopped me as I approached the kitchen, but I heard Ethan say, from the informal parlor where the staff was evidently being kept out of the way, "That's Charlotte. She works here. She's J. Rand's personal assistant. They must be back from their trip."

"Are you Charlotte Rumford?" the officer asked me. I nodded. "Sorry for your loss."

"Sorry for yours, too," I murmured. Officer Mike Emery had still been a member of Pine Haven's police department. "Chief Adams asked me to make coffee for everyone."

"Sounds good, thanks."

"Can I help her?" Ethan asked.

"Yeah, go ahead. Kitchen was cleared a few minutes ago."

Ethan accompanied me to the kitchen where all the lights were still on. "You guys got back pretty fast," he commented as I went into the pantry to start the coffeemaker. He leaned against the doorway as I measured the grounds into the filter basket, slid it into place, and then filled the water chamber. "Uh, you might want to turn it on." I made a face, pushed the button, and the brewer started heating up. "You okay?" I shook my head. "How's J. Rand?"

"Furious. Upset."

"Yeah, I bet. This is crazy. How did that thing get in the house? My room is right next to Kerry's. We swapped rooms last week because he was getting spiders in his and he's..." He shook his head, correcting himself. "He was afraid of spiders. Crazy thing for a gardener to be so scared of, right?"

"You switched rooms?" I frowned slightly. "Was that common knowledge?"

"Uh, no. Druce would have blown a gasket. You know how he is. No one can do anything without flying it under his nose first around here. But, there was a lot going on at the time. We really just moved our clothes to each other's rooms and figured we'd catch Druce once things settled down again and we'd get the change of rooms okayed."

"So, no one knew?"

"No. It was just between Kerry and me. Why?"

I shook my head. "I don't know. My brain is scrambled right now," I replied. I opened the breadbox and found some muffins left over from yesterday's breakfast. After giving them a quick reheating in the microwave, I arranged them on a platter. "I really don't know. It seems like certain people were targeted in this attack. Helen's been like a mother to me. And you've been like a big brother. You're also pretty close to J. Rand, closer than anyone else in this house is."

"Yeah, I suppose that's true. I was hired when he was in high school. I was just recently out of high school. He wasn't a happy dude, but he liked to work with his hands, so he'd come out and do stuff in the shed. Occasionally, we'd talk, you know, just about stuff. The house. Projects. He wanted to build things, big things. I guess what he was talking about were those clock towers. I had no clue. He and I would go out to the clock shop in the evening after dinner and we'd poke around. We found some cool stuff, but a lot of the old metal he'd load into his truck and we'd take it to the scrap dealer the next day. He was mucking the trash out of the place out. His father just needed a small area to work on his clocks, so the whole back area of the shop was full of scrap metal and junk. He got some decent money for the metal."

"So, basically, you're the only one who's anywhere near close to him in this house?"

"I guess so. He trusts me. We've been talking about this and that lately. Just things." His eyes fell on me as he stopped talking.

"Things?"

"Well, you know. Guy stuff. He likes you. Did you know that? He's not going to ask you to leave."

"You told the cop I was his personal assistant."

"I know. J. Rand told me he was asking you to stay on. I just..." He shrugged. "I assumed that, since he took you with him, that he'd asked you to stay on already and you'd agreed, that you'd gone off with him on business."

"We weren't on a business trip, Ethan," I said quietly, just to see what his reaction would be. "It was personal."

"Holy shit, Charlotte!" he said. And then his face, as pale and haggard as everyone else's around the house, lit up with a huge grin as he grabbed me and pulled me into a tight hug. I gave him a quick hug in return.

And then I burst his happy-bubble by pushing myself away and saying, "You and I are going to die."

"What!" His grey eyes met mine. "Why do you say that?"

"Because this beast wants to crush Julian. You're the closest friend he has here. I think you were the one who was supposed to die tonight, not Kerry. And I'm his girlfriend, the one person he loves more than anyone else in the whole world. I wasn't here, so it either went to Windsor when it was finished its terrible work here or it sent a, for lack of a better word, associate to Windsor to kill my mother and her husband. I don't know if it was supposed to have killed Mike or not, but Mike evidently woke up or managed to get away briefly. He grabbed his gun and took a couple of shots at it. The first one may have hit it, his second shot, probably fired as whatever rushed him, grabbed him, and killed him, went wide."

"You know this for a fact?"

"I can put two and two together from what I was told. I'm not stupid."

I started taking mugs down from the cupboard and handing them to him. He set them on the counter in rows. I then filled a thermal carafe with the freshly brewed coffee and started a second pot. "I need to get back to the study. Let everyone know there're coffee and muffins here in the pantry." I put a couple of muffins on a plate, grabbed three mugs and the carafe, plus one of the sugar bowls, a container of half and half, and some spoons then made my way back to the study where I put everything on the desk.

Chief Adams gave me a grateful look as I poured coffee into the three mugs. He was already eating a muffin by the time I set his filled mug down before him. Julian took his coffee from me. Silently, he sat back in his chair sipping it, holding the mug in both hands. I was worried that he would scald himself holding the cup like that, but apparently his hands were cold or he was even more numb with shock than I thought he was. "Be careful you don't burn yourself," I murmured as I sat down in the second chair with my own mug. He glanced at me sideways and nodded once.

Then, I jumped back up to close the door because I needed to tell them what Ethan had told me and I didn't want it being spread throughout the whole house. Both of them were looking at me curiously as I sat back down. "Ethan and Kerry swapped rooms one day last week. Kerry's room had a spider infestation. He was arachnophobic. They just changed rooms and didn't tell Druce or anyone else." I didn't need to say anything more because I caught Julian's reaction to this bit of unexpected information. I also saw

Chief Adams' eyebrows slowly rise as the implication struck him.

"So, do you think Ethan was the target, not Mr. Noble?" he asked us.

Julian set his mug down as he stood up and began pacing the room. His renewed rage was palpable in the room. His hands were clenching and unclenching. His jaw was rigid. He was beyond furious, just barely restraining himself from violence. "Yes," he finally answered. "Ethan and I are friends. Helen was like a mother to Charlotte. Caroline took care of Charlotte's suite."

"Were you and Caroline friendly?" the chief asked me.

"Yes, I guess so. We talked. She was younger than Rose. She was really kind to me after Ripley was killed. I was a wreck." I didn't have to remind them of my fifteen days in the psych ward. Both of them were well aware of that. "She was closest to me, besides Helen."

The chief and Julian exchanged glances again. "Then I'm inclined to agree with you, Rand," he said, although I could tell that everything that had happened was still troubling him on a deeper level. "I just don't know how a beast can be trained to attack certain people. I can see a master managing to break into a home and setting the thing loose, but how would it be able to open doors and differentiate between one person and another? That would take a lot of time and training."

Julian dropped back down into his chair. He glanced at me, letting me know that I was to keep my mouth shut. "Any animal can be trained. Didn't Charlotte tell you she saw the wolf, or whatever it was, walking on its hind legs in the antiques shop like a human being?"

The chief's eyes shifted to me briefly before he focused on Julian again. "Yes. I recall that she made that statement. But she was in shock at the time."

"I was telling the truth. That was what I saw," I said.

Again, his eyes met mine for a moment before he looked back down into his mug. I could tell he was trying to make sense of all this craziness. Wolves that walked upright. "It sounds like a campy horror novel, if you ask me," he muttered. "I can't think of anyone around here who would be keeping wolves and training them to kill like this. This isn't that big of a town. Someone would surely have seen or heard something about it by now. This has been going on for a dozen or more years. It can't be the same wolf that attacked you and your friends at Turkey Pond. That was an adult wolf. Wouldn't that be old, for a wild animal?"

"It could still be around," Julian said quietly.

The chief heaved a sigh, then reached for the carafe and refilled his cup. "We can't figure out how it got into this house. The doors were all secure according to Druce."

I saw Julian stiffen again at this piece of information and again his jaw went rigid, muscles bunching and twitching slightly. I didn't like that, either. I was bright enough to pick up on the fact that the beast had not broken in. It had already been in the house when everyone retired for the night.

But, how had it gotten in and where had it hidden itself until it snuck upstairs to the second floor to kill Helen and Caroline, and then up to the third floor to kill Kerry in his bed, although it had meant to kill Ethan in that same bed, was another question. Or had it killed Kerry first, and then realized that it had killed the wrong person? No. Kerry and Ethan looked enough alike that in the dark that they could easily be mistaken, one for the other. Unless it was all about scent? The wolf might have had Ethan's scent. After it had attacked him, had it realized that it had killed the wrong man? Wouldn't it have just gone to Kerry's room and killed Ethan, if he had been the intended target, tracking him by scent? Probably, but it was possible that there had been time constraints. It had other murders to commit, so it had gone to the second floor to kill Helen, and then Caroline, or vice versa. The clock had been ticking. Had the same werewolf then slipped out of the house and driven to Windsor to kill my mother and stepfather?

I nearly lost it. I wanted to burst out laughing at the mental image of a wolfman behind the wheel of a car, jaws all gory and smeared with blood, bloody paws gripping the wheel, as he tooled along Main Street heading toward Windsor. I bit back the laugh and found myself suddenly crying instead. "I'm sorry," I said. "I'm sorry!"

"It's been a long night." Chief Adams slowly rose from the chair behind the desk. "Look, you two kids go sit with the others. We'll be here another hour or so and then we'll let you get back to whatever it is you need to do. I can't say normal life, because none of us are living normal lives these days." He came around the desk. I stood up as he did so. He looked at me, and then he set his mug down on the corner of the desk and gathered me in his big, strong arms and gave me a long hug. "Don't you worry about the funerals for your Mom and Mike, honey. The Police fraternal organization will pitch in and help you with all that. Rand will have his hands full enough dealing with the funerals for his people here. What if I come get you tomorrow afternoon and we'll go over to Winslow and Waterman's and see what they can do for them?" I nodded and thanked him. "Rand, you okay?"

"Yeah. Thanks." They shook hands and the chief left us alone, closing the door behind him. "Fuck," Julian said. That about summed it all up.

Chapter Twenty-Two

Chief Adams was a huge help to me at Winslow and Waterman's. I more or less held it together in the funeral home while picking out matching gunmetal gray caskets, my mother's lined with a pale, blush pink satin, Mike's with traditional white. We chose verses for the memorial cards. Mike's card would have the American flag on it with sunlight streaming through the stars and stripes, a bright blue sky behind it. Mom's would have roses, in honor of the years that she was in the Garden Club. Neither of them had gotten around to picking out plots, so Chief Adams and I visited the cemetery manager's office and chose side by side plots in a nice area, then brought the signed contracts back to the funeral home and finished providing information for the obituaries. He treated me to lunch at the Corral Restaurant in Windsor because he'd taken me to the house Mom and Mike had bought so I could pick out clothes for them. The bloody bedroom had shaken me. He had shielded me as best he could from the gory mess still there, surrounded by yellow police tape. A Windsor cop had met us there to allow us inside to get the clothes for the funeral.

Lunch kind of calmed me down. Doing something ordinary distracted me, having to choose what I wanted to eat, even though I hadn't had any appetite when handed the menu. But, when the food came, my burger had been too tempting to ignore. I was still eating when he leaned forward, his eyes meeting mine. "I need to ask you a personal question, if I may?" I nodded. "Are you and J. Rand in a relationship other than employer and employee?" I stared at him. "The reason I ask is, he seems awfully protective of you. And I noticed the looks the two of you exchanged. I'm not being nosy here. I'm just trying to figure out why this stuff is happening to you guys."

"Yes, we are," I admitted.

He nodded, sat back, picking up a long french fry and swirling the end of it around in the puddle of ketchup on his plate as he thought things through. "Do you have any enemies?"

"I'm beginning to think that I do," I confessed.

"Any you can name for me?"

"No, I'm sorry. I can't put any names to what's going on. I don't know."

"I'm inclined to think that this enemy is the same one targeting Rand."

"That would appear to be true," I agreed.

"Charlotte, I need your help here, if I'm going to put a stop to this senseless slaughtering of human lives. The cattle, the goats, the deer, and wild animals in the woods, I can write that all off as the work of feral dogs. However, feral dogs do not break into houses and kill people in their sleep. They don't pull them into the woods from dark parking lots and murder them savagely." I had trouble swallowing the bite of burger I'd just finished chewing.

The Clockmaker's Son

"They don't slip into antiques shops and attack women. They don't pick up young ladies and hurl them tens of feet down the aisles, breaking their arms." His eyes met mine again. "There's something going on around here that is…shall we say, unusual?" I couldn't even blink. He nodded once. "I need your help getting a better grasp on this situation so I can do what I need to do to stop it from continuing. This bloody rampage has to stop. The residents of this community are getting more anxious and vocal about this. As the chief of police, I have an obligation to keep all of the citizens of this community safe. It's my sworn duty." He stretched a hand toward me, but did not touch me. He turned his hand palm up in a plea for assistance. "Help me to help the two of you," he said quietly, his eyes holding mine. "Please."

"You need to talk to Julian," I said, barely able to get the words out, feeling as if I was betraying the man I loved, knowing I wouldn't be able to live with myself if he was furious with me for this breach of his trust in me.

"J. Rand doesn't trust many people. And he's quick to anger. I don't want to step on his toes, but I think the two of you need all the help you can get to deal with this thing; whatever it is that's going on here. So, will you do this for me, honey? Will you find a few minutes to talk to him on my behalf? Let him know that I'd like to talk to him, in private. I could meet him at the shop even, away from prying eyes and listening ears. He can tell me the truth about what's going on here. I don't care what that truth is. I just…I just want to help you stop this before other people get killed. That's all I want to do. If I have to take my badge off to do it, so be it."

That was a mighty big statement for the chief of police to make. But, I was of two minds. He had always cared about me. But then again, other people had seemed to care about me, too. I had reached a point in my life where I didn't know who I could trust anymore. I knew who the big,

255

bad wolf in this town was, but I didn't know who that wolf might have made his rotten underlings, willing and able to do his bidding at any time. But, maybe Julian would know. He had better sensory perception about these things than I did. "I'll talk to him," I said. And then I stretched my hand a few more inches, bridging the gap. I slipped it into his big, meaty paw. I felt no prickly sensation, just warmth, and a few callouses, as he gently gave my slender, much smaller hand a squeeze.

Julian was not around when I got home from planning the funerals that I needed to deal with. I went up to my room to change my clothes, then ran downstairs, making my way to the kitchen where I found Lorraine sitting slumped at the table, head in her hands, quietly crying. "I'll help you make dinner," I said.

"I'm sorry, Charlotte…it's just more than I can cope with today."

"It's all right. I don't think anyone is expecting a five course meal tonight." I knew Helen planned the menus ahead for the week, so I went to her small desk in the corner where she kept her notebook, flipped it open, and read the menu she had scheduled for tonight. We would skip the soup course. I could throw fruit cups together. We would pass on the main entre tonight and make do with the fish course as the substitute. I'd put together a fresh salad. Mashed potatoes were easier to deal with than potatoes au gratin. "Here's what we'll do," I said, turning back to her.

Druce was standing in the doorway between the staff hall and the kitchen. His eyes were on me, watching me in a somewhat unnerving manner. "Lorraine can handle the cooking, Miss Rumford," he said.

"Lorraine is mourning the loss of her best friend," I snapped back. "The most she can handle today is slicing up vegetables and mashing the potatoes. I'll handle the rest of the meal."

"You are not the cook."

"I'm not a lot of things," I replied. "Most of all, I'm not a heartless asshole who can't find compassion in her heart for another person's suffering. Get the hell out of this kitchen and leave us alone!" His back stiffened and he seemed on the verge of telling me off, but Rose came into the kitchen from the back hallway and she was also weepy. "Sit down, Rose. I'm making tea for all of us." I shot Druce a hot look of anger before turning on my heel and going into the pantry to get what I needed to make tea for Lorraine, Rose, and myself.

Julian did not return for dinner. With Lorraine's half-hearted help, I managed to produce a fairly decent meal for the staff. There was plenty for Julian, too. I made up a salad bowl and a plate for him and scooped some fruit into a dish, putting it all in the refrigerator before cleaning up from our meal. Druce had joined us, but it was clear that he was not pleased with me. He was probably dying to pour vitriol into Julian's ear when he got home, but I didn't care. We all had to eat. We all had to keep this house running.

After dinner and clean-up, I helped Rose. The house had been left in somewhat of a mess by the police. We tidied up the first floor. We were not allowed to go into any of the rooms where death had come calling. There were padlocks installed by the police on those doors and they were crisscrossed with yellow police tape. I had no desire to go into any of those rooms. With all the miscellaneous cups and mugs we'd collected washed up and put away, Rose and I left the kitchen. Druce would make sure the house was secure for the night.

I went up to my suite, glancing toward the closed door to the west wing as I reached the top of the main staircase. I was now more concerned about Julian. I didn't know where he had gone off to or what he had been up to all day. All I did know was that he was angrier than I'd ever seen him before. I hoped wherever he'd gone that he was safe and not out doing something crazy and stupid without one of us whom he trusted backing him up.

I took a long, hot shower, put on my nightgown and crawled into bed. Reaching over, I wound up the little clock and then set it back down on the bedside table. I hadn't locked my doors. If the beast was coming back to take down the rest of us tonight, a locked door wasn't going to slow it down any.

I thought about slipping my nine millimeter pistol under my pillow. Mine didn't have silver bullets in it like Julian's did, but the bullets would more than likely wound the werewolf and slow it down some. I just hoped I wasn't so jittery that I shot and killed a person if someone else, like Rose or Lorraine, came into my room. If Druce came in, I really didn't give a damn if I shot him dead or not. I'd had my fill of his condescension today, his reprimands and reminders that I was just J. Rand's personal assistant. Well, I was of a differing opinion on that, but that was really none of his business.

I wasn't asleep yet, too restless to totally relax, when I heard the door of my bedroom open. One of the hinges needed oiling. "You awake?" a familiar voice I'd been longing to hear asked.

"Yes."

"You want to grab whatever first aid stuff you can find and meet me in the bathroom in my suite?" I sat up with a gasp, my heart suddenly racing. "I was at the shop doing some work and a section slipped. I got cut up a little, is all."

"I'll be there in a few minutes. Druce keeps a first aid kit in the staff hall. I'll grab that."

He left and I slid my feet into slippers, pulled on my robe and ran down the back service staircase to the staff hall. I found the first aid kit in one of the cupboards and then raced back upstairs via the main staircase.

The upstairs main house hall seemed shadowy and eerie as I reached the top of the staircase. Pausing and looking around, I noticed that the east hall door was partially open, the hallway beyond it dark. Before I could make sense of that, I realized that it was a candle flame that was casting the eerie light. The candle was sitting on a table. I had no idea why a candle would be there. It was rather dangerous to leave a candle unattended like that.

Narrowing my eyes, I made out a dark figure against the closed door of Mr. Beresford's sitting room. "It's late. What are you doing creeping around?" I demanded in an authoritative a voice as I could muster, not really sure who it was. Julian had just passed through here, or was he so badly hurt that this was as far as he'd gotten?

"I could ask you the same thing," came Druce's imperious response.

"J. Rand got banged up at the shop. He asked me to grab the first aid kit and patch him up. I'm doing my job." I started toward the door to the west wing.

"That's right. You've been busy servicing the young master like the red-haired whore that you are." I stopped dead, frozen in place by ice cold fury. How dare he say such a thing to me! "His kind is incapable of love. He will only take what he wants from you and give you nothing in return. When he tires of these woefully inadequate sexual services that you provide for him, you'll be gone. I give it another week or so at most." He moved away from the inset doorway, stepping out into the hallway. I turned my head and caught a glimpse of him, a flash of orange in his eyes from the candle's flickering flame.

"You're such a creep," I muttered.

"Let me give you one piece of advice. There is another master who would gladly accept your services, pathetic as they are. He would properly train you to please him. He would lavish gifts upon you. There is nothing in this house for you. There never really was. A sickly man, a traumatized boy who has grown up to be a damaged man. There is a much more virile and suitable master for you to serve."

I had no idea who he was talking about, but if he meant he would be my master, I thought that I'd rather drown myself than allow him to touch me in any way. "Maybe so. But, in this world, there is such a thing as free will. I freely serve the master of this house and I am not leaving until he throws me out." I wrenched the door knob, shoving the door open, passing through into the dark hallway beyond and then slamming the door shut behind me, stalking down the hallway in the nearly complete darkness, and slipping into Julian's sitting room.

I was muttering under my breath as I crossed the room and entered his bedroom. His bathroom light was on, so I continued to that room, pushing open the door that stood ajar. He was sitting on a bench against the wall, stark naked. There was a pile of bloody clothing on the white tile floor, bloody towels around his feet. He looked up at me, his face ashen pale. "Close the door," he said. The bathroom was cold and reeked of the coppery odor of blood.

"Oh, my God, Julian. You need to go to the ER." But then I saw what had really happened to him and nearly dropped the now seemingly inadequate first aid kit. "Oh…no," I said, barely able to speak.

"I'll be all right. I heal quicker than a fully human being. Just…I just need you to put some pressure on this one here. It's deep."

He had been fighting a werewolf or lycanthrope, or whatever, and had nearly lost. I was thankful it hadn't gone for his throat or we'd have been planning another funeral. I piled gauze pads over the nastiest of the gouges and then wrapped it tightly with roller gauze. He was breathing hard.

It sounded almost like he was panting, like a sick dog or a badly wounded and distressed animal would sound.

He remained slumped against the tiled wall while I clean more of his wounds and bandaged them as best as I could. "Was it Gunther?" I asked, my voice low and terse as I worked.

"No."

"Where were you attacked?"

"Outside, in the area behind the shop."

"I hope you gave as good as you got." My eyes rose until they met his. He was not wearing his glasses. His pupils were large and round with pain and shock. He started to look away, but stopped and returned his gaze directly to meet mine. "Did you?"

"I killed the sons of bitches," he said. I did not fail to notice the pluralization.

"Damn it all! How many were there?"

"Two. There was a third, but I raked it hard across the face. I think I tore one of its eyes. It took off into the woods howling." I struggled not to lose my partially digested dinner over that image. "The other two, I hauled them up to the pond. Not Turkey Pond. Big Pond. I weighted them with stones and dropped them from the cliff on the backside of the pond. It's deepest there. They're fish food now." I nodded as I lowered my eyes and resumed washing the last wound I needed to tend to on his hip that ran across his thigh. I'd put a hand towel across his groin. "Charlotte, I killed two people. I don't know who they were. They were in lycanthrope form. They didn't transform in death. Maybe they weren't quite completely dead yet. I don't know. I've never killed a lycanthrope before." I shook my head. I didn't know anything about that. "I murdered two people."

"I heard you!" I snapped. I sat back on my heels, my hand pressed against the towel covering his largest wound. "I heard you the first time you said it."

"I…I'm…"

I raised my head again. He had tilted his head back against the wall and closed his eyes, his face a mask of pain, shock, and grief. "In this damn world you've been thrown into against your will, it really is dog versus dog. We have the alpha dog out for blood. Your blood. If you lie down and roll over, exposing your belly and your throat, then you're as good as gone, Julian. And if you surrender to him, then you're going to be responsible for a lot more savage, brutal murders than those two already weighing your soul down."

"I'm already responsible for a lot more than those two dating back twelve years ago," he replied. "A whole fuckin' string of vicious, pointless murders have been committed. I could have stopped it back then, if I hadn't been such a goddam coward! I ran away, Charlotte! I ran like the coward that I am!"

"You were eighteen years old, Julian! You didn't even completely understand what had happened to you yet. You figured it all out in Germany, didn't you?"

"Yeah, but I could have come back and taken care of this. I could have fixed this sooner."

"You weren't strong enough for that yet."

"I don't even know if I'm strong enough for it now!"

"I believe that you are. And you've got back up, you know."

"Yeah, my little, redheaded bitch who hasn't even had a shoot…" I slapped him. Hard. His head snapped toward his right shoulder. He slitted his eyes, glaring at me.

"Don't you ever call me your bitch again! That's unacceptable! I'm your girlfriend!" My fury with Druce speaking to me as he had easily merged with my anger at Julian for calling me a bitch. I knew he meant the female dog kind, but I was not that either!

He was looking at me, and then he pushed himself upright. "Sorry. I'm sorry, Cherry. I hurt right now. I'm beyond pissed off. I say stupid things when I'm not at my best, and even then…" He shrugged. "I'm sorry."

"Let me finish patching you up," I said quietly, bending my head and removing the towel so I could wash the last deep gouge one more time and then get it bandaged up. My tears dripping onto his thigh alerted him to how deeply wounded and upset I was.

He raised his hand, pushing my hair back behind my ear, and then running the pad of his thumb across my wet cheek. "Do you know what I'm making for you in the shop?" he asked. I shook my head. How would I know such a thing? I'd only ever been in there one time. "I'm making you the full sized version of the sample clock tower in your sitting room."

"I don't think that will fit in my room."

"No, but when the suite I'm having renovated here is completed and you move into it with me, we'll be able to step out onto the balcony just before midnight and watch the clock come to life from there. I'm going to have it installed in the garden."

"Are you tearing out your mother's rose bushes?"

"No, of course not. I'm having the clock tower put in an area that will be full of violets and ivy. There will be some real rambling roses that will be allowed to climb the tower, and the ivy, of course will also climb it. I'll have to hire someone to keep it cut back, so it doesn't choke up the mechanical movements any. Every night, if you want to, we can go out there and watch the princess come out onto her balcony, the wolf leap from behind the tree to join her. He'll transform into a prince and kiss her."

"And then he'll transform back into a wolf and leave her weeping."

"Does that upset you?" I nodded. "What do you want him to do? Remain a prince, sweep her up in his arms, and carry her into the tower where he'll make mad, passionate love to her for the rest of the night?" I nodded. "But, that's not her story." I sighed a weepy sort of sigh as I closed up the nearly empty first aid box. "But, it can be your story, Cherry, if you want it to be."

I started gathering up all the bloody towels, tossing them into the laundry basket beside the bench. "I want to believe in that fairy tale, Julian, but my life has never been about happy endings."

"It's never a happy ending, Cherry. Not for them. However, it's a happily ever after that we're shooting for here, you and me" he said.

I glanced at him. "We need to add a few human allies, if you and I are ever going to reach that happily ever after part."

"We have Ethan."

"We need more."

"Okay, so who do you suggest? Who in this town can a lycanthrope place his trust in not to kill him?"

"Chief Adams," I replied. He opened his mouth to respond to that, but I covered his mouth with my still bloody hand. "Don't say anything. Hear me out first. Okay?" His eyes met mine, his pupils not as big and round anymore. He was healing. They were more oval now. "He already suspects there's something going on, something he probably won't comprehend, but he knows that you and I are the good guys. He wants to help, but he doesn't even know what's happening, other than people are being killed. He said he'll help us."

"You were talking to him about me?"

"No. I didn't say anything at all about the lycanthrope/werewolf thing. He's just figured out that it's focused on us, that we're both in danger. He doesn't want anything bad to happen to us, so he's offered to help us in any way that he can."

"Well, imagine that! The chief of police wants to save the life of a werewolf while others of my kind have been tearing his citizens to shreds over the years. Come on, Charlotte! He'll be so freaked out about this that he'll just shoot me on sight and tell Pine Haven that he's rid them all of the big bad wolf."

"But he won't have done that and they'll know it soon enough when the big bad wolf kills me and God only knows who else!" I stood up, looking down at my bloodstained nightgown and grimacing. "I don't get that prickly sensation when I touch him."

"You've been touching him?" His eyes narrowed.

"He took my hand to squeeze it in a gesture of reassurance. He cares about us, Julian."

"He most likely cares more for you than he cares about me."

"Maybe, but he knows that I care about you."

"Did you tell him that we're in a relationship? That we're lovers?"

"I didn't have to tell him. He figured that out on his own."

"Great." He pushed himself away from the wall, up onto his feet. The towel fell away from his groin. I lowered my eyes to make sure he'd sustained no damage there. I'd really just thrown the towel over him to keep from being distracted while washing and bandaging him. "See anything interesting?"

"You need to go to bed, Julian," I replied.

"Yeah, I do. So do you."

"To sleep!" I flared.

He laughed, shaking his head. "What did you think I meant?" That made me blush hotly. "Cherry, lose the nightgown, wash up, and come to bed. Both of us need to get some serious sleep." He limped past me into the bedroom. I stripped off my icky nightgown, threw it in the hamper, and then took a quick shower to sluice off all his blood. I toweled myself dry then went out into the bedroom. "I'm cold. Do you have a t-shirt or something I can put on? Sweat socks?"

"I have a fur coat you can wrap yourself in," he replied, his voice sounding strange. "Oh, my God, Julian! You didn't!" I snapped on the light and yelped. He was in his lycanthrope form. "I'll heal even faster like this. And I can keep you warm. Fur retains heat."

"You won't make a mistake and bite me, will you?"

"No, you're my girl," he said. I was glad he hadn't called me his bitch again. I'd have had to find his pistol with the silver bullets and shoot him for that. Instead, I switched off the light, carefully crawled onto the bed, and slid under the covers, snuggling against his furry belly. The bandages had more or less stayed in place on him.

I closed my eyes, heaved a weary sigh, and then reached behind me to find his big paw. I pulled it over my hip and held it between my breasts as I fell asleep, my hand holding his paw.

Chapter Twenty-Three

During the days leading up to and immediately after the funerals, there had been some changes in the household staff. Druce was summoned to the study and Julian lit into him, setting him straight on whose house it was, that his opinions about me were not welcome ones between these walls, and if he didn't like it, he could leave, he'd cut him a check right this minute and wash his hands of him forever, because, if truth be told, he'd never been as fond of him as his father had evidently been.

Despite the tongue lashing, Druce chose to remain. It didn't please me any that he was staying, but later Julian told me privately that he'd rather have him where he could keep an eye on him, than running around out in the community doing Gunther's bidding. Julian was able to exert some control over him by keeping him close.

During this meeting with Druce, he'd also set him straight about my place in the household. I was more than his personal assistant. I was his household manager; therefore my position was above that of a butler. Mr. Beresford had allowed the butler to lord it over the entire staff. Druce had abused his authority, but no one had ever complained, at least not until I'd become Julian's personal assistant. Then I had complained about Druce's treatment of me. He had been demoted and I had been promoted. It earned me a lot of dark scowls and somewhat snide remarks, but I'd tell him, in no uncertain terms, to fuck off, and he'd slink away, probably to call Gunther and tell him I was getting too big for own britches. Screw him.

Julian didn't want any new household members added right now, so Lorraine and I managed the cooking. I also helped Rose with the cleaning. Ethan took over the gardening, which wasn't much at this time of year with winter approaching. Sanborn also helped with the yard work and maintaining the house in good repair, since there wasn't much driving for him to do, although he kept the vehicles in perfect running order. He did not move into the house, but remained in the apartment above the carriage house, where he said he was comfortable and preferred to remain. Julian allowed this, although a new alarm system was installed out there.

Chief Adams met with Julian at the clock shop about three days after the last funerals had taken place. I wasn't allowed to go out there to meet with them, although I wanted to. I thought he should bring a buffer along, but he told me I might accidentally get shot, that one of us had to survive to finish the work that needed to be done.

I was extremely nervous about that meeting taking place on Clay Hill Road. If it didn't go well, then Julian might be shot and killed right then and there. If Chief Adams was skeptical and demanded proof of what Julian was telling him, my boyfriend was going to transform himself into his lycanthrope form right then and there as proof. I thought that was foolish and risky, but Julian had pointed out that we had no other proof of what we had to tell him to fall back on. Yes, he had the forensics reports, the autopsy reports, the tufts of fur they'd gathered at several of the sites where mutilation killings had occurred, and even the reports of an eyewitness, me, of a wolf that walked upright, but there was no guarantee that the pieces would all fall together in the right order to form a picture that was undeniable no matter how unbelievable it was in reality.

At three thirty, as the afternoon sun was beginning to wane, Julian called me on my cellphone and asked that Sanborn drive me out to the clock shop. He wanted Sanborn to drop me off and then return home. I asked how it was going and he evaded that question, just repeating what he'd said. I told him I'd be there as soon as I could.

I was left off at the front door of the shop. Chief Adams was in the front office and let me in, locking the door again once I was inside. "Hello, Charlotte."

"Hi." I was looking around nervously, as if I expected to be attacked. I didn't really know what to expect, but he placed his hand on my shoulder and nodded toward the corridor.

"Julian is in his office. Let's go there."

We walked the short distance to the office and he let me go in first. Julian was sitting at his desk. Chief Adams came in and closed the office door, drawing the old, somewhat brittle green shade down over the window. The blinds were closed over the two office windows that faced the road around to the back of the shop. "All right, son, she's here."

"What's going on?" I asked.

"I have to show him proof of what I've been telling him. I said I wanted you here," Julian replied. "If anyone can

269

stop him from putting a bullet through my heart, it's you." He stood up, already unbuttoning his shirt and shrugging out of it. His t-shirt followed.

"Uh," Chief Adams said, probably thinking we'd brought him out here for some sort of weird three-way sex.

"He has to get undressed or he'll ruin his clothes," I said as Julian continued stripping down. "Can I hold your gun?" I asked. He gave me a look which only confirmed that he was nervous about this, uncertain what was going to happen. "In less than a minute, my boyfriend is going to become a wolf and I don't want you reflexively drawing your weapon and shooting him out of some sense of honor or duty to protect me. I've seen this a couple of times already. I'm used to it. You're going to see something totally mind-blowing for the first time. So, please, let me hold your gun until he's back to normal again. For everyone's safety."

He glanced at me again, and then handed me his service weapon. I knew he probably had another gun on him, most likely strapped to his ankle, but he'd have to bend down to get it and I would hit him over the head with the butt of his service weapon if he tried that.

He leaned back against the door, even more wary now that Julian was naked and I was holding his gun. "You'd better sit down," I told him.

He glanced at both of us, and then shook his head. "I prefer to remain standing. Go ahead, son, but this had better be something that's not going to leave me doubting your word in the least."

"Oh, you're going to believe me one hundred percent," Julian assured him as he began stretching, his limbs lengthening. He was trying to control it, to slow the transformation down, but he really couldn't do that. He was nervous, apprehensive. It happened fast, so fast that the rapid change dropped him down onto all fours, growling in pain, panting.

"Holy shit! What the fuck!" cried the chief as he began to crouch down, reaching toward his ankle for his back-up weapon.

"Don't you dare shoot him!" I cried, literally flying across the room, throwing my arms around Julian's furry neck. "He needed to do this to prove to you that he wasn't lying. Neither one of us is lying to you! There are werewolves, lycanthropes, in Pine Haven. One transformed Julian when he was fourteen. It was the alpha wolf. He's wicked and evil! Julian fled Pine Haven after graduation because he didn't want to be like him." I spilled the whole story out as I slowly let go of Julian's neck and he rose to his full height on two legs. "The alpha wolf wants him dead because he rebelled. He's killing our loved ones, and now Julian's employees, to punish both of us. We have to stop it before it kills anymore people. It's going to kill me, Chief Adams. Then it's going to make Julian suffer horribly until he decides to rip his throat out and be done with him for good." I knew what I'd just said would pretty much coincide with what Julian must have told him earlier, before I'd been summoned here.

The chief was obviously in shock at seeing such an incomprehensible thing, a human being transforming into a wolfman. He was desperately trying to wrap his mind around the fact that this was real, that we hadn't slipped him an hallucinogenic drug and were messing with his mind. "I...I..." He shook his head. "I need to sit down." He staggered over to a chair with arms that were cracked, the stuffing leaking out of them. He leaned forward. Elbows propped on his knees, he held his face in his hands. Twice he peeked through his fingers as if hopeful the beast in front of him would no longer be there. "Julian, can you change back now? I've seen enough," he finally asked, scrubbing his face with both hands, rubbing his eyes and then his jaw. He carefully watched Julian transform back into a human being.

"All right, get dressed now. It's too chilly in here to be running around naked." His eyes shifted to me. I walked over and handed him back his gun, but stood between him and Julian, who was defenseless while getting dressed. "Young lady, you and I need to spend some time on the shooting range," he said to me and I nodded. "Sooner rather than later."

"You need to get some silver bullets made to fit your gun. Julian might know how to do that."

"I have some bullet molds at the station. I've made my own ammo in the past." He looked at his Glock. "I'd rather use my forty-four for hunting werewolves though. Or maybe the shot gun?"

"We can figure that out at our next meeting," Julian replied as he finished dressing.

"Now that I've seen the truth of it with my own eyes, can you tell me who we're going after?" he asked. Julian shook his head. "Why not?"

"Because the fewer people who know, the better. When the time comes, one of us will tell you and you'll just have to trust us."

"I'd like to know now." Julian shook his head again. "Rand, how can I protect the citizens of this community, if you keep secrets this big from me?"

This was a reasonable enough argument. I looked at Julian and he seemed to be thinking about it also. Finally, he said, "I'll tell you, but you absolutely cannot let on that you know or you're as good as dead if you do. We can't afford to lose you and I'm not just talking about Cherry and me. I'm talking about the whole damn town and all the surrounding communities here."

"Okay, now, let me try to get this as clear as I can in my own head. This guy, this lycanthrope, he stalked you kids up at Turkey Pond and he killed the Peck boy and the Underwood boy, but he didn't kill you. Instead, he infected

you with this...this...whatever...and you became like him?"
Julian nodded. "Why'd he leave you alive?'

"He was making others of his kind. Think of it as a
wolf pack. A pack of killers that he holds dominion over."

"So, what you're telling me is that there are others
like you?"

"I have no doubt that he's made others. I don't think
there're a whole hell of a lot of them because, if that was the
case, then there would be way more killings going on, more
mutilated and dead livestock and wild animals being found.
To protect himself, he's only created a few. Maybe he's
created more than just a few. If they were weak, or proved to
be difficult to control, then he would have killed them pretty
quickly because they would pose a threat to him. I think
there may a lot of bodies buried in the vicinity of his home
and you'll discover that more of those are male than female.
Some of the female bodies that you've found, I think they
were girls that he let his pack practice on. The ones like
Chase and Ripley, the ones that meant something to
Charlotte and me, he's doing that himself and he's not being
nice about it." I made a sound and he glanced at me. I went
and sat down in the other chair beside the chief.

"It's all right, honey. It's okay. We're going to take
care of this. We'll put an end to it." The chief took my hand
and held it in his. "Give me this son of a bitch's name,
Rand," he said.

"Joseph Gunther," Julian replied without hesitation.
I felt the chief's response through his hand.

"I've heard some things about that guy ever since he
moved here after taking the job as the new gym teacher. It's
all been rumor and conjecture, nothing concrete that I've
been able to build a case on. I've been out to his place, that
swank cabin past the Renegade Club, nearer to the
swampland, a dozen so times. It's in a nice, remote location.
I've heard there've been some parties out there, but I always

273

hear about them after the fact. By the time I get there, the place is clean as a whistle. That one is as slick as oil." He shook his head. "I've been wanting something more concrete on this bastard for fifteen years."

"Well, you're going to have to wait a little longer. We have to kill him when he's in his wolf form or else I'm condemned to remain like this for the rest of my life. I'm really not anxious to do that."

"What do you mean?" Julian explained. "I see." He turned his head and looked at me. "No, I don't imagine this little lady wants to tie herself down with a werewolf for the rest of her life."

"I would if I had to, but I'd rather he be all human again."

"Now, that's love, son. You'd better hang onto this little gal."

Julian's eyes shifted to me. He had removed his glasses to transform and now reached for them, remembering that he should put them back on. That made me think of something. "How come Mr. Gunther doesn't wear dark glasses?" I asked.

"He wears special contact lenses."

"Oh." I frowned. "Then how come you've never gotten contacts?"

"It's easier to take a pair of glasses off than it is to pop contacts out and try to find a place to put them so they don't dry out. I guess I'm just more economical minded than he is. He probably buys them by the gross or something."

"Rand, am I allowed to ask you questions?" the chief asked.

"Yeah, sure."

"Have you ever killed anyone?"

Even I was aware of the hesitant pause before Julian replied, "No."

The pause before the chief asked his next question was even lengthier. "Is there anything you want to tell me?"

"Not right now."

"They attacked him," I said. "He came home all torn up. You must have seen the scars on him. He's healed, but he still has the scars."

"I noticed the scars," Chief Adams replied. "I take it that they fade fairly quickly?" Julian nodded. "Then would you mind undressing again so I can take a few shots of the damage you took? If I wait to do this, the scars will fade and there will be no proof that something like this ever happened to you, just your word and Charlotte's which, without evidence, would be difficult for any jury to believe, if it ever goes that far."

"I'd rather that we handle this business outside of the realm of jurisprudence," Julian replied as he stood up and slowly undressed again. Chief Adams documented the scars up close, and then took a full frontal and a full back side shot of Julian, which he did not especially take kindly to, but the chief said it was necessary to show who bore all those scars. "I feel like I've been violated," Julian muttered as he redressed.

The chief chuckled. "At least no one has actually laid a hand on you."

"You'll delete those pictures when this is all over, won't you?"

"Yes, I will. I give you my word on that."

"I don't want any naked pictures of me showing up on the internet."

"Rand, I'm an officer of the law. I shot some photos as evidence. That's all it was. I'm not into getting off on pictures of naked young men. I was married for twenty-seven years to Alice Farnum. After she died, I dedicated my heart and soul to my job. Occasionally, if I need to reconfirm that I'm a man, I take Nancy Tucker to dinner and we go to her place for the night. That's about the extent of my sex life right there in a nutshell."

"Thanks for sharing."

"I've been intruding on your private lives here. Now we're on level ground again." He stood up, slipping his phone back into his pocket. "I'm heading back to the station now and I suggest you take this little lady home. I'll try a shot of whisky before bed to ward off the nightmare I feel coming on already."

"You had to see it to believe it," Julian pointed out. "I told you it would change your life."

"Yes, you certainly did, and it has." He walked over to where Julian was now sitting on the corner of the old desk. "I'm in your corner, Rand. I've always cared about that young lady over there, from the very first time I saw her skipping down the sidewalk on her way to grade school holding hands with that cute little Forbes girl. One of them died a gruesome, horrific death because of my ignorance. I'm not inclined to see the same thing, or even worse, happen to Charlotte. I promise you, I'll have your back on this."

"Thank you," Julian said quietly. "I appreciate that more than you know."

The chief then turned to me. "Have Sanborn bring you downtown every day at one-thirty. We'll go down to the shooting range in the basement and I'll show you how to handle that powerful little nine millimeter of yours. We've got ear protection and goggles at the range."

Julian went to let him out, making sure that he got safely into his vehicle and out onto the road. He stood at the door, watching to see if any cars would follow the chief back to town, but after five minutes no vehicles passed by. "You ready to go home?" he asked me. I was more than ready. "Or would you like to see your clock tower first?"

"It's dark. We need to get home. Lorraine has probably started cooking. She's nervous about handling dinner on her own."

He agreed then went back, shutting off lights and locking the doors. We went out, got into his truck, and headed home. "We've either gained an ally or, when all this actually sinks in and he realizes that I'm just as much of a monster as Gunther, then he's going to come gunning for me."

I gnawed my lip the rest of the way home, hoping that Chief Adams would be able to accept it like I'd accepted it, although I still didn't like it. He wouldn't like it either. However, if he had any hope at all of stopping Gunther, then he had to put his trust in J. Rand Beresford, the eccentric, reclusive son of R. Hollis Beresford, the beloved clockmaker of Pine Haven.

Chapter Twenty-Four

I began my firearms lessons in November. Winter was brutal with several nor'easters shutting down Pine Haven. Julian was restless. I opened up the ballroom workshop and tinkered with clockworks to keep my hand in it. Occasionally, if we were snowed in, he'd join me. By February, he was fabricating clock cases for me and I was ordering parts and carefully making some of my own pieces, not very skillfully at first but, as April arrived, I was definitely getting better at it.

I still helped with the cooking and cleaning. Julian spent a lot of his time in the clock shop. Allyson Gray had brought in a crew and they'd begun the renovation work in the west wing in March, so that wing was off limits. If Julian wanted me, he had to come to my room. He didn't come as often as I hoped he would but, when he did, what existed between us blazed back to life in a matter of moments and it was better than it had ever been.

Druce skulked about the house watching everyone as if he suspected we were slipping poison into his bourbon. He also seemed increasingly more restless and frustrated. I began to realize that his frustration and restlessness arose from the control Julian was exerting over him.

As my twenty-third birthday approached at the end of May, Druce left the house one day and did not return. When Julian came home from the clock shop that evening and discovered that the butler had done a disappearing act, he wasn't happy. He went into the study and made several phone calls.

When he finally came into the dining room where I was poking at my food, sat down, and began eating, I just looked at him. "The shit's going to hit the fan any day now," he informed me.

"That's nice dinner table talk."

"This isn't Masterpiece Theater."

"No, it's more like Monsterpiece Theater." I put my fork down. "I'm a fairly decent marksman now." I flipped over the piece of paper that was near my right elbow and fired it down the length of the table toward him. He slapped his hand down to stop the paper before it flew off his end of the table and then looked down at it. "I passed the department's firearms qualification test."

"Good job, Cherry. I'm proud of you. I have a few clips loaded with silver bullets for you. It's time to put one in your pistol and keep it there. Don't go wasting the bullets taking pot shots at squirrels out in the yard."

"I won't. I'm saving them for wolf hunting." Our eyes met down the length of the table. His father had told me that Grace Beresford had always sat on his right hand side. My eyes still on his, I picked up my place setting, placemat and all, and moved it to the seat to his left. I had sat at his father's left hand side. But, as I went to pull out that chair, Julian shook his head, moved his right hand and tapped the place to his right, indicating that I should move my place setting to his right side. This made my heart wobble a bit in my breast. Before I could sit down, he jumped up and pulled out the chair for me. I sat down, but he didn't push the chair in. Instead, he dropped down onto one knee beside the chair. "What are you doing?" I asked.

"I'm giving you your birthday present a couple of days early," he replied.

"Well, can't you do this upstairs?"

"I could, but I'm giving you something else upstairs," he replied, lowering his head, looking at me over the tops of his glasses.

"Hold on!" I cried as he dipped his hand into his front pocket. "Wait a minute!" I turned toward him in the chair, and then I took his glasses, lifting them off his face, folding the stems, and laying them on the table. "I want to see your eyes."

He took my left hand in his, and then began to slip a ring onto my finger. "Charlotte Louise Rumford," he said, making me jump. How on earth had he discovered what my middle name was? "I never thought I'd be doing this but before he died I made a promise to my father during one of our talks together and I'm determined to keep that promise. I've thought about backing out on it, but then I realized that I don't want to do that. I want to give my father the daughter that he'd always wished for, the one that he chose for himself. I chose you before he did, although not as a daughter or a sister. I chose you as the only one I could ever give my heart to. You're so sweet, Cherry. I didn't think I deserved anyone as good as you, but you've accepted me for what I am, for who I am. You didn't crush my heart under your heel. You embraced it and gave it a home right there in your breast beside your own heart. Tonight, I want to say something that I haven't yet said to you. I want to tell you that I love you. I have always loved you. I will always love you. Will you do me the great honor of agreeing to be my wife?" I nodded, tears spilling down my cheeks, unable to speak. He slid the ring the rest of the way onto my finger. It was blurry, but I knew it would be beautiful once I could see it clearly. "You want to give me a kiss, maybe?"

"Yes." I managed to say. Yes, I would marry him. "Yes." Yes, I wanted to give him a kiss.

He stood up, taking my hands and pulling me up out of my chair and into his arms. We were in the midst of a very passionate kiss when Lorraine came into the dining room. She nearly dropped the tray on which she had brownie sundaes ready for our dessert. Those sundaes would never taste as sweet as the kisses Julian and I were sharing, but we broke apart and resumed our seats. She cleared away our plates and set the dessert dishes down before us. "Rose and I will clear tonight, Miss," she murmured before leaving the dining room.

I smiled at Julian and he winked at me. We were going up to my room to finish celebrating our engagement. I ate my sundae, but had trouble tearing my eyes off my now sparkling and crystal clear diamond ring. "Eat up, buttercup. You can admire your ring all you like while I'm ravishing you in the bedroom." This was the most relaxed and playful that he'd ever been. I turned my head to look at him and, in that moment, I saw a normal, happy, twenty-six year old young man. He was smiling.

From a distance, we'd look like any ordinary newly engaged couple, flushed and smiling, both shy and teasing with one another. But, if you came closer and looked into his eyes, the pupils would be rather alarming. They were slits in the bright light from the chandelier. I was thankful that his eyes had been closed as Lorraine came in with dessert or else she'd have dropped the tray and run screaming out of the house. He had kept his gaze down as she'd cleared the table, and then slipped his glasses on again before looking at her.

We went upstairs and fell into my bed, undressing one another between kisses and fondling one another. Finally, we were naked and the lovemaking began in earnest. We were a little wild in the heat of the excitement of our new relationship status. I had to put my hands up over my head and grip the headboard because I was afraid he was going to push my head right between the iron rods that supported the ornate top piece. "Julian!" I panted. He growled. "Julian!" He raised his head, his wolf eyes meeting mine. "You're hurting me."

"I'm sorry," he said.

"Don't stop, just, take it down a notch or two, okay? I want to do this again with you tonight, not be too sore to do it."

"I'm just…happy."

"I know you are." I smiled at him. "I'm glad you're happy. I am, too. I'm happier than I've ever been in my life because you have always been the only one I could ever love like this. You're the only boy I ever wanted to be with." I let go of the headboard to grab his head and pull his face to mine. I kissed him as passionately as I could, relishing the growl at the back of his throat that told me that he liked my kissing him like that. "Continue," I commanded in a throaty whisper. He obeyed. Tonight, I had control of this wolf. He was all mine.

But, I wasn't allowed to have him all to myself for long. A phone call at quarter past one came through on the house phone. Ethan answered it, and then came to my suite where he knew Julian was because renovation work was in full swing in the west wing. "Rand?"

"What do you want?" Julian answered drowsily.

"The police are on the phone for you."

Julian groaned as he got out of bed, feeling around in the dark for his jeans and pulling them on as he made his way to the door. He opened it a crack. Ethan put the cordless phone in his hand. "This is J. Rand. What's going on?" He listened, and then he cursed. "Yeah, I'll be there in about twenty minutes." He disconnected the call, handing the phone back to Ethan. "So much for celebrating, Cherry. The shop's been broken into. There's a fire up in the woods behind it. I'm heading over there." He flipped on the bedroom ceiling light. I threw my arm up to shield my eyes. He looked around, spotted his glasses on the bedside table, came and slipped them on. "Have to keep up appearances."

"What do you want us to do?"

"Call the chief on his personal cell and tell him this is it. He's done toying with me. Tonight, when I'm the fucking happiest I've ever been, he's going to take me down and crush that joy right out of me. I knew this would happen. I'm not surprised. If the three of you want to hike up into the woods as my backup, that'd be great, but it might get you killed."

"Aren't we all going to be killed anyway, unless we can stop him?" I asked.

"Yeah, that pretty much sums it up. Ethan, you know where to go?"

"Yeah, boss. I'll be there as fast as I can."

He looked over his shoulder at me, then came back to the bed, bent over and gave me a lingering kiss. "Love you," he whispered. "If at all possible, let's meet here again soon and continue the party."

"Love you, too, and yes, we'll do just that." I injected as much confidence as I could into my voice, but in my gut, I didn't have much hope of that happening.

Ethan went to get dressed. I scrambled out of bed and pulled on clean clothes. I raked a brush through my tangled hair and pulled it back into a ponytail. My face was a little red from all the kissing I'd done with my scruffy-jawed fiancé. My breasts were tender and I was a little sore, but those would be reminders to me of how much he loved me and would increase my determination to survive.

Julian was gone by the time Ethan and I got downstairs. Ethan hadn't wanted to leave Lorraine and Rose home alone, so he'd woken them up, made them get dressed, and we were dropping them off at the police station on our way out to Clay Hill Road. Sanborn was going to stay at the house and stand guard with a shotgun. I hadn't liked that idea much, but he'd assured me that he'd be fine.

I had my nine millimeter with me with extra clips stuffed into my jacket pockets. Ethan had his sniper's rifle and scope in a bag, and most likely had a back-up weapon as well. If Julian had his gun with him, it would more than likely be left behind wherever he shed his clothes when he transformed. I'd have to keep an eye out for that and grab it, if we came across it.

The chief was at the station when we got there. He, of course, recognized Lorraine, Rose, and Ethan. He came outside, having been briefed by his desk sergeant as to what was happening out at the clock shop, the break-in and now the fire. It seemed every piece of equipment in town had been dispatched to the scene.

Chief Adams followed us to the scene. I jumped out, but was prevented from getting closer to the shop by a police barricade across the driveway. It wasn't until just after Ethan had taken off to go to his sniper's perch via a back route that I noticed that Julian's truck was not in the lot, nor was it among the vehicles lining both sides of the street. "He's not here!" I cried, pulling out my phone. I tried calling him but his phone went straight to voice mail. "Damn it, Julian Rand Beresford!" I shouted angrily. I was terrified that he had lied to us, that he had been planning on taking on the alpha wolf all by himself all along.

"What's wrong, Charlotte?" the chief asked, making his way back to where I was standing.

"Julian's not here! His truck isn't here."

"Maybe he parked farther down the road." I shook my head. "Have you tried calling him?"

"His phone went straight to voice mail."

He frowned. "Can you reach Ethan?" I touched the contact number for him and sent the call. When he answered, I handed the phone to the chief. "Chief Adams here. Where are you?" He listened. "Did you, by any chance, notice Rand's truck up that way? Do you remember passing it before you dropped Charlotte off?" He listened again. "I have a bad feeling about this. I have a feeling this is all smoke and mirrors to distract us from the location where Gunther is actually meeting Rand." I said that Julian would probably have been able to sense that and he'd gone off to wherever Gunther was. "Where do the two of you think they are?"

It was then that I saw a figure staggering out of the woods by the rotating red beacons of the fire engines in the lot. "Oh, my God! Look!"

"Hold on, don't disconnect!" He handed the phone back to me before ducking under the police tape and running toward the figure. I wriggled under the wooden barrier, managing to escape the grasping hands of the cop who tried to stop me. I bolted after the chief.

The man had collapsed on the ground. The chief was on his knees next to him, bending low, trying to hear what he was saying. I skidded to a stop when I recognized Druce. His face was deeply gouged. I recognized him by his nose, the penguin man. He was in tattered clothing that was bloodstained, but something was wrong with the whole picture. He seemed too whole for having been attacked by a werewolf in the woods. And how would he have managed to escape?

And then it came back to me, slamming hard into my brain. The prickly sensation whenever he'd accidentally brushed against me or vice versa. It was the same as when I touched Julian, when Gunther touched me! "No!" I screamed as I saw his hand and wrist lengthening beyond the sleeve of his torn jacket. "He's transforming!"

The chief looked back at me instead of down at Druce. I pulled my pistol out of my pocket and aimed it at Druce. "Charlotte, no!" Chief Adams shouted, but then he was howling with pain because Druce had raked him with his claws, hard. The chief fell back and Druce began to rise up. He was going to lunge down at him and tear his guts out, and then his throat!

"You goddam son of a bitch! Your master's going to go straight to hell tonight! Go hold the gate open for him!" And I fired a bullet into the base of his skull. Almost simultaneously, another shot, more muffled, rang out.

Police officers were running toward us. "Put your gun in your pocket, Charlotte, and step away," Chief Adams panted from beneath the body of the wolf.

I slid my pistol into my pocket and turned away, scared to death that he was going to die. Officers shoved me aside in their haste to get to their fallen leader. I heard their cries of shock at what they found, but they heaved the wolf off Chief Adams and helped him to his feet.

He had bloody wounds on his shoulder. His jacket and shirt were torn open, but he had a Kevlar vest on beneath his shirt. Although Druce had been trying, he hadn't been unable to dig his claws into the chief's belly to tear him open.

I realized there was a distant voice yelling. It turned out to be Ethan. I brought the phone to my ear. "What?"

"Jesus Christ, Charlotte! I heard gunshots! What happened?"

"It was Druce. He attacked the chief."

"Did he kill him?" he shouted into the phone.

"No. We got him." I'd realized, when they'd flipped the wolf off of the chief, that he had managed to get his gun free and he had shot it through the heart. And, in that moment, my mind made several quick leaps. The heart of the wolf. The heart of a home. Gunther was proud of his home, his lair. He committed all sorts of crimes there that he had been getting away with for over a decade now. "Holy shit!" I cried. "Julian's at Gunther's! Gunther's going to kill him and dump his body in the swamp where he'll never be found! This is all a distraction, a diversion! Ethan, do you know where that bastard lives?"

"I've got it on my GPS. I'm back at the truck, heading over there now!"

"Be careful! If you shoot a wolf, you'd better make damn sure it's not my wolf!"

I turned around and saw three officers staring at me. Chief Adams came over to me, slipping his arm around my shoulders. "I'll take her to the ambulance. The three of you, keep your eyes open for any additional wolves. You have the ammo I issued?" They nodded. "Only shoot if the wolf is lunging at you. Aim for the heart or between the eyes, whichever you can hit first." They nodded again, licking their lips nervously. "Come along, Charlotte."

He steered me back down the driveway toward the road. "Julian's at Gunther's cabin," I said.

"Yes. Is Ethan on his way there?" I nodded. "We'll just be a minute or two behind him."

We got into his SUV and he pulled away, heading further down Clay Hill Road. I was shaking with adrenalin and nerves. I was fairly vibrating in the passenger seat. He reached over and patted my arm. "We'll be there shortly. If there's anything we can do, we'll do it. This ends tonight." I nodded. "Honey…it may already be too late for…"

"Don't say it!" I cried. "Please…don't tell me that."
I held my left hand out, the next streetlight we passed under
causing the diamond on my ring finger to flare brightly.

"When did this happen?" he asked.

"Tonight at dinner. He proposed just before dessert."

He pressed down harder on the accelerator, but did
not turn on the lights and siren. If Gunther heard the vehicle
approaching, he would think it was only drunk kids leaving
the Renegade, which had been hopping when we'd passed it
a few moments ago. I was fairly sure the road through the
swamp was a popular shortcut for people leaving the bar
who wanted to get back to Windsor and nearby Tylerville.

We almost missed the driveway. If he hadn't caught
the flare of Ethan's taillights through the trees, we'd have
missed it completely. He applied the brakes, reversed, and
pulled into the long driveway with just the running lights on.
Ethan was a dark shape at the back of his truck.

As I went to get out, I heard and sensed what
sounded like a large animal running across the ground
nearby. Ethan raised his rifle and, without even pausing,
fired two rapid shots. I heard a yelp of pain and then felt the
thud of a body hitting the ground. I ducked around the front
of the SUV, not wanting to know how close that body had
been to me. I had sensed the heat of the bullets passing me.
"One down," Ethan muttered. He then began rummaging
around in a bin in the back of his truck. "Here, you two. Put
these on." He handed us each a pair of goggles—night vision
goggles as we soon discovered. Immediately, we were able
to pick out the cabin, the trees, a car, and Julian's truck
parked at an angle off to the side of the house. Beyond it, I
could see some scattered lawn furniture and a gazebo.

"Over there!" Chief Adams said in a low, terse
voice. "I saw the flash of eyes, just at the corner of the
house." Ethan slowly moved further down the driveway to
try to get a better angle, but the thing came rushing toward

him. I pulled out my gun and fired as it leapt at him. Another shot followed mine and the wolf dropped heavily to the ground and lay still.

"That's two," Ethan said. Moving his gun from the holster on his hip to his left hand. "Ambidextrous," he said, giving me a goofy grin. "Nice shootin', Charlotte."

The sound of howls and yelps came from the wooded area behind the house. Cautiously, we began making our way around the side of the house on the driveway side. There were no lights on. It was even darker in the back yard.

With a snarl, another wolf leapt toward us, taking Ethan down. He screamed with pain. As the wolf pounced on him, a shot stopped it from killing him. Blood sprayed from the massive head wound the Glock had inflicted. Ethan kicked and shoved his way free, but he was limping as we resumed our slow advance toward the woods. "Three," I murmured because Ethan had not said it.

"Yeah," he said, through clenched teeth.

"How bad's the leg?" the chief asked.

"Bleeding, but he didn't hit the femoral artery."

The chief nodded. "Let me take the lead now. You hang back. You've got better range with that rifle. Charlotte, you stay between us."

We headed toward the woods where the sounds of fighting animals still raged. Julian was outnumbered. I was heartsick thinking that we wouldn't arrive in time to do him much good. The only satisfaction that I might walk away with tonight was, if I survived, knowing that we weren't leaving until Gunther was dead.

We came upon a horrific sight. There were two dead wolves in a clearing, and four more circling one another, all four of them bleeding heavily from terrible wounds, panting, growling. They were tired, but none of them were backing down. I had no clue which one of them was my fiancé. They all looked alike in the near darkness.

Two wolves suddenly lunged at one another and were quickly locked together, snarling and grunting. They rolled on the ground, teeth gnashing, claws ripping. I had no idea which one was Julian, but knew that he had to be one of them. "Let them fight," Chief Adams said quietly, stilling my shaking hand. The other two wolves slowly circled the fighting pair. It confirmed to me that Julian definitely had to be one of the wolves locked in that deadly battle; therefore, the other two wolves were not him. I whispered what I thought to the chief and he nodded. "But we can't be sure," he whispered back.

"I can't just let him die! The odds are against him!"

"Shh!"

One of the fighting wolves yelped and then went still. The one underneath almost seemed to be convulsing, and then it heaved the heavy body off itself and scrambled, somewhat unsteadily onto all fours, head lowered, eyeing the other two circling wolves as if taking their measure. One of the two suddenly lunged at it and they both rose onto their hind legs, snarling and swiping at one another.

My heart was hammering with fear and I felt sick. "Charlotte! How good to see you!" came a familiar voice from somewhere in the darkness ahead of us. "We'll take care of your companions momentarily. I wouldn't want to interfere in this fight."

"This is so unfair! You're wearing him down making him fight these other wolves! You're a goddam coward is what you are! You have to tire him out before you fight him! You're despicable!"

"I'm simply teaching him who the alpha wolf of this pack is and who is the disobedient pup. Keep shouting like this. You're distracting him, making him lose his focus. When they've finished playing with him, I will then show him that I am his master once and for all. I will take his bitch right in front of him. It won't be pleasant for you, Charlotte.

I'll be in wolf form. I'm afraid you're going to experience a level of pain that you can't begin to imagine. It may just stop your heart." He laughed cruelly. To my right, Ethan went down with a soft grunt. The chief moved to do what he could to protect me, but he was also taken down.

The two wolves that had come up behind us tried to grab me, but I was smaller and more agile than they were, I darted to one side, dropped to the ground, rolled behind a log, popped up, and shot them one right after the other. This attracted the attention of the wolf waiting his turn at Julian. It began to walk toward me, but suddenly stopped with a jolt as if it were on a choke chain. "Put the gun down, Charlotte, or I'll make things much worse for your lover!" One of the wolves fighting howled in pain. "You see? He's much weaker now, I can get to him!" There was a sick glee in his tone. "Put the gun down or I will have my wolf tear his throat out right now!"

I dropped the gun. I was ordered out from behind the log. Slowly, I stood up and came around the log. I passed Ethan and the two dead wolves I'd shot, and then I dropped to my knees and vomited. I sort of collapsed near the chief's feet. A gleeful howl came from the darkness.

I stayed where I was, pretending that I'd passed out. I was regrouping, thinking. Behind my back, I heard another strangled yelp and knew that one of the two wolves fighting was dead. Immediately, the other wolf jumped on the survivor. Julian had killed another one, but I didn't know how much strength he had left in him.

I squeezed my eyes shut because I couldn't bear to see him torn apart and killed. And then I screamed when I was easily lifted off the ground. "Here's my little prize!" Gunther barked. "I have her now, Julian. I have your pretty little bitch! It's my turn to play with her now! You've had all the fun you're going to have with her. I've waited a long time to get my paws on her!"

He was transforming. I could feel it happening. And then he was tearing at my clothes, literally ripping them off of me. The night air was humid and chilly. I was shivering. And then he dropped me onto the ground, hard, grabbing me, putting me on my hands and knees. "I'm going to take your bitch now, Julian! You're going to hear her scream! I'm going to make her scream and beg for mercy, but I will not show her any mercy whatsoever! This is what you get for disobeying me! This is your punishment for running off to Europe! I am your master!" I screamed. The wolf howled, well, both wolves howled. I couldn't hold back the blood curdling scream of pain as he tried to mount me.

I raised my head, wanting my last sight to be of Julian. The two wolves were locked together still, but not moving. And then I saw that one of them was transforming, resuming his human form. I recognized the matted long hair. I saw the glisten of scars on his shoulders. He was wounded, bleeding heavily. "Charlotte," he rasped.

I didn't say anything. My teeth were clenched as the alpha wolf made another attempt to enter me, but I was squirming. He dug his claws into my hip and rib cage. With every ounce of strength that I had left, I flung what I held in my hand underhanded toward Julian. I saw that he'd caught it and did what I had to do next. Gathering every ounce of strength that I had, I pushed myself upright, slamming as hard as I could into the wolf behind me. Then, I just dead dropped to the ground. He was startled by my unexpected actions and raised his head, looking around, trying to figure out what was happening.

My fiancé, with his wolf eyes, aimed the throwaway pistol that I had pulled out of Chief Adams' ankle holster and put three quick bullets into the throat and forehead of the alpha wolf and two more dead center into its chest. It fell heavily on top of me, pinning me down. I couldn't draw a breath, he was so heavy, but then the weight was shifted to one side and I was dragged out from underneath the still somewhat furry body. He had begun to transform back into his human shape.

I was sprawled naked across Julian's lap because he had dropped to the ground. He was hurt badly—bleeding, breathing hard. But, he managed to lift me up high enough so he could duck his head and give me a coppery flavored kiss. I'd bitten my lip, so I was guessing it was my blood. It didn't really matter at that point. It was still a very a sweet kiss despite that blood.

It was Ethan who gave me his flannel shirt. It was a little cold and damp with his blood, but it was better than being naked in the chilly woods. The chief had also come around and was back on his feet. He had a Maglite on his belt that he shown around the clearing, illuminating each body, for they had all reverted back to their human forms. It was a gruesome sight, one that I didn't think I'd ever forget.

Julian had gone off, located his clothes, and had managed to get himself dressed. He added his sweatshirt jacket on top of Ethan's shirt. I still had my socks on, but my legs were cold and I was shivering hard. "Ethan, take her up to the yard, put her in your truck with the heater on, and keep an eye on her. Rand and I have a few things to take care of and then I have a couple of calls to make before we can join you," Chief Adams directed.

"Do you know who these men are?" I asked through chattering teeth.

He gave me a long look and then turned his head away, staring off into the swampland to the left of the clearing. "I recognize most of them. I've arrested several of them any number of times at the Renegade Club and at the other local bars. Vagrants, drunks, homeless men. Swamp men living rough out here in makeshift shelters. He created his pack of werewolves from the throw-away men in our community. It's pretty damn sad, when you think about it."

"Why's that?" People had choices, I thought.

"These bums are gonna be known as Pine Haven's heroes from now on. I'm going to have to announce that I'd assembled a group of volunteers to scour the swamps where I'd determined the pack of feral wolves had made their lair. I'm going to have to create a fiction out of this that will satisfy the community and my superiors. I need to set their minds at ease about this whole wolf situation." He sighed. "And then we've got the loss of the popular high school gym teacher to deal with. Another cover-up. Another tragedy on top of everything else. We'll be a community in mourning for some time as we all recover from this whole nightmare." He turned back to us. "The four of us will always know what really happened out here. We're going to have to live with that truth and keep it an absolute secret." I nodded, completely understanding that and agreeing with him. "You and Ethan go on now. Go warm up in the truck. We'll take care of a few things here and then I'll make the calls I need to make. We'll be with you shortly." He focused on Julian, who wasn't in the best of shape. "You gonna make it there, Rand?"

"Julian. My name is Julian," he replied. "And, yeah, I'll be okay."

We were already at the hospital in Pittsfield when we heard that a propane explosion had occurred at Mr. Gunther's cabin close to dawn. The house and the surrounding woodland had rapidly become a blazing inferno. The story we heard later that same morning was that the cabin's owner had never woken up, that he had burned to a crisp in his home.

Later, when Julian and I were more fully recovered, we took a drive out there. There had been nothing left to the cabin, just a charred cellar hole full of charred, brittle debris and a blackened, stone fireplace. The woods behind the cabin were blackened also, right down to the swampy pond.

The skeletal remains of the charred "heroes" had been recovered and they'd all received proper burials. What caught me by surprise was the report of five charred wolf skeletons that had also been found where the fire had been its fiercest. I'd asked Julian about it and he'd just winked at me. That night, I'd tackled him in bed and gotten half an explanation from him when he'd revealed that it hadn't been just clock tower sections in those shipping containers from Germany that he'd been so anxious about when he'd moved back to Pine Haven.

Mr. Gunther's funeral had been attended by hundreds of former students, but, curiously enough, very few teachers or school staff. We hadn't gone, had just spent a quiet day at home. That night, Chief Adams had joined us for dinner. After we'd eaten, he and Julian had gone to the study to talk in private for a couple of hours.

We'd had Druce, who had no close family, buried quietly in Tylerville, but none of us had attended the burial.

The fire damage in the woods behind the shop was cleaned up. Fortunately, the fire had not spread down the hill to the shop, but had been contained to the area around Turkey Pond. Julian brought in a bulldozer to clear a one lane road up to the pond, and then he'd had acres of white sand trucked in, creating a crescent-shaped beach up there. The land was still posted *No Trespassing*, but the high school kids still snuck up there. If they were going to swim and make-out in the woods like many generations of teenagers had previously, at least it was a nicer place now and a lot better than that den of iniquity that had corrupted a lot of teens when Julian and I were growing up.

Three months after my twenty-fourth birthday, my incredible husband, Julian Rand Beresford, unveiled the full-size version of the miniature clock tower he'd installed in my former sitting room in the garden behind the house. It was visible from the balcony of our larger and more comfortable private suite. It had taken him a little longer to complete the clock because he had wanted to add one additional tiny movement to its mechanical action sequences. This additional mechanical action occurred at three o'clock in the afternoon, the time I usually took a break from clock making in the former ballroom, which was now my studio, went upstairs, and had tea on the balcony with my husband who was usually home. He liked to get up early. He worked from five in the morning until two in the afternoon and then he would come home to see what I had accomplished that day. Sometimes, after dinner, he joined me in the workshop to work on a special clock with me, if we received an order from royalty.

But, at three o'clock, the roses on the clock tower bloomed, the birds trilled, and the tower doors opened. The red-haired princess emerged onto the balcony in a green dressing gown with a tiny violets pattern all over. Behind her emerged the bare-chested prince. It was left to the viewer's imagination as to what they'd been doing in her tower bed chamber. (I had a very vivid imagination.) They kissed more passionately than they did at noon and midnight, and then danced on the balcony to the birdsong all around them before retreating back into the chamber with the violets and ivy painted on the walls beyond the doors. Once inside, the prince turned and appeared to lean out to pull the doors shut behind them, but before they were completely closed, if you watched very carefully, (you needed binoculars to see this), he winked.

Susan Buffum

About the Author

Susan Buffum resides in western Massachusetts where she works as a medical secretary and writes as a hobby. She shares a mountainside home with her husband, John, and their daughter, Kelly, who also writes. They are owned by two literary cats— Revere and Riley Beans.

Susan has self-published a number of novels and story collections including *My Magical Life, Miss Peculiar's Ghost Stories, Volume I, The Subtlety of Light and Shadow, butterscotch-a collection of stories, Black King Takes White Queen, The Hanging Man and Other Stories,* and *Out* among them.

Susan welcomes your comments and feedback. She can be contacted at sebuffum415@gmail.com

Susan writes an author blog at susanbuffum.blogspot.com

www.ingramcontent.com/pod-product-compliance
Lightning Source LLC
Chambersburg PA
CBHW071232250626
47163CB00001B/142